HIDDEN TRUTHS

MARY D. BROOKS

AUSXIP PUBLISHING
WWW.AUSXIPPUBLISHING.COM

Copyright © 2015, 2022 Mary D. Brooks

Third Edition

All rights reserved. No part of this publication may be reproduced, transmitted in any form or by any means, electronic or mechanical, including photocopy, recording, or any information storage and retrieval system, without permission in writing from the publisher. The characters herein are fictional and any resemblance to a real person, living or dead, is purely coincidental.

ISBN:978-0-9944765-6-2 (Paperback)

Edited by Rosa Alonso
Cover Design by Mary Draganis
Interior Design by Mary Draganis / AUSXIP Media

Published by AUSXIP Publishing
www.ausxippublishing.com

ACKNOWLEDGMENTS

Rosa Alonso – Super Editor, awesome friend. Thank you for your tireless work in making this book the best it can be.

Lucia Nobrega - Your incredible generosity and talent touches me greatly.

Arielle Strauss - Thank you for your generosity of spirit and for making me laugh!

To my readers who have encouraged and supported my writing over the years! To the many who said 'is it ready yet' and 'when is the next book'! It's what every author wants to hear.

CHAPTER 1

January 20, 1950

Sydney, Australia

The melodious tones of Yiannis Hatzopoulos drifted across the backyard, which was bathed in the most brilliant sunshine that only a Sydney summer could provide. The baby blue-colored sky was devoid of any clouds as far as the eye could see—just a vast blue expanse. It was a typical Sydney summer's day with a hint of the muggy humidity that would soon descend on the Emerald City.

Yiannis serenaded the group of friends sitting around on the deck chairs on the lawn overlooking the Pacific Ocean. A small barbeque with its simmering coals was being fanned by Earl Wiggins, a blond-haired man wearing an apron over his white cotton shirt and long tan shorts, wooden tongs in one hand and a magazine in the other to fan the coals.

The wooden wraparound porch was decorated with streamers, and a huge Happy Birthday banner with little cartoons and splashes of color adorned the banister.

Zoe Lambros glanced around at the small, rowdy group and laughed along with a joke that Earl had made. She didn't find the joke as funny as Earl's delivery of it. He told lame jokes, and she suspected the language barrier had something to do with it.

Sweat trickled down the side of her face, and she pulled a handkerchief from her pocket and wiped away the moisture from her sweaty face. She leaned back in her wicker chair and smiled. The love of her life was in the kitchen, which overlooked the backyard, cutting up some fruit, and from where she could see, it looked like Eva was also preparing some more refreshments.

You take my breath away, Evy.

Eva's long black hair was tied in a ponytail, which revealed a long, graceful neck. Eva wore a dark pink blouse with little-embroidered butterflies that Zoe found extremely cute. Eva stood at the window for a moment, looking out into the ocean and playing with her gold cross, which hung around her neck.

What are you thinking, my love?

"I'm so glad this baby will come in the middle of winter and not summer."

Zoe turned her attention to Elena Jacobs. Elena was twenty-two, the same age as Zoe, and she had brown hair and deep, dark brown eyes. She was Zoe's best friend and a survivor from the hellish war. They shared a bond that neither could understand. Elena wasn't looking too comfortable at that moment.

"You should have crossed your legs," Zoe teased.

Elena gently slapped Zoe on the arm. "Ha, Ha."

"So, has she stopped playing soccer?"

Elena put her hand on her belly. "She is rather active. By the way, how do you know it's a girl?"

"My mama used to say that if you carry the baby high, it's a girl, and it's a boy if you carry it low," Zoe explained. "You are carrying the baby high."

"I hope your mama was right. I want a little girl."

"Freddy wants a boy?"

"Of course." Elena laughed as she turned to find her husband, who was talking to their friends. She turned back to Zoe, who was giving her an affectionate look. "One day, we will be having this conversation when you have children."

"I'll need to change my name to Mary." Zoe leaned in. "Somehow, I don't think Eva is very skilled in that area."

Elena ruffled Zoe's red hair playfully. "Yes, hmm. Sorry."

"Not to worry, my friend. I'll be playing with your little one soon."

"How are you feeling?" Elena asked.

"I'm good, just a little tired, but good. I'm thrilled the cast is off my leg." Zoe tapped her injured leg with the cane. "I'll be even happier to get rid of the cane."

"We would be happier if it never happened again."

Zoe looked up towards their friend, David Harrison, who was sitting on the other side of the porch chatting with Eva's father, Panayiotis Haralambos. "Have you ever heard of a Power of Attorney?"

"What does that have to do with your accident?"

"It has a lot to do with it." Zoe smiled. "David said that if we sign one, then if either of us gets sick, we have the legal right to make decisions for the other."

"That makes sense and practical. Just don't go hurtling into cars to test it out."

"I'll try not to," Zoe replied.

The door opened, and Eva, the birthday girl, walked out. She wore black pleated shorts that stopped at the knee. Two buttons were undone on her shirt, and her gold cross was visible.

Zoe sighed on seeing Eva. Having Eva to herself had been a rare commodity these past few weeks, but that was going to change from this evening on.

Eva handed Earl a plate of sausages for the barbecue near the kitchen door, and her gaze fell on Zoe. Zoe smiled when Eva blew her a kiss.

Eva smiled as she put another tray down and joked with the people around her. *She's lost weight,* Zoe thought.

Eva approached Zoe and dropped to her haunches beside her chair.

"You are gorgeous," Zoe whispered, getting a shy smile from Eva. She resisted kissing Eva in front of everyone. She took Eva's hand and kissed it instead. "I love you. Are you enjoying yourself?"

"I am." Eva nodded, her ponytail bopping up and down. "How are you feeling?"

"I'm good," Zoe said with a slight smile. Eva looked dubious. "I'm a little tired, but it's alright."

"You're going to bed after all of this. You need to rest up." Eva interlocked her long fingers with Zoe's smaller ones. "Promise?"

"Uh-huh," Zoe responded solemnly. Out of the corner of her eye, she saw Eva's father looking at them and mentally sighed at not being able to kiss her. Father Haralambos accepted them for who they were, but Zoe was still uncomfortable with him seeing her kiss Eva. He was, after all, a priest, and Eva's father. She had no qualms about showing her love for Eva and would declare it to the whole world if she could, but was reserved about expressing her love around him.

Eva looked up at Zoe, a tiny smile playing on her lips as she gazed into Zoe's eyes. There was no barrier there, and Zoe felt as if no one else was around her. The look she was getting from Eva was rarely seen in front of other people. She reached down and brushed Eva's dark hair. "I'm not going anywhere," she whispered. "I'm feeling better than I have been since the accident."

Eva broke eye contact by taking a deep breath and dropped her head down as Zoe kissed the top of her head.

"Are you alright?"

Eva looked up and nodded. "I am," she responded softly. She cleared her throat and rose to her full height. "Remember-"

Zoe leaned in. "I'll go to bed, I promise." Eva's smile widened. "I promise, promise, promise."

Eva laughed lightly. "I believe you." She kissed Zoe's hair and walked toward the kitchen.

CHAPTER 2

Eva leaned across on the kitchen bench and waited for Zoe to look her way. When she did, Eva blew her a kiss, and mouthed "I love you." She smiled, knowing Zoe was going to be in the kitchen shortly.

Moments later Zoe walked through the doorway and snaked her arms around Eva's waist. Eva closed her eyes, smiled at Zoe's touch, and sighed. She put down the cup in her hand and turned in Zoe's embrace.

"Hello," she said and leaned down for a gentle kiss on Zoe's lips. "I wondered how long it would take you to come inside."

"Did you now?"

"I did." Eva tweaked Zoe's chin, which was a reversal of what Zoe usually did to her.

"How is my old lady today?"

"I have the most beautiful woman in my arms, so it's perfect now." Eva gazed into Zoe's sea-green eyes. "I love you."

Zoe sighed, hugged Eva, and rested her head on her

chest. "I love you, my little Fraulein," she said in German, much to Eva's delight.

Zoe looked up with a twinkle in her green eyes and smiled. "Help me up."

She kissed Eva lightly and then rested her cane against the kitchen cabinet. She faced Eva, and they smiled at each other as Eva helped Zoe maneuver her way up to sit on the bench top, so they were the same height.

"Now just one more thing." Zoe wrapped her legs around Eva's body to bring her close and captured her lips for a long, passionate kiss. "Hmm, I like this."

They gazed at each other and laughed.

"I do love it when you sit here."

"I love it when I sit here too," Zoe mumbled as Eva nuzzled her neck. "You have to stop worrying, Evy. I saw it outside. You were doing it again."

"I'm scared of losing you. I nearly lost you on that stupid motorcycle."

"I know you're scared, but I have to do one thing before I give it up."

Eva sighed deeply and closed her eyes. "Do you have to?"

"Yes. It's for me. I want to prove to myself that I'm not scared of getting back on."

Eva remained silent for the longest time. She wanted to give a voice to the fear but also knew that Zoe wanted to face her own fears and exorcise them from her mind. "Can I ask you for one favor?"

"Do you want to ride naked in the sidecar with me down Legacy Road?" Zoe quipped and grinned. "So it's not that." She shrugged. "Name it, and I'll do it," she said after a beat.

"This will be the final ride?"

"Yes. I promise I won't ride Mabel again."

"Thank you," Eva whispered before she leaned into Zoe and placed a gentle kiss on her lips.

"I love that song 'I gaze into my love.'"

"That record you keep playing and the one I want to destroy?" Eva giggled. She must have heard it a thousand times in the last six weeks. If Zoe loved a song, she would play it until she got tired of it, and then it would disappear for a few months only to resurface again. Eva had entertained the thought of stomping near the record player to make the needle jump and scratch the record. Then she would have some peace, but she knew Zoe would go out and buy the recording again.

"Yes, that one," Zoe said as she leaned in for a kiss. "There's a line that says...my heart goes flitter flutter when I gaze into your eyes." She gazed lovingly into Eva's eyes. "My heart goes flitter flutter for you."

She traced her finger down Eva's full lips, and then trailed down her cotton shirt, unbuttoning two buttons and exposing Eva's lacy bra.

Zoe followed her fingers with feather-light kisses. "Flitter flutter all night long."

Eva sighed at Zoe's touch.

The kitchen door swung open.

They stepped away from each other and looked at the door, which swung back and shut.

Zoe quickly closed Eva's shirt with a frustrated groan.

"Soon, love, soon," Eva whispered and gave Zoe a kiss. "It's a little warm in this kitchen."

Zoe grinned and opened Eva's shirt again. "Ah, the promised land," she whispered into Eva's chest. "Just a little while longer, Heidi and Helga." She kissed the top of Eva's breast and grinned as Eva rocked with laughter. She cupped

Eva's face and kissed her lightly. "I can't wait to get you alone. I've missed having you to myself."

"Heidi and Helga have been missing you." She laughed at Zoe's penchant for naming things. This time it was her breasts, which had taken on personalities according to a very bored, bedridden Zoe. Zoe was also frustrated at not being able to make love to her, so she had decided to tease her instead.

"I know." Zoe lightly cupped Eva's right breast and sighed. "I touched Helga this morning."

"Yes, she told me."

"Hmm." Zoe leaned in for a kiss. "She was delighted to see me."

"Heidi wasn't impressed," Eva quipped, and they laughed. "I want to make love to you so much that it hurts," she whispered.

"Soon," Zoe whispered. "Father H is going back home tonight. I'm going to ravish you."

"You are?"

"I am." Zoe grinned. "All. Night. Long." She punctuated each word with a kiss. "You know what I missed while I got acquainted with my bed and not with your body?"

"What's that?"

Zoe brought Eva's hand up to her lips to kiss her knuckles and gazed into her eyes. "I missed hearing my name as we made love."

"I missed touching you and loving you every single minute of the day." Eva sighed. They hadn't made love in over six weeks, and that was frustrating both of them. Having her father in the house was great because he cared for Zoe while Eva was working, but it also caused Zoe to feel very uncomfortable.

At first, she couldn't because of the pain, and then the knowledge that someone else was in the next room killed the desire. Their libidos were willing, but Zoe's shyness won. Zoe was a passionate woman who loved her and didn't care who knew it, but she just couldn't get past having Eva's father in the house while they made love. They tried soon after Zoe's cast was removed but quickly stopped when Zoe heard her father-in-law in the next room. The walls were not soundproof and that killed any more lovemaking.

"You know what I love when we make love?" Zoe ran her fingers through Eva's hair and kissed her again.

They parted with a smile.

"Oh, yes." Zoe nodded and unbuttoned Eva's shirt. She reversed course and buttoned up Eva's shirt when Earl walked into the kitchen.

"Did you get tired standing?" Earl tousled Zoe's hair. He glanced at Eva, who was looking down at their intertwined hands. "Was I interrupting?"

"Yes," Eva growled.

"Oh, good." Earl laughed and picked up another pair of tongs. He played with them with a satisfied grin. They smiled at each other before Earl leaned over and kissed her on the cheek. "I think it would be a good idea if the fire were out there and not in here." He scampered out the door.

"We have to, don't we?" Zoe asked.

"Yes." Eva helped Zoe down from the bench top. She watched Zoe pick up her cane and sighed. "Zoe-"

"I'm fine, Evy. Really I am. Can you please stop worrying?" Zoe took Eva's hand and held it. "You can't worry all the time. I'm fine. I'll prove it to you later."

Eva put her arm around Zoe's shoulders. "Only if it doesn't tire you out," she said half-joking.

"Oh, no." Zoe shook her head before gazing up. "It won't tire me out at all, but I'm not sure about my old lady." She chuckled as they left the kitchen and re-joined their family and friends outside.

ZOE WAITED IMPATIENTLY as Eva escorted Father Haralambos down the driveway. She could see the smile on Eva's face and her less than a leisurely walk back. Eva entered and closed the door. Zoe snaked her arms around Eva's waist and smiled.

Eva graced Zoe with a tender, lopsided smile and placed a gentle kiss on her lips.

They looked at each other for a long time. "I love you so much," Eva said hoarsely. "You are the best birthday present anyone could have given me."

"God, I love you." Zoe traced a path with her soft lips across the proud chin, teasing the dimple she loved so well. Eva took Zoe's hand and led her to their bed.

The look of lust in Eva's eyes made Zoe's heart nearly stop. She quickly unbuttoned Eva's blouse and let it fall to the floor, followed by her bra, pants, and panties.

"Time for me to show you how well I've recovered!"

CHAPTER 3

"I DO LOVE THOSE EYES," EVA SAID.

"You do?" Zoe asked.

"Oh, yes...I have a thing for them."

"You don't say."

"Hmm. Always had. Green eyes make me weak at the knees." Eva kissed Zoe. They parted and smiled at each other. "I've got another secret you may not know about—redheads are my weakness." She nuzzled Zoe's neck, causing Zoe to laugh and squirm off her. Eva turned sideways to face Zoe and gently kissed her again. She wrapped her long arms around Zoe's naked body, closed her eyes, and sighed contentedly. Zoe watched Eva intently and for a long moment, wasn't sure what Eva was doing.

"Evy, what are you doing?"

"Lying naked here with you." Eva opened her eyes and smiled.

"Why did you close your eyes?"

"I was praying," Eva admitted.

Zoe blinked at her. "You pray after we make love?"

"No, but I wanted to thank God for not taking you from me." Eva stroked Zoe's face tenderly.

"Have you ever wondered what God thinks every time we make love?" Zoe asked.

Eva shook her head slowly. "No, I don't think I've ever thought about that. Have you?"

"Oh, yes. I wonder what He thinks every time He hears 'Mein Gott! Zo...hiccup... eeee.'" Zoe grinned. "Do you know that when you're aroused, your eyes go the most amazing deep shade of blue?"

"I can't see myself when I'm aroused, so I'll take your word for it," Eva responded a little shyly.

"It's true." Zoe smiled and brushed Eva's hair off her face. "They go a shade darker, but I remember in Larissa, your eyes were almost navy blue and I couldn't figure out why."

"You saw my eyes change color?"

"Yes, they were almost navy blue rather than light blue. It must have been the light or the angle I was sitting at."

Eva gazed down at Zoe with a puzzled expression. "I was just allowing myself to think how beautiful you looked there, half-naked on the floor."

"I wasn't half-naked on the floor. It was a hot day."

"I had hoped you would take your shirt off," Eva admitted and giggled. "Now, if you had done that, I would have been a sobbing mess on the floor, but that didn't stop me from thinking about it."

"Was that the first time you allowed yourself to do that?"

Eva shook her head. "Yes. I would stop before I thought about doing anything like think of you naked. That was too much."

"I've never seen your eyes that color again, but when we make love, they nearly get to that color."

"Oh," Eva replied. "I thought if I tried not to look, I would be alright. It was very difficult not to pay attention."

"It was hard not to look at me since I was your maid."

Eva rolled over and put her arm across Zoe's bare waist. "That's why it was hard. It was hard to watch and not let the feelings I was having for you take over my mind."

"So that day we went up to Athena's Bluff was the day you finally surrendered."

Eva smiled and nodded. "I surrendered to my feelings that day knowing what it would bring. I've told you that before."

"You have, but every time I think about it, I remember the look you had in your eyes when I was taking your hose off and feel silly that I didn't recognize it for what it was."

"How could you, love? You were young and didn't know anything about the aversion treatments and what touching me like that would do to me. I allowed you to do that, so it was my choice."

"You made a choice to let me touch you like that and allow your control to slip. I'm in awe of your strength, Evy. Knowing what I know about the aversion torture, I would never have done that."

"It was worth it." Eva smiled. "If I close my eyes and think back to that day, I can still feel your hands, and I get this bubble of happiness inside me."

"I think that was the first time I flirted with you, and I didn't know how to flirt so..."

Eva laughed and kissed Zoe tenderly on the lips. "Oh, you were doing an outstanding job of it."

"I remember that day, and it was just so beautiful.

You were gorgeous. You were wearing a light blue dress, and two buttons were undone, which showed off your gold cross. You had a white belt and white gloves. You wore your hair up that day, which was just so beautiful."

"I sometimes forget what a great memory you have."

Zoe giggled. "I didn't understand why my body was reacting the way it was to you. I felt funny."

"You were heading into heavy like."

Zoe nodded. "I finally understood why none of the boys that Kiria Despina would want to introduce me to was of any interest to me."

The two women looked at each other for a moment. "Because we don't like boys," they said in unison and laughed.

"I had never felt that way before about anyone. When you kissed me for the first time, it made sense."

"As first kisses go, that wasn't the way I wanted it to pan out."

"You knew what was going to happen if you did kiss me."

Eva nodded. "I knew but did it anyway. Kissing you was worth the pain," she replied quietly. "It was worth every minute of it." She leaned in for a passionate kiss.

"Oh, like that," Zoe said breathlessly. "No one can kiss like you. Not that I have anyone to compare it with, but I don't need to compare. When we made love for the first time, I thought my heart would explode."

"Just had to wait for a little bit of time," Eva admitted. "It was worth the wait. Making love to you for the first time was just..."

"I know, Evy." Zoe leaned over and kissed her tenderly on

the lips. She rested her head on Eva's shoulder and sighed. Eva looked down at her with a smile.

Zoe traced the scar on Eva's shoulder. "So who was your first?"

"My first what?"

"Lover."

"Why are we talking about this?"

"Because I want to know."

"I knew there had to be a good reason," Eva quipped and tenderly kissed the top of Zoe's hair. "Not who you think." She wrapped her arms around Zoe and looked down at her.

"You mean it wasn't that she-demon?" Zoe rolled over Eva and looked at her between her breasts. Eva tried to capture Zoe's mouth, but Zoe moved her head away. "Ah. No kissing until you tell me."

"Oh, Zoe..."

"No kissing." Zoe kissed her fingers and put them gently on Eva's lips. "You talk first."

"Do I have to?"

"Yes, you have to."

Eva looked into Zoe's eyes and smiled. "If I must."

"You must. I thought you said the she-demon was your first?"

"She-demon? Greta was my first female lover, but she wasn't my first."

"Really? Wow." Zoe blinked. "Do you want to share?"

Eva laughed. "It's not romantic in any way."

Zoe looked down at Eva and grinned. "Now you have to tell me."

"Why?"

"Because I'm your wife, and as your wife, I have a right to know who's had sex with you. That's why," Zoe stated and tweaked Eva's chin. "There's also this matter of having a fondness for green-eyed women."

"Redheaded and green-eyed. Oh well, in that case." Eva put her hand behind Zoe's head and pulled her down for a long passionate kiss. They broke and smiled at each other. "Okay, I'll tell you."

"That was sneaky, Miss Eva. Now let me get comfortable." Mindful of Eva's back, Zoe shifted from on top of Eva to lie beside her, her arm wrapped around Eva's waist.

"Why did you move? I was enjoying that."

"Your back won't like me being on top of you like that." Zoe shifted and hitched herself up on her elbow to look at Eva.

"My back is fine."

"It won't be if I'm sitting on top of you. Now tell me. I have a better understanding of how painful it is after these past few weeks, so don't tell me it won't."

Eva turned sideways and faced Zoe. She intertwined her long fingers with Zoe's smaller ones and smiled. "I was thirteen years old, and I had an inkling I didn't like boys."

"What was the inkling?"

"I had a huge crush on this girl that I just couldn't stop thinking about."

"Ooh, was she pretty?"

"Not as gorgeous as you."

"Oh, you are a smooth talker," Zoe teased. "So you had a crush on this girl. Who was she?"

"Do you remember my friend Wilhelm?"

"Willie? Yes, but he isn't a girl."

"No, but his sister was. Very much a girl." Eva smiled. "Leila. She was just so cute, with red hair and the most amazing green eyes..." She stopped and stared off into space.

"Hello, Eva." Zoe snapped her fingers in front of Eva's face.

Eva burst out laughing.

"You sneak, I thought you had just drifted off down memory lane."

"You're jealous."

"No, I'm not."

"Yes, you are. You don't have to be—she wasn't interested in me."

"Stupid girl. Why not?"

"I was this thirteen-year-old pest, and she was this most elegant creature."

"How old?"

"Eighteen." Eva smiled. "I was always at Willie's house. I sometimes practically lived there. Aunt Marlene even gave me my own room."

"Aunt Marlene?"

"Not my real aunt, but she might as well have been," Eva explained. "I would go over there, and instead of listening to the gramophone with Willie, I would be following Leila around like a puppy."

"How utterly adorable."

"How utterly silly." Eva chuckled. "It got quite noticeable, and Willie asked me what I was doing."

"And you told him?"

"I didn't have any secrets from Willie," Eva explained. "We were inseparable. Our parents thought we were going to get married. Everyone thought we were going to get married when we were old enough."

"Wow."

"Except us." Eva smiled. "Willie and I were best friends, and we loved each other, but our love wasn't sexual. I didn't feel that way about him."

"Why not?"

"He was a boy."

"Did Willie know?"

"That he was a boy? I think he had some idea." Eva chuckled along with Zoe. "Willie told me."

"Willie told you he was a boy?"

"No, that I was a lesbian."

"You cannot be serious. Willie told you that you were a lesbian? You didn't know?"

"Of course, I knew, but I wasn't going to admit it. He wanted to know why I was over at his house without him being there, and I made some sort of excuse, which of course he knew was a lie."

"Because you're a terrible liar."

"I wasn't very good at it." Eva smiled. "It's like you and Elena. Our friendship was so strong sometimes I could tell when something was wrong with him even when I wasn't with him. I just could feel it. It's the same feeling I get when you're not feeling well. I don't know what it is, but it's only ever happened with Willie, Henry, and with you."

"Because you love us?"

"Doesn't happen with Earl, and I love him like a brother."

"Does Willie have green eyes?"

Eva shook her head. "No. Blue."

"And blond hair?"

"Thick, curly blond hair," Eva replied. "I used to tease him that he looked like a blond French poodle."

"Blond, blue-eyed, and now the other missing part of your boy type. Was he tall?"

"Yes. Taller than me, broad-shouldered, and very handsome."

"Your type."

Eva looked indignant. "There you go again with the type. I don't have a type."

"Deny it all you want, but I know the truth. You do befriend tall, blond, blue-eyed men. Look at all the men in your life." Zoe held up her fingers to count them off. "David—tall, blond, and blue-eyed. Earl—tall, blond, and blue-eyed. Your father—tall, blond, and blue-eyed."

"My father has brown hair. Well, he did before it went that salt-and-pepper look."

"No, he didn't. I've seen pictures of him, and he had blond hair."

"Henry hasn't got any hair, and he has green eyes."

"Henry is the exception to the rule."

"Hmm, all right, but I don't understand why this is important."

"It's important. You like one particular sort of man. So getting back to your story. Willie told you that you were a lesbian?"

Eva nodded. "We were sitting down in the park after school, and he wanted to know why I was following his sister around. After going through several excuses, he said he knew why. I challenged him, and he said, 'you're sweet on my sister.'"

"What did you say?"

"I said the sun had got to him and he needed to rest." Eva chuckled. "I tried to deny it, of course."

"You were thirteen, and he was?"

"Same age."

"Hold on a minute, back in Larissa you told me that you figured it out when you were fourteen," Zoe said. "I remember that so clearly."

"Of course, you would remember that." Eva laughed lightly and kissed the top of Zoe's head. "Well, I would have scared you if I had said thirteen."

"No, you wouldn't have." Zoe shook her head. "If you had told me you were a lesbian at thirteen, it would not have been scary. Having the Nazis in my home is scary; lesbians don't scare me."

"Nazi evil she-demon lesbians do."

Zoe laughed. "So back to your story. Now, tell me who...oh...it was Willie?"

Eva smiled and nodded. "I said to him that he was wrong and that I just hadn't met the right boy yet. He pointed to himself. 'Well, I'm a boy.'"

"Good point."

"Indeed. I said if I met the right boy then fireworks would go off in my head and all the other romantic things they said in the movies."

"Not fireworks." Zoe shook her head. "Atomic bombs."

"Well, that was before atomic bombs," Eva joked. "Willie told me he was a virgin, which I knew because if he wasn't, he would have told me. He knew I was a virgin, so he said, 'why don't we find out if you are a lesbian?'"

"He was smitten with you." Zoe rolled on top of Eva and grinned down at her. "What a clever boy. I never thought of doing that. I should have said, 'Fraulein Muller, let's make love and see if I'm a lesbian,'" she said in German.

Eva burst out laughing.

"So did you?" Zoe asked.

"Hmm, we did."

"And?"

"We were both quite clumsy, and it was funny."

"Were you embarrassed?"

"No. Willie had seen me naked before."

"Do tell."

"We went skinny dipping in the lake each summer," Eva said. "We grew up together, so it wasn't a shocking thing."

"Losing your virginity was..." Zoe raised an eyebrow. "Didn't Greta say that she was your first lover?"

"She liked to think she was, and for whatever reason, it made her feel something. I don't know what, but then I didn't understand her at all."

"I really despise that woman."

"I know. So did Willie."

"Why?"

"He hated her passionately." Eva nodded. "We had a fight over her after I told him. We didn't stay mad at each other for very long, but he told me that he didn't trust her and she was a pompous, egotistical prostitute."

Zoe's eyebrows shot up in surprise and then she laughed. "Oh, my goodness, I love this boy!"

"He was right about Greta, and he was right about a lot of things."

"What happened to him?"

"The last time I saw him was at his farewell party after he joined the army." Eva sighed. "I never saw him again."

"He volunteered?"

"Yes. His father was a high-ranking officer, so it was expected of him. All the men in his family were army men. His uncle was an officer in the Nazi Party."

"Oh." Zoe nodded.

"Willie wasn't a Nazi, Zoe. Not all Germans were."

"I didn't say he was."

"You were thinking it. He knew that when he was the right age, he would be in the army. It is destined, he would tell me. I hated the idea but there wasn't much either of us could do about it."

"When did he leave?

Eva took a deep breath and exhaled slowly. "November first, 1938. He looked so grown up in his uniform." She put her arm around Zoe's shoulders and brought her closer. "You would have loved him, Zo."

"You think so?"

"Yes. He was a funny, kind, gentle man. You remind me so much of him. Accepted the fact I was a lesbian without questioning. I wasn't normal, but that was alright by him." Eva smiled.

"He sounds like he was a perfect friend."

"He was and still is because I don't believe he is gone. Unless I see his grave, I won't believe it." Eva buried her head against Zoe's chest. Zoe put her arms around her and held her. "I was lucky to have a friend like Willie, and I'm extraordinarily lucky to have found you."

"Luck had nothing to do with it. We were destined to be together."

"You don't believe in destiny."

"I do when it comes to you," Zoe replied taking Eva's hand and kissing it. "So tell me more about Willie?"

"We used to sit in the park and watch people. He would point to one girl and tell me why she wasn't good enough for me or what I needed to say to talk to a girl. I reminded him that I was a girl and I knew what to say."

"Did you know?"

"Of course not." Eva laughed. "I was this tall, awkward teenager. I was tongue-tied talking to boys, and talking to girls...that was never going to happen because of who my family was."

"So what happened to his redhead, green-eyed sister?"

"Back to the girl, I see?"

"Of course. Remember I have a one-track mind."

"Leila got married to a handsome German officer, and well, I got married to a gorgeous redheaded, green-eyed Greek." Eva grinned and kissed Zoe tenderly. "Willie was right, and I will wager that he would approve of you. Now, Miss Zoe, didn't you ever have a crush on a girl?"

"I had this huge crush on one girl."

"Really?"

"Oh, yes," Zoe replied and then looked up at Eva for a long moment. "I married her."

"I was your first crush?"

"Before you came, no boy ever made me feel anything, Eva," Zoe said. "I liked them, but none of them made me giddy like some of my friends were when the boys looked at them. After we starred at each other-"

"You mean after you hit me with the rock and then you stared," Eva gently teased.

"Yes, well...the strange thing was that when I went back home, all I drew was your face, which was a little odd."

"You were drawing me?"

"Hm, well, yes. Before we had that first meeting, I used to watch you from the window every morning when you went off to the church with Henry and that other idiot. Like clockwork. You were up at sunrise, drudging up the hill to the church."

"How did you manage to wake up so early?"

Zoe poked out her tongue at Eva. "Ha Ha, I'll have you know that I can wake up early when it involves watching a beautiful woman passing by my window." She giggled as she met Eva's gaze. "I would sit at the window and watch you go and watch you come back. You always wore that cloak so I could never see what you were wearing underneath."

"Muller thought that walking to the church would be good for me."

"It was. Little did that fool know what you were really doing, but I didn't mind since it allowed me to get closer to you."

"Ah, yes, *the* plan."

"My plan did not include falling in heavy like." Zoe giggled. "It's funny now that I think about it. My mama would have been laughing if she had seen me. Me, a maid."

"You were an excellent maid with soft hands." Eva smiled as she held Zoe's hand and kissed it.

"I used to avert my eyes when my cousins stayed with me, and they would change into their nightgowns. I didn't want to look at other naked people—it made me uncomfortable."

"Why?"

"I was shy about my own body, and I thought it was improper." Zoe shook her head. "I must say that my cousins didn't look anything like you, and I just couldn't stop looking at you."

"You were looking at me? Like that?"

"I surprised myself when I found that it really didn't bother me and that I wanted to see you." Zoe smiled and looked away for a moment.

"I didn't think anyone would want to see me naked and look at me that way again," Eva quietly confessed.

Zoe leaned in for a kiss, this one intense, longer, and much more passionate. "You can't see what I see, and that is you are the most beautiful woman I have ever or will ever see. Inside and out. You were my first love and my only love." She traced a path with her lips across Eva's proud chin.

CHAPTER 4

June 12, 1950

"It is a happy day, Eva."

Eva leaned back in her chair and smiled at the gray-haired older woman sitting in her office. Her position as an interpreter in the Immigration Department gave her the ability to use her language skills to help the constant stream of migrants. In this case, Mrs. Fenstermacher, who had become a regular visitor to the section, would only speak to Eva.

Mrs. Fenstermacher leaned over in her chair and tapped the newspaper on Eva's desk. She pointed to the article that she had circled with a pen. "This is a happy day, Eva, a happy day. Read that to me, please?"

Eva nodded. "Your justice has arrived, Mrs. Fenstermacher."

"Ach, such formality from a pretty girl like you. I keep telling you to call me Louisa."

Eva smiled. "Ah, that's a little hard to do."

Mrs. Fenstermacher reached out and clasped Eva's hands. "You have shown me great respect. Thank you. Is your mother still alive?"

"No, my mother died in 1938."

"Ah." Mrs. Fenstermacher leaned back in her chair. "We have lost so many, so many. Today we celebrate their life, yes?"

"Yes, ma'am." Eva picked up the newspaper. She knew her stepfather's name would be in it. She quickly read the brief article about the Nazis that had been caught and had been tried for crimes against humanity. The report noted the names of those who had been executed previously, some she knew personally like her stepfather's friend, General Rhimes.

"I see your father's name."

Eva looked up in surprise. "How..."

"There're not many secrets in our community, are there?"

Eva shook her head. She fully understood how the Germans congregated together, sharing news and waiting on the many lists with names of survivors even so many years after the war had ended. Miracles occurred, but they were few. "How long have you known about my stepfather?"

"Your stepfather was Hans Muller? He wasn't your father?"

"No. My father lives in Greece and is the village priest." Eva surprised both herself and Mrs. Fenstermacher. She hadn't planned to reveal that information, but she felt the need to disown Muller.

"Well, that is interesting. Muller's name appeared in the paper when they captured him. Your photo was there too, and I recognized you when you first arrived to work here."

Eva nodded. "And you still wanted me to help you?"

Mrs. Fenstermacher patted Eva's hand. "The sins of the father do not get passed on to the daughter. Even the sins of the stepfather. It is not your fault that man was a *momzer*."

Eva had heard the word many times with her Jewish clients. The bastard was too good a word for what her stepfather had done and for those who committed such acts of brutality against innocent people.

"That describes him very accurately." Eva looked down at the newspaper.

"I rejoice that justice has been done, but I can see this is hard for you," Mrs. Ferstermacher said quietly.

"It's not hard for me, Mrs. Fenstermacher."

The old woman took Eva's hands and smiled. "Yes, your lips say the words, but the heart knows the truth. He was your stepfather, and he loved you once. Before he became a monster, he loved you. He raised you to be a beautiful young woman. That is why I say, I'm sorry for your loss."

Eva was moved by those heartfelt words. "It's very rare to find compassion for those who murdered your family, Mrs. Fenstermacher." Eva shrugged a little when Mrs. Fenstermacher shook her finger at her for not using her given name.

"What can they do to me now? Nothing. What they have done, they have done. If I get mad, I get mad at myself. They are not here for me to take out my rage upon them." Mrs. Fenstermacher sighed. "If my Sylvie had lived, she would have been thirty with a child of her own."

"You think of them often?"

"Ach, yes, of course, every day." Mrs. Fenstermacher nodded slowly. "Every day I wake up and hope it was a big bad dream. You know, like the dreams we all have of someone's big black dog that is after you, and you're running and running, but you can't escape it." She sighed. "The black dog was real, and his bite was painful. We can shoot the dog, but the bite remains."

"I've never heard it described that way before."

"Ach, yes, there were lots of black dogs." Mrs. Fenstermacher took out her handkerchief and dabbed the tears from her cheeks before she looked up at Eva. "There are many like me, Eva, too many."

"Yes, there are many."

"You understand better than the others. I can see it in your eyes. You show compassion, and this is more than a job for you."

"I have a friend who was in Bergen-Belsen as well..."

"A man?"

"No, a woman."

"Ah, what is her name?"

"Elena Mannheim. She got married and is now Elena Jacobs."

"Elena...hmm, I don't recall that name," Mrs. Fenstermacher replied. "Elena Mannheim...she lives here?"

"Yes."

"Hmm, I should ask my friend Helga. She will know. It was very difficult for the women, very difficult." Mrs. Fenstermacher stopped and gazed at nothing for a moment. "Some days it seems like a lifetime ago and other days it feels like yesterday."

"I know what you mean."

"Indeed." Mrs. Fenstermacher nodded, lost in her thoughts. "They say..." She paused then looked up at Eva. "They say it's wrong to wish someone ill, but I hope those *momzers* died slowly and painfully."

Eva swallowed the lump in her throat and looked down at the newspaper. She once loved her stepfather dearly. Eva mourned the loss of the man she loved, not the monster that he had become. It wasn't something she could understand or talk about with Zoe. It was something that she needed to work out for herself without burdening Zoe about it.

"I know you mourn, Eva, and I'm sorry for upsetting you, but..."

Eva took Mrs. Fenstermacher's wrinkled hands. "You have every right to feel this way, Mrs. Fenstermacher."

"I lost everyone, everyone...all gone."

Eva didn't have to wonder how the woman coped with such a loss. She knew. Living with Zoe gave her insight into how such a loss impacted one's soul. It affected every part of her life. Everything she did was influenced by the murder of her mother and the rest of her family. How Zoe managed to live through the horror was something Eva couldn't begin to comprehend. She knew Zoe would have dearly loved for her to kill her stepfather when he came looking for Eva and attacked them in their apartment. Zoe was ready to exact vengeance on him, but it was Eva who held the poker in her hand, and it was Eva who chose not to kill him. The remarkable thing was that Zoe understood why Eva didn't do it. Zoe's love for her overcame the desire for revenge.

Eva gazed at the photo of a smiling Zoe, together with Henry, Elena, Friedrich, and Earl, which sat on her desk. "I believe we will see them again."

"Ach, maybe one day." Mrs. Fenstermacher patted Eva's hand and smiled. "Now, we live in the here, and now so we have to make the best of it, yes?"

"Yes." Eva nodded and smiled.

"I am going to go home and frame this newspaper. Even

though I don't understand what it says, I know it talks about justice."

Eva folded the newspaper and handed it back to Mrs. Fenstermacher. She led her out of the office and down the corridor to the central waiting area.

"Thank you, Eva." Mrs. Fenstermacher clasped Eva's hand and chuckled as Eva bent down. She gave Eva a kiss on the cheek and walked out of the building.

"Mrs. F is happy?"

Eva turned to Debbie Harrison, their receptionist, and smiled. "Fenstermacher."

"I can never say that name," Debbie said.

"Is Haralambos easier?"

Debbie shook her head. "Not really. You should change your name to Smith. Did she come in for this?" She brought a copy of the newspaper to her.

Eva looked down and nodded. "Gunther Koch was captured, and Mrs. Fenstermacher is overjoyed."

"He sounds like a proper bastard." Debbie poked at the photo of the captured man.

"Hmm." Eva nodded and walked back into her office and closed the door.

"A proper bastard," she said and shook her head.

CHAPTER 5

Quiet. Peaceful. It was a lazy spring day, and the jacaranda trees were in full bloom. Those descriptions ran through Zoe's mind as she rode her motorcycle through the deserted street. The sound of the bike and its sidecar made a rumbling noise, with the occasional engine splutter joining the throng of cicadas in the trees.

The giant jacaranda trees that lined up on either side of the street created a canopy of purple and Zoe gleefully glanced up and laughed with joy. This was her favorite time of the year. Not too hot or too cold, but just so perfect.

Legacy Road was one of Zoe's favorite routes on her way home. The artist in her marveled at the color, the aroma, and the beautiful vista of the trees. Riding Mabel, her motorcycle, after her accident was a sheer unadulterated joy.

This was the day Zoe would ride Mabel for the last time. It was the road when she had her accident, and when she passed the spot where she had collided with the car, she threw back her head and roared to the heavens as she sped off.

This was her redemption; her way to prove to herself that she could do it. Eva had been apprehensive, but she hadn't tried to dissuade her. Now that she had achieved what she set out to do, Zoe would honor the promise she had made to Eva that she would no longer ride Mabel. There would come a time when the motorcycle will once again be used but for now, for Eva's sake, Zoe chose not to.

The old motorcycle rounded a bend and went into a cul-de-sac which was also lined with jacaranda trees. At the end of the cul-de-sac was her oasis. Zoe maneuvered the motorcycle up a grassy driveway, past the postman who was delivering mail next door.

Zoe practically jumped off the seat, then took off her leather helmet and shook her long red hair. She ran her fingers through it a few times in a useless attempt to bring order to chaos.

She jogged up to the gate, leaned on it, and waited for the postman to approach. "Good afternoon, Mr. Smith, anything for us?"

"You're going to kill yourself on that thing one day," Mr. Smith replied, the same comment he made every time he saw Zoe on the motorcycle.

"Nah, Mabel is not going to kill me." Zoe looked back fondly at the old motorcycle. "Speeding cars will kill me," she muttered under her breath.

"I don't know, young lady, the way you zoom about on that thing..."

"Mr. Smith, you worry too much."

Mr. Smith grumbled good-naturedly and handed Zoe two letters. "You be careful now."

"I will." Zoe watched Mr. Smith walk back down the sidewalk to continue his route.

As she walked the sandstone-paved walkway to the front steps, she patted her jacket to see if she had the house keys.

She stopped to admire the jasmine that Eva had planted near the steps leading up to the house. The climber was steadily growing and was soon going to wind itself around the wooden porch. With its two large jacaranda trees and the beautiful garden in the front, she loved the house that was nestled away from the road. It had a lot of character. She wasn't sure what that meant, but that's what the real estate agent had told them.

Zoe glanced at the letters in her hand. The familiar handwritten address on the top envelope was going to please Eva. Eva's father, Panayiotis Haralambos, had recently returned back to Greece due to his deteriorating health.

Eva was heartbroken to find out that her father was going back to Greece, but in the end, they both knew it was for the best. Father Haralambos wanted to live in Greece even though his only daughter was thousands of miles away. His health overruled his heart.

Zoe stared at the other envelope for a long moment. She recognized the handwriting and was acutely aware of the contents. She sighed deeply and shook her head as she walked up the stairs of the house. She was met by Ourania, her blue-eyed, black-and-white cat, sprawled out on the welcome mat.

"Well, aren't we lazy?"

Zoe went down on her haunches and scratched Ourania's belly. She laughed when Ourania rolled and offered her more of the furry belly in response.

"I want to come back in the next life as a cat, Ourania. You have got it way too easy."

The cat meowed and curled back up, leaving a very

bemused Zoe to gingerly step over her and enter the house. She dropped her keys on the small table in the hallway, then took her jacket off and placed it on a hook near the door. She dropped the letters on the side table near the front door. She looked down to find that Ourania had come inside and was rubbing against her leg.

"Ourania, I've got work to do," she said.

Ourania totally ignored her.

Zoe went to the bedroom and hummed to herself as she replaced her shirt with her painting shirt—one of Eva's shirts that Zoe had taken to paint in. It was overly large for her small frame, but she loved the baby blue color. Eva called it the splodge shirt because it had every color in the rainbow.

"She's just jealous, isn't she, Ourania?"

Ourania was sprawled on the bed.

"Just because I stole it from her..." Zoe turned towards the door at the footsteps on the floorboards. "Hello there."

Elena appeared in the doorway. "Was that Mabel I heard rumbling down the street?"

"You could hear that?"

Elena put her hands on her hips. "You can hear that motorcycle all the way across the harbor."

"Well, now you are just exaggerating. Mabel was not that loud."

"I also heard your hollering."

Zoe grinned. "I was happy."

"What? But..."

"Yes, yes, yes, Mother hen." Zoe waved her hand. "I know, but I had to do it."

"No, you didn't. What about Eva?"

"Eva knows what I was going to do today. It's done, and

now Mabel can be retired. Stay calm and don't try to get excited or the baby will come."

"Oh, no, that is what I want to happen. I'm very ready to have this baby." Elena put her hands on her belly and smiled down, and then she sighed and exhaled slowly. She looked back up at Zoe, who was laughing.

"You look beautiful," Zoe said.

Elena looked back at her in disbelief.

"You do, El. You look beautiful."

"I'm bloated like a whale."

"Whales aren't bloated," Zoe replied with a small smile.

"Okay. I'm bloated like a puffer fish," Elena amended.

Zoe nibbled her lip and then shook her head. "No, you don't look like a puffer fish either." She knelt beside Elena. "You look radiant. You're tired from carrying Baby No Name. This too shall pass."

Elena scowled. "You have no idea what this is like."

"No, I don't," Zoe replied quietly and took Elena's hand. "But I know what I see, and I can see a woman who is going to give birth to a beautiful baby girl..."

"You're going to be changing nappies for this little girl." Elena smiled.

"I'm up to the task and so is Eva." Zoe smiled.

"Does Eva know?"

"Of course." Zoe giggled. "We both will."

"And babysit?"

"Absolutely." Zoe nodded. "Eva even wants early morning feedings."

Elena laughed and ruffled Zoe's hair. "You are good for me, Zo."

"Of course I am." Zoe chuckled. "It's in the contract I signed."

"Don't ever change, my friend." Elena crooked her finger, and Zoe rose a little to get a kiss on the cheek. "So, what were you doing speeding down Legacy?"

"Thought I had distracted you."

"What would have happened if you had had an accident?"

"I didn't. I wanted the last ride, and that's it for a while."

"Was Eva drunk when she agreed to that?"

"No. Eva knows I needed to do this," she said as they left the bedroom.

Zoe opened the door to the room at the front of the house and ushered Elena through the doorway. The room was Zoe's project. Eva called it their Journey Room. The room was bathed in sunlight that streamed through the white lace curtains over two ornate windows and fell upon a mural of Sydney Harbour with a passenger liner in the dock, which took pride of place between two other paintings. On the left was the Brandenburg Gate, Berlin's landmark icon, set against a blue sky. On the right was Athena's Bluff overlooking the valley below and Mount Ossa.

A murky orange sofa was in the middle of the room. The color didn't fit into the decor and stood out, but the couch had sentimental value. A side table stood nearby, and an orange-colored flokati rug lay in front of the couch.

"That sofa makes my eyes ache," Elena teased as she stood in front of the Germany mural. "I still can't believe you dyed that beautiful white flokati rug into the murky color."

"Well, I wanted it to match the sofa."

"It's a waste of a beautiful rug." Elena turned to the artwork of the Brandenburg Gate. "This is beautiful. Your attention to detail is incredible."

Elena then turned to the next panel, which depicted Sydney Harbour with the docked ocean liner. "I like how you centered this image and had the sunshine on it."

Zoe grinned. "That was Eva's idea. She said that the light was shining where it should."

Elena turned and smiled at Zoe. "Very poetic." She stood in front of the Greek mural. "This is an odd scene to paint. I was wondering what it meant when you were painting it."

Zoe went to the painting of Athena's Bluff and put her hand on the rustic cabin that lay meters from the cliff face. "That's my brother's house."

"Why this cliff face? Why didn't you paint the Acropolis?"

Zoe gazed at the vista for a moment. "This is the place where Evy told me she loved me." She felt herself blush a little. She turned to find Elena smiling at her.

"That's romantic."

"That's Mount Ossa." Zoe pointed to the mountain. "I would sit on Athena's Bluff for hours and wonder what was beyond the mountain. What adventures I could have, what art I would create."

"You found out."

"The hard way," Zoe replied quietly and raised herself on her toes to look closer at the top of the mountain, but the artwork was taller than she was. "I'll get Eva to redo that bit of the mountain," she muttered. She turned to Elena, who was looking at her with some amusement. "Eva had to paint the top of the mountain. I couldn't reach it without stepping on a ladder. She was a little overprotective after the accident."

"A little?"

"Well, a lot," Zoe amended. "I think she's at the point where she doesn't wake up every time I move."

"She's a sensitive soul, isn't she?" Elena asked and sat down on the creaky sofa.

Zoe stood in front of the mural for a long moment, not looking at the painting. Her mind went back to 1942 and the constant animosity she held for the German major's daughter. "Eva is extremely sensitive. Sometimes I think she can read my thoughts with the way she acts."

She sat down on the floor and brought her knees up against her chest while she rested her back against the wall that had the mural of Athena's Bluff.

"I used to make her so angry." Zoe frowned and looked up to meet Elena's inquisitive eyes. "I couldn't kill her so I figured I would hurt her with my words."

"You were enemies. It wasn't as if she was your best friend."

"I was provoking her, really trying to niggle her into showing some emotion." Zoe sighed. "I thought she was a cold bitch."

"Eva is a master at being that."

Zoe flashed a look of irritation at the unexpected response.

"I mean she looks and behaves aloof, not the bitch part," Elena added quickly.

Zoe pursed her lips and shook her head. "What you think is coldness is just shyness. She's not cold or aloof."

"It's a little difficult to know with her, Zo."

Zoe let her head rest back against the wall and closed her eyes. "I was her maid, and I would help her bathe and other duties. One day I heard that the Resistance had succeeded in blowing up the train lines again. Every time they blew them up, the Germans would rebuild them. This time Muller rounded up some villagers just outside of Larissa and shot them." She stopped for a moment. "That morning I was helping Eva bathe. I was mouthing off, and I was rough with her." She wiped the tears that had tracked down her cheeks. "She was in such poor health, but I didn't care."

"Zoe..."

"No, it wasn't right, El." Zoe held up a hand. "I was the one being a bitch. Eva was helping the Resistance, but that didn't matter to me that morning. I hurt her with my words. She didn't say anything; just endured it. I kept at it for most of the morning. Eva was trying really hard not to let my words get to her, but they hurt her."

"She had her aloof face on?"

Zoe nodded. "The angrier I got, the calmer and quieter she got, until she couldn't take it anymore." She glanced up and sighed. "When I stopped my tirade to catch my second wind, I saw that Eva's hands were white-knuckled balled-up fists."

"She exploded?"

"Yes. She dropped the facade that my words were not affecting her and screamed at me. I didn't understand a word she was saying, because she was speaking so rapidly in German, and I was shocked into silence. A part of me was transfixed by the sight of this woman losing complete control and screaming at me. Good thing no one was in the house at the time or else I think we would have had all the guards come up and shoot me."

"Isn't that what you wanted, for Eva to lose control?"

"Yes, but not like that. I wanted to see some emotion; something to make me think she had a heart."

"Ouch."

"Eva didn't have any control over her life," Zoe said. "She had nothing. Her stepfather had her watched, and the villagers hated her. She couldn't go outside without armed guards. She wore this ugly hooded black cloak everywhere she went."

"She still wears it."

Zoe sighed. "Yes," she said. *She still wears that thing, but I'm not going to make her stop. She needs it.*

The two friends were silent for a few minutes until Zoe looked up at Elena. "Eva is not an easy person to get to know, El. Don't judge her because she looks like a cold bitch. She isn't."

"I didn't say she was a cold bitch."

"She is protecting herself. That cloak she wears... only makes her stand out more. She's over six feet, and that made her stand out as well. In Larissa, everyone knew who the woman in the black cloak was. They didn't need to see her. They called her 'The Hooded Nazi' amongst other taunts. Not many tall women in Larissa."

"What did you call her?"

Zoe looked up for a moment. "I called her a cripple bitch."

"You called her a cripple? To her face?"

"I didn't care. The last thing I cared about was her feelings. She had to endure this for three years from the villagers. Then there was me. She had to endure my hatred all the while she was risking her life by helping the Resistance and Father H."

"That would be impossible to deal with."

"She did it, and I never let go of the idea of killing her, so she must have worried that one day I was going to carry out my threat. I said it often enough."

"What did she do once she stopped her tirade against you?"

"She cried and told me she was tired of all the hatred directed at her. She thought I was her friend, and all I did was make her angry." Zoe's voice caught. "I barely stopped myself from blurting out that I wasn't her friend and what I really wanted to do was kill her."

"You didn't..."

"No, I didn't blurt it out." Zoe shrugged. "I told her to stop crying because cold heartless Nazis didn't cry."

"What did she say to that?"

"She said she wasn't a cold, heartless Nazi." Zoe grimaced. "She then put on that stupid cloak and walked out into the midday heat to get away from me."

"How long was that before she told you how she felt about you?"

"A year." Zoe smiled at the memory of that special night. "We learned that Father H was going to be sent on the same train that the Resistance was going to blow up. I got so angry that I just ran and yelled at the world."

"That's so unlike you, Zoe," Elena teased.

Zoe replied with a crooked grin. "Eva found me, and we talked a little in church before we went back to the house, but in my anger I traipsed mud into the house—a god-awful mess. Eva told the housekeeper to have a bath ready. We went upstairs." Zoe's grin widened. "She was so worried about me catching something."

"She really cared about you."

Zoe nodded. "She was anxious that I was going to get shot and then worried I would catch something and be sick. She was so surprised when I told her that she wasn't a boy and that I didn't like boys. You should have seen the look on her face. That's the night she kissed me for the first time. She paid a terrible price for that."

"What happened at Athena's Bluff?"

"She told me she loved me and that she will face the wrath of her stepfather because of it if he ever found out."

"Which he did?"

Zoe sighed. "He did, but we got through it. Athena's Bluff is where I realized I wanted to live more than wanting to kill as many Germans as I could and then die."

"That's an incredible story."

"She's an incredible woman." Zoe smiled. "All right, I've had enough of this going down memory lane. I need to cook dinner for my incredible woman."

Elena tried to get up from the sofa, but after a couple of attempts she held out her hand. "Help me up. This sofa is going to eat me."

CHAPTER 6

Dusk descended quickly, and the pink sky darkened as Eva drove her white car, affectionately nicknamed Aresti, down the jacaranda-lined street, and turned into the driveway. She scowled when she caught sight of Mabel. The presence of the motorcycle reminded her of Zoe's accident.

What she really wanted to do was take Earl's hammer and break it into little pieces, but she stopped herself. That contraption belonged to Zoe, and she had no right to do that. She parked the car and sat inside for a long moment. Despite not wanting to think about her stepfather's death, it seemed fate had conspired against her. She sighed. Well, she couldn't just run and hide from the world like she had been trying to do. Shaking her head at her own melancholy, she got out of the car.

Eva looked at the house. It was more than a house. It was a real home—a safe haven amidst a world that didn't understand them or would want to.

Whatever had happened during the day, she knew she

could leave it behind when she stepped through that door, but sometimes it wasn't what happened during the day that haunted her dreams. It had been a tumultuous few years, and the woman inside the house was the only reason Eva was still alive.

Sighing deeply, she straightened to her full height. "Stop this right now."

She stopped to take a sniff of the jasmine, which always reminded her of home, and then climbed the stairs to the front door. As she entered, she was greeted by the sound of Greek music and a pleasant aroma coming from the kitchen. She put her handbag down, took off her jacket, and hung it up.

She quietly made her way to the kitchen and leaned against the doorjamb. Zoe, oblivious to Eva's presence, was dancing and singing to the music while stirring the pot.

Eva snuck up behind her. "I could ravish you, and no one would hear you," she whispered in Zoe's ear as she put her arms around her and nuzzled her neck.

"Oh, my...please, no. I mean, yes!" Zoe said.

They laughed. Zoe turned in Eva's embrace and looked up into her eyes. "So, you want to ravish me?"

"That's the plan," Eva said, waggling her eyebrows.

"Well, I have to let you know that the love of my life is due to come home at any moment."

"Is that so?"

"Uh-huh. And you know, she is the jealous type."

"Is she now?"

"Oh, yeah. She is also the most beautiful creature God put on this earth." Zoe grinned and caressed Eva's cheek before teasing her dimpled chin.

"Can't be. I'm staring at the world's most beautiful

creature," Eva replied, getting a tender kiss from Zoe. "Hmm, I should remember that line. It gets me kissed."

Zoe playfully slapped her arm and giggled.

"So, Madame Froo Froo, what have you been up to today, apart from letting a strange woman attempt to ravish you?"

Eva thought the name was hilarious. She had earned it after they had visited the state fair and a woman claiming to be a fortuneteller wanted to predict Zoe's future. Eva didn't know where Zoe got the name Froo Froo from, but when the woman asked her name, Zoe came out with Madame Froo Froo. The fortune teller predicted that Zoe would find the man of her dreams, who would be tall, dark, and handsome. He would give her what she really wanted. She didn't finish the prediction because Zoe was laughing so much they had to leave.

Zoe was gazing up at her, and Eva knew right then that her attempt to hide the tears was a mistake. Zoe always knew.

"You've been crying." Zoe brushed Eva's cheek. "Why were you crying?"

Eva swallowed and tried to clasp Zoe's hand. "How do you know?"

"Well, your eyes are red, and I know when you're upset."

Eva didn't respond for a moment. She wasn't going to lie to Zoe, who knew her all too well, and there was no point in it. "Reality came and sat on me today."

Zoe looked into Eva's eyes for a long moment, took her hand, and kissed it. "Why don't you go and sit down, and I'll make us some tea?"

"To ease the blobs?"

"To banish the blobs."

"Okay." Eva leaned down and tenderly kissed Zoe's lips before she walked out of the kitchen.

Zoe sighed as she watched Eva leave. She wondered if someone at work had mentioned Eva's stepfather.

Zoe put the kettle on and picked up two cups. She heard Eva go into the bathroom and run the water for a few minutes. Family was important to Eva, and lately, she had begun to tell her about her childhood and growing up in a wealthy family in Germany. Little by little, the pieces of a giant puzzle were coming together. Zoe knew there were wonderful memories intermixed with the bad, and at some point those happy memories resurfaced. Zoe was glad that they had. Eva's childhood was so different from her own. She would dearly love to hear stories and see photographs of that time.

Zoe smiled at the memory of a picture of a very young Eva with her grandparents that used to be on the wall in Eva's room. The look on Eva's face made Zoe smile.

The kettle whistled, startling Zoe out of her thoughts. She put the cups down, the tea into the pot, and then put the kettle and the cups on a tray.

Eva came out of the bathroom and into the living room just as Zoe entered with the tea.

The living room was decorated with a mixture of both their artistic endeavors. On the walls were paintings by Zoe and photographs taken by Eva. On the mantle above the fireplace were photos of their family—Eva's father, Henry, their friends Elena and Friedrich, Earl, and David with his wife, Debbie.

Eva sat down on the deep burgundy sofa that dominated the room, opposite a massive fireplace, and stretched her long legs out on the white flokati rug that contrasted with the deep brown of the floorboards. To the right of the fireplace was a second-hand oak bookcase overflowing with books.

On the other side of the fireplace was a small table with a gramophone and a tidy stack of records—a mixture of Greek musicians, English jazz, and German operas.

Zoe put the tray down on an oak end table with white lace doilies next to the sofa and poured one cup of tea. She put a dash of milk just the way Eva liked it. She glanced up to find Eva smiling at her.

Zoe handed Eva the tea and watched as she sipped it. She decided not to make herself a cup of tea just yet and curled up against Eva.

"Why did you get the attack of the blobs?"

Eva sipped the tea for a moment. She put the cup down and looked at Zoe. "You know how I've been avoiding the wireless and the newspaper?"

Zoe nodded. "I did notice."

Eva closed her eyes and leaned back against the headrest for a few moments. She opened her eyes.

Zoe nestled her head against Eva's chest.

Eva smiled and kissed the top of Zoe's hair. "I had a client today who reminded me I was living in the real world."

"You were living in a make-believe world?"

"No." Eva shook her head. "I was trying to avoid the news."

"That doesn't work very well."

"Well, it does if everyone else is playing the same game, but Mrs. Fenstermacher wasn't playing the game."

"Ah. She showed you today's newspaper."

"Have you seen the paper?"

"I saw it at Mr. Harris' shop," Zoe replied. "The game worked for a while."

"I always play a different game."

"Not always. You just have a way of wanting to shut out the real world."

"What do you call that?"

"Survival."

Eva smiled and kissed Zoe's lips. "You're much too kind."

"It's how you got through Aiden. It worked then, and it works for you now."

"It works until reality hits me on the head." Eva shrugged. "Can I ask you a question?"

"Of course,"

"Is it wrong?" Eva gazed at Zoe with a lost look that Zoe hadn't seen in a very long time.

Zoe threaded her arm around Eva's arm and waited.

"Is it wrong to mourn for him?" Eva asked. "Even though he was a monster?"

"Even though he was a monster, later on, he was still your father. I don't think it's wrong." Zoe took Eva's hands. "It can't be wrong to mourn someone you love."

Eva sighed deeply and put her head on the headrest. She closed her eyes. "I'm torn between mourning him and knowing my mourning him is a betrayal to you."

"What?"

Eva opened her eyes, glanced at Zoe, and stared into the unlit fireplace. "I feel like I'm betraying you, your mother, the others that suffered and died...I'm betraying myself."

"Because you mourn for your father?"

"Yes."

"Tell me about him."

Eva turned to Zoe, looking confused. "You already know a lot about him."

"No, tell me something I don't know. Tell me something that he did when you were young."

Eva took a moment and then smiled.

Zoe wanted to shout for joy at the look on Eva's face. "Want to share it?"

Eva smiled. "When I was ten years old, I wanted to speak Italian because my father, my uncles, and my grandmother spoke it, and I thought it was such a beautiful sounding language." Her smile broadened. "I went to Papa and begged him to teach me." She laughed. "It was so much fun. We would sit at the dinner table, and he would say the word in German and then in Italian. I would go around trying out phrases and speak to the housekeeper only in Italian."

"How did that go?"

"It was confusing for Frau Milano...poor woman put up with me."

Zoe laughed.

"I'm sure she wanted to laugh at me, but she played along. When I could string several phrases together that made any sense, Papa decided to surprise me by taking me to Rome. I was in absolute heaven."

"Is Rome as beautiful as they say?"

"It's beautiful, and you would love it—so rich in history, and the artwork is just glorious." Eva put her arm around Zoe and pulled her closer. "I'm going to show you Rome one day."

"That memory is special to you, and you should treasure

it. Mourn for that man, the one who taught his daughter how to speak Italian and showed her the beauty of the country. Not for the man who was a monster."

Eva swallowed. "Thank you."

"*Ti amo, il mio amore,*" Zoe responded in the little Italian that she had picked up from Eva. She lovingly gazed up at her. "I will always love you," she said in Greek and then grinned broadly. "*Meine Liebe.*"

Eva rocked back and laughed. "You are just..."

Zoe brought her down for a passionate kiss to follow up her declaration of love.

"Incredible," Eva whispered as they gazed into each other's eyes. "Incredible."

"You know there is something you can never do."

"What's that?"

"Betray me or our love. So I don't want you to think that mourning your father would betray me or my mother or the others. You should mourn for him, Evy."

"Thank you, my love." Eva kissed the top of Zoe's head and hugged her.

CHAPTER 7

Eva hummed along with the third movement of Vivaldi's *Winter* coming from the gramophone in the living room. The third movement was her favorite, and she closed her eyes and smiled at the memories of sitting with her mother in a concert hall and marveling at the talented violinist who, without his knowledge, entranced a teenager with his talent.

She sighed. The warm water and soap on her hands from washing the cooking pot at the sink were her reality at the moment.

She was quite happy to leave the cooking to Zoe, who enjoyed it. The few times Eva had cooked were a culinary equivalent to allowing a tone-deaf singer into the Vienna Boys Choir. That was how Zoe had described it after she had valiantly tried to eat a German stew Eva had cooked. Her analogy of the tone-deaf singer had stung at first, but then she had to laugh because it was true. Zoe couldn't eat it even if she did love her dearly.

Eva wore light tan long shorts that reached down to her

knees and a lime green shirt, and she was barefoot. It was perfection itself to be out of her work clothes and not wearing shoes. She could go barefoot in the house, even in winter, if it weren't for Zoe's obsession with wearing slippers and worrying about catching a cold. Eva wasn't sure how catching a cold and not wearing shoes were related, but after trying to tell Zoe many times that she couldn't get a cold that way, she relented and wore slippers in the winter.

Zoe walked into the room, humming the music.

Eva turned around and smiled. "*Ciao, Bella.*" She flicked a bit of the soap suds on her hands at Zoe.

Zoe dodged the spray, came up behind her and put her arms around her waist. She rested her head on Eva's back. "Italian is such a beautiful language when you speak it."

"Isn't it normally?"

"It is, but no one sounds as sexy as you."

Eva smiled. "Are you going to help me with the washing, my Bella?"

"No, that's all yours."

Eva squirmed in Zoe's arms and giggled as Zoe tickled her. "I'm going to drop the pot." She held it up.

"No, you won't." Zoe lifted Eva's shirt slightly and slipped her tape measure around Eva's waist. She mumbled something that Eva couldn't quite decipher.

Eva turned around. Zoe sat down at the table, picked up her pen, and wrote something in her sewing book.

"Ooh, look." Eva dropped the pot into the water-filled basin, making the water splash over the sides.

Zoe half-turned and shook her head. "Do you want some dessert?"

"What did you make?"

"Baklava." Zoe went to the refrigerator and pulled the door open.

Eva couldn't quite get used to this addition to their kitchen. Their new refrigerator was more substantial than its predecessor and bright red. Zoe's favorite color was red, so as soon as she saw it, it was destined to go into their kitchen. Eva wasn't all that enthused with the salesman's sales pitch, but Zoe was sold when she saw the eggcups in the door crisper and ice trays in the freezer at the top.

Zoe held out the tray of baklava.

Eva snagged a small piece. "Hmm, this is good." She licked her fingers and gazed at Zoe as she put the tray on the table. "I love it when you do that."

"Do what?"

"That little hair tuck behind your ear," Eva replied and mimicked tucking her own hair behind her ear.

Zoe's red hair had grown over the winter months, and when she was in the sun, the red-gold highlights illuminated her face. Eva loved it so much she had persuaded Zoe not to cut it, not an easy task since Zoe liked her hair shorter. To her surprise, Zoe had agreed on the condition that Eva grew hers longer as well. She knew she had been out-maneuvered so she'd also relented.

Seeing Zoe with her long flowing locks made coping with her own long mane worth it. "The baklava is scrumptious."

Zoe looked up and grinned. "You say that about everything I do."

"Not everything."

"Really?"

"Hmm?"

"What don't you like about me?"

Eva nibbled her lip and tried not to smile at Zoe's look of mock outrage. "You crack your knuckles."

Zoe put her hand over her mouth in mock horror. "Oh, dear." She grinned and proceeded to crack her fingers, which made Eva wince. "You don't like that, eh?"

Eva grabbed Zoe's hands. "No, I don't, but I love everything else about you. *Come, sei bella.*" She repeated it in German and Greek, which earned her a kiss.

"Multi-lingual sweet talker."

"That's me, the female Don Juan." Eva turned to finish rinsing the pot.

Eva turned to say something but stopped when she spotted Zoe was rubbing her thigh. She turned back to the sink for a moment and then decided she wasn't going to ignore it. She placed the dripping pot in the dish drainer, dried her hands on the towel, and got down on her haunches next to Zoe so she could be eye to eye with her.

"*Ciao, bella.*" Zoe smiled and cupped Eva's cheek. "It doesn't sound sexy when I say it. Can I have a kiss?"

"Oh, no, you're very wrong. It sounds very sexy." Eva kissed Zoe on the lips. She rested her hand on Zoe's thigh. "Is your leg hurting tonight?"

"It's a dull ache that won't go away. How did you know?"

"You were rubbing it," Eva replied quietly as she put her hand on Zoe's knee.

"Woke up this morning feeling a little sore but it's all right."

"You didn't say anything. Remember what we agreed..."

"Evy, do you tell me every time you get up in the morning that you're feeling sore?"

"I don't have to; you already know."

"Not all the time."

"Is it annoying to you that I worry about you?"

"No." Zoe shook her head and took Eva's hands. "I know you worry about me because you love me, but you will give yourself an ulcer if you worry every time I get on Mabel."

"You na..." Eva stopped. What she was going to say wouldn't be the right thing to say. "You worry about me all the time as well."

Zoe smirked.

Eva sighed in resignation. "Is there any way I can get out of this with my pride intact?" She gave Zoe her best puppy-eyed look.

Zoe laughed. "You know that works on me every time."

"Does it really?"

"You know it does. Those sad, droopy, blue eyes. How long did it take you to perfect that look?"

Eva just smiled. "It comes naturally." She stood up, gave Zoe a quick kiss, and went back to the sink. She smiled when Zoe followed.

"Good girl, now don't slouch."

Eva shook her head and stood to her full height.

Zoe went down on her haunches next to her to measure her.

"Zoe..."

"Oh, come now, Evy, it's taken me weeks to create this pattern, and I want to see you in it."

"Zo, we can go—"

Zoe looked up at Eva. "Yes, we can go to the department store and buy you a new outfit, but it won't be the one I'm fantasizing about." She got up, put the measuring tape on the table, and turned back to Eva, who was grinning at her. She put her arms around Eva's waist and looked up. "I want to see you in something I've created, and it's going to be very beautiful." She stood on her toes and kissed Eva lightly. "I need a better view. Help me up."

Eva helped Zoe up onto the bench top. Zoe opened her legs and captured Eva's body and brought her close.

"Comfortable?"

"I am now." Zoe cupped Eva's face and stared into her eyes. "When I was confined to my bed, I drew all sorts of outfits for you."

"Like little girls do for their cut-out dolls?"

Zoe chuckled and nodded. "Yes, but I have a living doll. Some of my designs are just...well, let's just say you can't wear them outside our bedroom."

"Zo...you see me naked all the time."

"Yes, but what does that have to do with it? It's my fantasy."

"Your fantasy?" Eva couldn't quite believe it, but a blush traveled up Zoe's neck to light up her face. "Are you blushing?"

Zoe grinned. "I've had this fantasy for a long time. I've drawn it, but it's not the same. I want to see the real thing. You dressed in a fire engine red costume with horns and a tail—a cute demon. Oh, my goodness, I got all hot and bothered just talking about it." She fanned herself with her hand. "I've drawn it, now I have to see you in it."

"I won't have to wear it outside?"

Zoe's gently tapped Eva's cheek and said, "Don't worry, only you and I will see it."

Eva shook her head and laughed at Zoe's vivid imagination. It had led to some unusual situations, and none of them was her idea.

Eva took Zoe's hands and held them for a moment

before she brought them up to her lips and kissed them. "You still fantasize about me?"

"What do you mean do I still fantasize about you?"

"There's nothing left to fantasize about," Eva said quietly, unsure why she was feeling insecure at that very moment.

"What?" Zoe asked. "Do I still fantasize about you?"

"Yes."

Zoe sighed. "I've been fantasizing about you since we met."

"Well..."

"All right, maybe not since we met," Zoe amended and smiled. "Maybe a few days after we met. I fantasized about you when I wasn't even sure why I was fantasizing about you. I've had dreams about you; I've had daydreams that would set off the fire alarms in a dozen theatres."

"A dozen?" Eva asked, feeling a little goofy for even voicing one of her most profound concerns.

"At least," Zoe replied.

"Are the dreams good?"

Zoe cocked her head and regarded Eva for a moment. "No. Reality is much, much better."

They gazed at each other for a long time.

Eva took in a deep breath. "Wow."

"You didn't know that?"

"I...um...I..." Eva didn't quite know how to give voice to the little doubts in her mind or if they even made any sense.

"You don't feel the same way?"

"Oh, I do, I do..." Eva rushed the words out, not wanting Zoe to think she had any doubts about her. "It's me."

"What?" Zoe shook her head. "I sound like one of those scratched records."

"Zoe, I'm thirty."

Zoe grinned. "Yes, I know. I planned your birthday party."

"And you are twenty-two."

"Yes, I know that too. Thank you for reminding me."

Eva nibbled her lip and wondered if Zoe hadn't thought about the age difference before. "Um."

"What is going on up there?" Zoe gently touched the side of Eva's head. "What is going on up there that has been going around and around for a long time, if I know you?"

"I'm a lot older than you."

"Yes, we have already established that."

"I'm...you...may..."

"What are you talking about?"

"I have this fear that one day you will wake up and will see and won't..."

"Stop!" Zoe grabbed Eva by her shirt and brought her closer. Eva stared into her wide green eyes. "Do not tell me that one day I'm going to wake up and have fallen out of love with you."

"I—"

"Don't utter those words; don't even utter a syllable." Zoe gently put her fingers over Eva's full lips. "There is never going to be a world where I won't be madly in love with you. There will never be a time when I open my eyes and the eyes gazing back at me won't belong to you."

"Z—"

"Shhh," Zoe admonished. "You love me, don't you?"

"Yes, I love you." Eva's voice broke a little, and she tried not to let the tears come. "It's nothing."

"Shhh. If you love me and I love you, what is the problem?"

"You are missing out."

Zoe's head fell backward, and she looked up at the ceiling. With a sigh, she looked back at Eva. "You must be out of your mind."

"What?"

"You have gone totally insane. I think we need to call that mental asylum..."

"That's not even funny." Eva scowled.

"Oh, stop that." Zoe smoothed out the crease between Eva's eyes. "You are out of your mind. I have no idea how long that's been going on in your head, but it does need to stop. Yes, I am younger than you. Yes, you are eight years older. So why is this a problem other than the reason you have cooking up in that pretty head of yours?"

"I don't know," Eva said as she put her arms around Zoe. "I don't know. I just feel something is going to happen."

"It is going to happen."

"What?"

Zoe grinned and looked sobered. "Life will happen, Evy. Life will happen like it's happened to us. Some good, some bad, some downright unbearable. It's happening."

"I don't want anything to change."

"You don't have a say," Zoe responded, much to Eva's bemusement. "It's out of your control."

"What if..."

"What if my green eyes turned blue? I don't think that's possible."

"Zoe, be serious."

"I am serious. I'm not going to wake up one morning and not want to be with you."

"How—"

"Holy Mother of God," Zoe exclaimed. "Good God,

woman, you just have to look at me, and I fall to pieces. Don't you understand?"

Eva nodded, trying not to cry.

"You love me, don't you?"

Eva nodded.

"All right now. I love my old lady, and that isn't going to change. I'm not sure why you are feeling so unsure about my love for you. Was it my teasing that you are my old lady?"

"No." Eva shook her head. "It's not that. I have this bad feeling something is going to happen to us."

"What?" Zoe asked and shook her head at using that word again. "I think it already happened, love. Remember...Me, motorcycle, tree."

"It's not that. I don't know. I just have this feeling."

"Well, we don't know what that feeling is, but can we talk about it in the living room where I can cuddle up on a nice sofa rather than this hard bench?"

"I thought you liked it up here."

"I do, but I think this needs cuddle time to go with it."

Eva kissed Zoe before helping her down off the bench. She watched Zoe for a moment and then took her hand and led her into the living room.

CHAPTER 8

The evening breeze fluttered the lace curtains in the living room and brought the hint of impending rain. The temperature had also dropped a little but not by much. Eva stretched out on the sofa and Zoe lay beside her with her head resting on Eva's shoulder.

Zoe looked up and smiled as she lightly traced Eva's dark brows with her fingertip and kissed her softly.

"Is it going to rain?"

"Yes, it is, and I would love to talk about the weather but... Evy, what's going on up there?"

"A lot of thoughts rumble up there."

"You overthink."

"Isn't that what God made it do?"

"I think He gave you an extra dose of the thinking portion," Zoe gently teased. "I think I know what's going on."

"You do?"

"You hit thirty, and you think I'm going to run off."

"No."

"If it's not that, then what is it?"

Eva closed her eyes before she looked down to see Zoe's steady gaze. "I can't give you what you want."

Zoe blinked. "What do I want that I don't already have?" She scowled when Eva didn't answer. "What don't I have?"

Eva sighed deeply and looked up at the ceiling. "Children."

"Er..." Zoe was stumped. Children were the last thing on a list of things that might be wrong. "Children?"

"Yes."

"Evy, hmm." Zoe shifted to where she could see Eva's face. She gently tipped Eva's face towards her. "I don't think you are capable of giving me, children." She tweaked Eva's dimpled chin.

"I'm serious, Zoe."

"I know you are, but who said anything about wanting children?"

"You."

"Me? I said to you that I want you to give me children? Did I do that when I was on my pain medications? Because if I did, then I was out of my mind."

"No." Eva shook her head. "It was at the party. You and Elena were discussing babies and..."

"Oh, that." Zoe mentally slapped herself for being so stupid. She had seen a flash of something on Eva's face. She thought nothing of it until now.

"Do you want children?"

"Do I want them? Yes, I'd love to have children. Can I have them? No," Zoe said honestly. "If it were possible to have them, I would have a dozen, but I'm afraid it's not possible."

"What if it was?"

"You are now being silly."

"I'm not.".

"Yes, you are," Zoe insisted. "I don't believe we are even having this conversation."

"Why?"

Zoe mentally rolled her eyes. Most people thought she was stubborn, but they had never encountered Eva's stubborn streak. She could latch onto a topic and never let it go until she dissected it into oblivion. "Other than the fact that we are both women?"

"Zoe—"

"Other than the fact that having sex with a man would be tantamount to me jumping off the Harbour Bridge?"

"Just—"

"Evy, are you serious? Do you want me to have sex with a man?"

"No!" Eva's voice rose.

Zoe blinked in surprise at her vehemence and volume. "All right then. No sex with a man and that is the only way this woman is ever going to have children."

"There are other ways."

Zoe hitched herself up on her elbow and stared at Eva. "You are out of your mind. What in the hell is going on up there?"

"I want you to have what you want."

Zoe groaned and slapped herself on the head. "Ow. Nope, I'm not asleep. This would be a crazy dream if I were. So let me understand this. You want me to have children, but you don't want me to have sex with a man."

"Yes."

"My name is not Mary, and there won't ever be an

Immaculate Conception part two, so there." Zoe nestled back down. Eva's body shifted, and a very light laugh emanate from her. *Bingo!* She mentally gave herself a slap on the back for getting Eva to laugh.

"Zoe, it is possible."

"No, I don't think the Immaculate Conception part two is possible...why would it be? He's already come once; how many more times does He have to come down to earth?" Zoe continued, knowing full well what Eva was saying, but it was an area that wasn't going to be any good for either of them.

Eva turned to her side and regarded Zoe with a half-smile. She cupped Zoe's face tenderly. "I know what you're doing."

"What am I doing?" Zoe asked and smiled.

"I want you to have everything you have ever wanted."

"I already have everything I've ever wanted. Even when I didn't know what I wanted, I had it. Can we please stop this? I want you to stop thinking about this. It's upsetting me. I already got angry today."

"At me?"

"No, not at you, but you thinking I want to have children and be unfaithful to you makes me sick to my stomach."

"I'm sorry." Eva put her arm around Zoe and brought her in for a kiss. "It's just..."

"I know how you are feeling, but it's time to stop, all right?"

"Yes." Eva nodded. "What upset you?"

"I got a letter from Thanasi today." Zoe reluctantly let go of Eva and rolled off the sofa onto her knees and quickly went to where she had scrunched up the letter. She came back with a very crumpled note and smoothed it out against her thigh before she sat down.

"What did he say?" Eva asked.

"You got a letter from Father H, and I think it might be better to read that first before I go off on my tirade against the Greek golden boy."

"Oh, dear, all right. Do you want to read it?"

Zoe went to get the letter, settled back next to her, and ripped it open. "*My dear daughters, I hope this letter finds you both well and happy. I pray every day that Zoe hasn't crashed Mabel again.*' What a funny man."

Eva chuckled.

"'*I'm feeling better each day. The weather has been good for my health, and the change in climate is just what I needed. I'm going to Trikala for a dip in the artesian waters, which should help my leg a bit. I am blessed with two daughters who have made me a pleased old man. I love you both, more than you will ever know. Here I am, crying like a baby. I have some exciting news to report—Thanasi is getting married!*'"

"Is that what upset you? Thanasi getting married?" Eva asked. "Go on."

Zoe scowled and then went back to the letter. "'*I never thought I would see the day. His fiancée is a lovely young woman. Her name is Althea, and I have enclosed some photographs of the lovely couple. The wedding is going to be a huge event here. Larissa loves her hometown heroes, and all the town will be at the wedding. It will be a wedding to remember for a long time. Give my love to Henry, Earl, Elena, and Friedrich. I keep both of you in my prayers every night. I love you both. Love, Father.*'" Zoe sighed. "I miss him."

"So do I, but I think the Greek climate is better suited to his health. Why are you angry with Thanasi?"

"I'm not angry with Thanasi. I'm angry at the news he brought me." Zoe held the crumpled letter. "The government has passed a law that says landowners have to reclaim their property."

"Alright."

"Thanasi wants me to go back to Larissa and make sure the fields, Thieri's cabin, the house, and the farm are all claimed."

"Look at you—I married a wealthy woman," Eva teased.

"Your wife won't be a wealthy woman in a few months."

"What do you mean?"

"I'm not going back." Zoe crumpled the letter and threw it in the direction of the fireplace. It missed and landed on top of Eva's stack of books.

They looked at each other and smiled.

"You have to, Zoe, this is your inheritance."

"My inheritance can go rot. I'm not going back."

"Zoe, come on." Eva got up, bringing Zoe with her. "You have to go back."

Zoe scowled at Eva and shook her head. "I'm not going back. I don't want to talk about it now."

"All right but..."

"Evy, what did I just say?"

"You don't want to talk about it." Eva put her arm around Zoe as they settled back down on the sofa.

Zoe glanced at Eva and mentally shook her head. *There is no way I'm taking you back to hell. Mama and Papa will understand, and even if I lost everything, she is worth more to me than anything Larissa has for me.*

"Zoe..."

"Yes?"

"I love you."

Zoe looked up at Eva's face in the semi-darkness and the smile that reached the blue eyes. "I sure hope so. You're stuck with me."

CHAPTER 9

July 03, 1950

Elena sat on the veranda sipping a cup of tea. She had been feeling out of sorts all morning with twinges that she thought were contractions but were false starts. She was sure she had been quite challenging to live with, but her husband was a saint. He never complained, even when he was woken in the middle of the night to get Elena a drink of water or chocolate.

Elena's patience had evaporated with each day that passed. She was tired of being pregnant, tired of her sore back, tired of her sore legs that gave her all sorts of problems. Pregnancy did not agree with her. Despite that, she was eagerly looking forward to seeing her baby.

"Hey." Zoe came around the corner from her house and sat on the steps opposite her. "How is the mama-to-be today?"

Elena put her hands on her belly and grimaced. She

crooked her finger, and Zoe rose a little to get a kiss on the cheek. "I'm hot and bothered. How are you?"

"I'm alright."

"Are you over being irritated with Eva?"

"I'm not irritated with her; I'm just annoyed she won't let this go." Zoe nodded. "She doesn't understand, El."

"Being irritated is the same as being annoyed, Zo. I'm on Eva's side on this. I don't understand it either. That's your home; that's your inheritance."

"I know it is."

"Ah." Elena nodded. "So why have you been having an argument with her for the last two weeks?"

"We are not having an argument. She is insisting I go and I'm insisting I'm not going. That's not an argument, that's-"

"Sounds like an argument to me."

"Evy wants me to go to Larissa, and I don't want to go. It's a simple case of stubbornness on her part."

"Her stubbornness or yours? Why don't you want to go back?"

"Because."

"Because is not an answer."

"You sound like a mama."

"I'm getting some practice being one with you at the moment."

Zoe smiled. "I don't want to go."

"You are a stubborn old goat. Let's not play this game. Just tell me why you don't want to go."

"I'll have to leave Eva here."

"She's a big girl, and she can handle you being away for a few months."

"What?"

"Eva wants you to go back to Larissa."

"No."

"Hasn't she been telling you she wants you to go?"

"She wants me to go and get the job done."

"So what is the problem? I don't understand."

Zoe stayed quiet, making Elena think she may not answer. "I can't leave and go away without her."

"That's not a problem, Zoe. Take her with you. Is it the money? I know it's expensive and you have been off work for a while. Freddy and I can lend you the money-"

"No, money is not the problem. We have enough for the both of us to travel." Zoe shook her head. "I can't take her back to Larissa."

"I don't understand why you don't want to go back with Eva if money isn't the issue. Please, help me out here and tell me why. Are you worried about what the village will say?"

"What? No," Zoe replied vehemently. "I'm not ashamed of Eva, and I don't care what Larissa thinks of me."

"If it's not that, then what is it?" Elena put her weight on the table to get up. She felt a searing pain shoot through her, and she sat down again. "Argh, that wasn't good." She grimaced as a second jolt hit her. "Oh boy, not good at all."

"What's wrong?"

"I think Baby No Name wants to come early." Elena exhaled in relief as the pain receded once again.

"Oh, no, she can't." Zoe stood in alarm. "No, no, no."

"Yes, yes, yes." Elena almost chuckled. Another contraction hit. "Oh, Zoe, I think we'd better go to the hospital."

"Oh, the hospital." Zoe got up and disappeared around the corner, leaving Elena still sitting on the chair.

Elena shook her head and tried to get up herself.

A moment later Zoe rushed back, looking very sheepish. "I forgot to get you."

Zoe held Elena's arm and helped her up. Elena leaned against Zoe for a long moment, and they slowly made their way down the path from the backyard to the front, where the car was parked.

"Oh, this isn't good," Zoe muttered and helped Elena sit in the front.

"Zoe." Elena put her hand on Zoe's arm to get her attention. "You want to stay calm a little."

"I am calm," Zoe replied and fumbled with the keys to the ignition. "Oh, yes, really calm."

"I can see how calm you are," Elena mumbled as Zoe swore under her breath when the key fell.

She picked it up and inserted it into the ignition. She then stopped and swore loudly in Greek. "I can't drive," she muttered in disgust. "You have to."

Elena gave her a look and then pointed to her belly. "I don't think so, Zoe. Call a taxi." Another contraction hit her. "Oh, boy."

"Oh, a taxi won't get here fast enough." Zoe's head fell on the steering wheel. After a moment she looked up. "I got it."

"Please, don't give it to me. I've got enough to worry about," Elena mumbled.

"Don't go anywhere." Zoe raced out of the car and disappeared down her own driveway.

Elena took deep breaths and counted until Zoe came back.

Zoe quickly came back out of the driveway on her motorcycle with the sidecar.

"Oh, no."

"Come on." Zoe hopped off and ran around to Elena's side and helped her out of the car. "I've cleared away everything in the sidecar, and it's going to be perfect."

"You said you weren't riding Mabel again. You promised Eva! The perfect way to kill us." Elena scowled at the sidecar. "Don't go fast."

"I promise to drive really carefully, and Eva will understand."

Elena shook her head, took Zoe's hand, and let her help her get into the sidecar. It was a very tight fit.

"Zoe."

Zoe strapped the leather helmet to Elena's head, patted her belly, and put on her leather gloves.

"Yes?"

"Forget what I said about going slow okay?" Elena grimaced as another jolt of pain hit her.

"Oh, okay." Zoe fumbled with her keys again. "Damn it." She started the motorcycle.

She gunned it, and they roared off down the road with Elena clutching the sides of the sidecar for dear life.

CHAPTER 10

"How long have you been waiting?"

Zoe turned towards the woman seated next to her and sighed. "Six hours."

The woman knowingly smiled. "Ah, early days. My name is Jenny."

"Zoe Lambros." Zoe extended her hand. "Early days?"

Jenny shook her hand. "Six hours is nothing. Is this her first?"

"Yes."

Jenny rolled her eyes and chuckled. "Oh, my goodness, that might take longer. I remember when I had Henrietta. Well, goodness me, that took well over twenty-four hours, and I remember the poor lady who was next to me, well, she had twins."

"How long did it take her?" Zoe asked, not really wanting to know the answer but feeling it necessary to ask.

"Oh my, how long did it take?" Jenny pursed her lips in thought. "Oh, I think that was longer. Two precious babies."

"Is this Henrietta?" Zoe asked as a young girl sidled up to Jenny with a drawing in her hand.

The child looked at her with a broad smile. Blonde curls framed a heart-shaped face with bright blue eyes, and a sprinkling of freckles made Zoe smile.

"Indeed it is. This is Henrietta Louisa."

"Hello, my name is Henrietta Louisa Anderson," the child said with no trace of shyness, which surprised Zoe. "What's your name?"

"Zoe Lambros," Zoe replied. "How old are you?"

"I'm four!" Henrietta replied and held up four fingers. "Look!" She gave the piece of paper she was holding to Zoe.

"Oh, goodness, this child hasn't got a shy bone in her body," Jenny exclaimed as Zoe took the paper.

Zoe smiled. The artwork was a giant sun, and that was about all Zoe could discern. "That's great."

"You like it?"

"I like it."

"You can keep it," Henrietta exclaimed.

Zoe nodded. "Thank you."

Henrietta looked pleased with herself. She gave her mother a smile and then went back to her drawing.

"My daughter, the social butterfly," Jenny proclaimed and laughed.

"You know they're Freddie's babies because they're taking forever to get here."

Zoe looked toward the sound of the voice echoing down the corridor. Moments later Henry, Earl, David, and Eva walked in. Earl carried a giant bouquet of flowers.

"Hey." Zoe waved to Eva.

She stood up and, mindful of the people around her, deliberately toned down her welcome for Eva. They looked at each other for a brief moment before they hugged. She went to Henry, Earl, and David and gave them a hug.

"Where is the daddy?" Earl asked as he put his arm around Zoe.

"They came and got him about an hour ago. Let's go outside," Zoe said quietly to Eva.

Zoe and Eva walked a few yards down the corridor and out the door to an empty balcony that faced the quiet road. Eva sat down in one of the chairs and waited for Zoe to drag over the other chair and sit next to her.

"What I wouldn't give to kiss you right about now," Zoe whispered.

Eva gave Zoe a very chaste kiss on the cheek. "That's all I can give you, my little hero."

Zoe giggled. "I'm so glad you are here."

Eva lit up a cigarette, took a drag, and exhaled. She offered the cigarette to Zoe, who took it, took a puff, and then handed it back. Zoe didn't smoke but would occasionally take a puff of Eva's cigarette. It was a habit she had just recently begun, much to Eva's delight, Zoe had discovered. Smoking was Eva's way of relaxing.

"Are you alright?" Eva asked. "Debbie said you called when I was out and I couldn't come sooner."

"I know. She said you were in a meeting. I'm good now," Zoe replied. "Elena's waters broke, and then I was going to take the car."

"But you can't drive."

"Yes, I remembered that." Zoe chuckled. "So the only way was to get Elena into the sidecar. I promised you I wouldn't ride Mabel again, but we had no way of getting to the hospital in time-"

Eva gently placed her finger against Zoe's lips. "It's alright, and I understand."

"You're not upset?"

"No, I'm not upset. You had to take Elena quickly, and you were careful. It's good that you rang me after you were at the hospital for my own peace of mind, but I'm not upset."

Zoe sighed with relief and smiled. "Time for me to learn how to drive a car."

"If you want to. It's far safer than a motorcycle."

"Would that stop you from worrying?"

"No," Eva admitted, a slight smile playing on her lips. "I worry anyway."

"Less so in a car. Want to hear about our adventure with El in the sidecar?"

"That must have been a rough ride."

"Well, it wasn't easy. We got stopped by the police."

"What?"

"I was speeding down Legacy, and you know that police car that sits there just around the corner? Well, he saw me, and the sirens went on, and we got stopped."

"Oh, dear." Eva put her hand on Zoe's shoulder. "What happened?"

"Well, Elena was in pain and speaking German, I was panicked and speaking Greek, and the policeman was confused until he realized what was going on." Zoe giggled. "We got Elena out of the sidecar and into his car, and he sped away."

"That baby is going to have quite a story."

"What was your meeting about?"

"Something," Eva said cryptically and took a drag of her cigarette.

"Something?"

"Hmm, work-related."

"Really?" Zoe noticed Eva had turned away from her and was looking out at the traffic. "Evy, look at me."

Eva turned back to Zoe. "Yes?"

A light tap sounded on the window behind them. They turned around to see Earl beckoning them inside.

Eva stubbed out her cigarette, and they went back inside to find a beaming Frederick handing out cigars to everyone in the waiting room.

"Boy?"

Frederick shook his head. "Just as good—a little girl."

"Aren't cigars for boys?" Earl asked as he took one.

"I don't care, my friends," Frederick exclaimed and slapped Earl on the shoulder.

"How is Elena?"

"Tired, but she wants to see you."

"Me?" Zoe asked.

"You and Eva. I'll take the boys to see my little girl," he said and put his arm around Zoe's shoulders. "Thank you for being there."

"You've already thanked me. A few times," Zoe replied and was taken aback when the usually reserved Frederick kissed her on the cheek.

Zoe and Eva were ushered into the room where Elena was resting.

"I have a baby," Elena exclaimed as Zoe and Eva hugged her.

Eva sat on the nearby chair, and Zoe sat on the bed, holding Elena's hand.

"We heard," Zoe said.

"You haven't seen her yet?" Elena asked.

"No. Freddy told us you wanted to see us."

Elena regarded Zoe with an exhausted smile. "That was hard work." She made a face, which caused Zoe to giggle. "This was going to be a surprise for later, but I couldn't wait, so I wanted to tell you now."

"What's that?"

"Well, as you both know, we don't have any family other than you, Henry, Earl, and David. In the Jewish tradition, we don't have godmothers as you do."

"You don't?" Zoe asked.

"No, but Frederick and I want our girl to have someone who can look out for her and love her in case we are not around." Elena looked at them. "Life is so fragile. We want both of you to be their legal guardians if the worst happens."

Zoe glanced at Eva, who was sitting ramrod straight, and saw her look of utter shock. Then a huge smile creased her face.

Eva got up and stood next to Zoe. "I don't know what to say." She took Zoe's hand. "We're not Jewish."

"Frederick and I know that if anything happened to us, you would care for her."

"Of course," Zoe answered and felt Eva's hand tighten.

"We want to make this legal, and when I get out of here, Frederick is going to draw up the documents."

"You are serious, aren't you?" Zoe felt a little lightheaded that Elena was entrusting them with such responsibility.

Elena nodded. "Very serious. You do want to do this? I can give you time to think about it?"

"No," they said in unison.

Zoe looked up at Eva. "We would be honored."

"I'm so glad. I have something else to tell you." Elena

grinned broadly. "Well, when you go down to the nursery, you need to say hello to Rebecca Jacobs."

"Thank you." Eva kissed Elena on the cheek.

Zoe sat back on the bed and took Elena's hand.

"Zo," Eva said after a few moments. Zoe turned around to meet her gaze. "I think we should let Elena have some rest."

"Oh, yes, indeed." Zoe hugged Elena again, and they left the room to head down to the nursery.

Eva took Zoe's hand and held it for a long moment. She brought Zoe's hand to her lips and kissed it. "This is quite an honor."

"Yes," Zoe responded as they walked down to the nursery.

When they got there, Henry, Earl, David, and Frederick were congregated in one area.

Frederick greeted them with a kiss on the cheek. "Elena explained everything? Good. Now come and meet my little girl."

Sleeping soundly in her bassinet was baby Rebecca with her dark hair peeking out from her pink bonnet.

"Oh, my goodness, she is so cute." Zoe put her face to the glass and grinned broadly.

CHAPTER 11

THE TRAM STOPPED AT A RED LIGHT, AND THE standing passengers took a collective lurch forward, then back. The afternoon was hot, and the last thing any of them wanted was to be stuck on a tram with dozens of their fellow citizens.

Eva wrapped her arm around the metal pole, feeling the coolness of the metal against her cheek, and closed her eyes. She shook her head and wondered why she had to go into work today, a Saturday no less. An influx of new migrants had arrived, and the interpreter department was utter bedlam, which meant everyone had to go to work.

"Excuse me, love."

Eva made room for people to get off the tram and resumed her spot against the pole. She hated taking the tram, especially on hot days, but Aresti refused to work that morning.

The tram lurched to a stop, and Eva realized it was her stop. She made her way to the door and down the two steps to the pavement. She looked up into the cloudless heavens and sighed.

She was thankful she wore sensible shoes as she rushed down the street and into the cul-de-sac. Earl drove his car up into the driveway just as she neared her house.

"Ah, my adorable Evy, the love of my life." Earl smiled broadly and blew her a kiss.

Earl was, for all intents and purposes, Eva's boyfriend or fiancé, depending on who was doing the asking. They made a show of it every time they appeared together outside. It was to both their benefits. Earl was a teacher, a well-respected man in the community. Eva went to school functions as Earl's girlfriend, and Earl attended functions with Eva as her boyfriend. The long-standing joke in the neighborhood was that Earl was gun shy and wouldn't commit. Eva played the long-suffering girlfriend.

Earl took a couple of strides towards the end of the driveway and waited for Eva to catch up. Eva was about to give him a peck on the cheek.

"Mrs. Walkins is watching us. Kiss me," Earl whispered.

Eva smiled, took one step into his arms, and kissed him on the lips. They parted and looked at each other. "Is she still looking?"

"Yep," Earl said and leaned in for another kiss. "Your kissing is improving."

"Ha." Eva cupped his face and looked into his eyes. "Your beard is annoying. Shave it off. Still looking?"

"Nope, gone." Earl chuckled. "I'm keeping my beard. It makes me look professorial."

"Makes you look like someone who doesn't want to shave," Eva teased.

"Leave my beard alone. So, why are you walking?"

"Don't know why, but Aresti refused to start." Eva gazed into her driveway at the vehicle. "I'm hot, I'm tired, and my gorgeous girl is home without me."

"Was she babysitting?"

"She was until the morning when Elena picked up Rebecca."

"So the love of your life is home alone, just waiting for you? Bet she had other plans."

Eva laughed and gently slapped him on the shoulder. "Good thing the love of my life isn't here to hear you. Are you free tonight?"

"Let me check my dancing card." Earl tapped his bearded chin in thought, much to Eva's amusement. "Why, yes. I am free. Are we going out?"

"No, you're coming to dinner."

"Are you cooking? I'm fully booked if you're cooking."

"Oh, funny man." Eva threaded her arm around his bicep, and they walked the short distance to her house. "No, we need to talk about a boyfriend for Zoe."

"All right. Why?"

"We're getting more and more invites to attend functions, and with Zoe's presence at the gallery, she needs one."

"How do you feel about it?"

"I would rather pluck out my eyes than see Zoe with a man," Eva admitted. "Even if that man is a pretend boyfriend."

"Have you talked about this with Zoe?"

Eva pursed her lips. "I have, and she has resisted."

"But?"

"As much as I hate this, the work she does at the art gallery will mean she will have to attend functions. You know how those places are. If she doesn't have an escort, it looks odd."

"Hmm, I know," Earl replied. "Patrick is in the same boat. He's going to be moving to the same school as me, and he will need a girlfriend for the many and varied, lovely functions we need to attend."

"I hate this charade," Eva said in exasperation.

"I know." Earl put his arm around Eva and kissed the top of her head. "What about Patrick and Zoe?"

Eva smiled despite her frustration at the current predicament she found herself in. "How serious are you about this boy?"

"Very serious."

"Do you think he will want to be Zoe's pretend boyfriend?" Eva would have laughed at the stupidity of the situation, but couldn't shake the unease she felt. The thought that Zoe was going to be kissed by someone other than herself made her stomach churn.

"He will have to be. He needs Zoe too."

"Alright, boyfriend, bring Patrick over for dinner."

"It's a date, m'lady." Earl bowed and tipped his imaginary hat to her. He straightened, gave Eva a quick kiss on the cheek, and walked back to his neighboring house.

"I do love that man, but he must shave off that terrible beard," Eva mumbled. "I hate beards."

Eva made her way up the paved walkway to the stairs. She entered to find the house unusually quiet. She put her bag down and took off her hat. She walked down the hallway and into the living room. Her eye caught the telegram on the table. She picked it up and scowled. *Come on, Zoe. How many more of these are you going to ignore?*

Need you to come to Greece. Urgent matter to clear up Zoe or else the State will own everything.

Zoe's inheritance. The government's new laws collided with Zoe's stubbornness. At the moment Zoe's legendary stubbornness was winning.

This is going to change. Determined she was going to sort this out today, Eva went looking for Zoe in the kitchen only to find it empty. The back door was open, and she caught sight of Zoe out in the garden.

Zoe got up from where she was kneeling and took off her hat. Placing a mud-covered hand on her back, she straightened from weeding the garden and wiped the sweat from her brow. She was dressed in one of Eva's shirts, which hung long and covered her white shorts.

"She does have a very cute behind," Eva said and chuckled. Ourania jumped onto the counter and rubbed up against Eva. "Don't you think so, Ourania?" She picked the cat up and gave her a cuddle. "Time for another cuddle." She put Ourania down on the counter.

She washed her hands and picked up a watermelon near the new icebox. She quickly cut into it and scooped it out.

"Zoe!"

Zoe turned and grinned. Eva came down the stairs with the cut-up watermelon in a bowl.

"Just in time." Zoe greeted her with a kiss. "Ooh, watermelon."

"So, are you going to come inside or wait until you get sunstroke?"

Zoe grinned as she ate the watermelon, the juice flowing down her chin. "Sunstroke sounds nice. Then you'll have to give me some tender loving care."

"I'll give you that even if you don't have sunstroke." Eva put her arms around Zoe.

"I know." Zoe waggled her eyebrows.

Eva laughed. "Let me go and change. I have to tell you what happened today."

"Busy?"

"Very busy."

"I'll finish up here."

Eva gave Zoe a quick kiss before she turned to go back inside. She nearly stumbled over the water hose and got an idea as she bent down to coil it up. She looked back at Zoe, grinned, and turned on the water. She crept to the kneeling Zoe and put the hose down the back of her shirt.

Zoe yelped in alarm and shot up. "Ugh!"

Eva squealed. She ran for the stairs to escape and tripped on the hose.

Zoe caught her and brought her down on the grass. "You are going to pay for that, Miss Eva."

"Oh, no. Have mercy on me," Eva beseeched.

Zoe, dripping wet, laughed, brought the hose closer, and put it under Eva's shirt.

Eva yelped and tried to fend off Zoe's hands and the hose. "I surrender."

"Okay, you live to fight another day." Zoe threw the hose into the tomato patch.

"Oh, Zoe, I'm wet."

Zoe leered at her and then giggled.

They lay on the wet grass, staring up at the cloudless blue sky, their fingers interlocked.

Eva turned and smiled at Zoe, who wore a smile that she could never tire of seeing. "We need to get up and get changed."

"We do."

Eva nodded and remained where she was.

"You're going to catch a cold if you don't."

"You don't catch colds like that."

"*You* do." Zoe sat up and gazed down at Eva. "Come on, remember the last cold you had..."

"That wasn't a cold. It was bronchitis." Eva sat up and watched Zoe get up from the grass and turn to pick up the hose. Her shorts were transparent from the wet.

"Evy, stop looking at my ass and get up."

"Why? I like the view from here."

"You are going to catch a cold sitting on the damp grass and in those clothes."

Eva took Zoe's hand and brought her back down on the grass. "Zoe." Eva hesitated. "You received another telegram."

"I did. I don't want to talk about it."

"We have to."

"No, I don't want to talk about it. It's my inheritance, isn't it?"

"Yes." Eva sighed. "But—"

"But nothing. I don't want to talk about it."

"Alright," Eva said, already resigned to the fact Zoe was not going to change her mind. "There's something else we need to talk about."

"What?" Zoe asked a little tersely.

"I asked Earl to come to dinner and bring Patrick with him," Eva said and steeled herself for the explosion. "Earl and I thought that Patrick would be a good boy—"

"What?" Zoe angrily asked and stood up.

"You need a boyfriend." Eva finally said the words she

dreaded saying to Zoe, knowing how emotional Zoe was about the issue.

"No." Zoe shook her head. "There is no way on God's green earth I'm going to have a boyfriend to please people, or God for that matter, who I don't particularly like."

"Zoe—"

"No," Zoe replied. "I will not do that."

Eva sighed. "You know why we have to do it."

"I know why, but I don't want to. Not now, not ever. I understand why you have to be with Earl, and I fully support that. I just don't like it." Zoe looked up and met Eva's gaze. "I don't like seeing you kiss Earl, and he acts like you're his trophy."

"He doesn't act that way, love."

"I know it's not the real Earl, but that's how it looks. It's like, 'look at my beautiful girlfriend.' What rot."

"You know Earl needs his school to know he is a man with a girlfriend."

"I know."

"People—"

"All those people," Zoe punctuated the air with her hands at the imaginary people, "can kiss my behind if they think I'm going to kiss some boy because they want me to."

Eva knew that Zoe was now thoroughly steamed and anything she said was going to get her into trouble, or more to the point, get her into even more trouble than she was in.

"Zoe, Patrick is—"

"I don't believe you are begging me to go kiss a boy."

"Oh, love." Eva put her arm around Zoe's shoulders and kissed her cheek. "I'm not trying to do that. I would rather pluck out my eyes than see you with anyone else."

"Welcome to my life." Zoe sighed. "Every time Earl kisses you, I just feel like screaming."

"I don't enjoy it."

"I know you don't, but I can't help myself."

"I know."

"No, you don't." Zoe shook her head. "You don't know what it's like. I've lost count of how many times I've wanted to hold you as he does in public. He kisses you, Evy, and that just infuriates me." She balled her fists. "I'm going inside before I say anything else that will hurt you. I'm going to change since we have company."

"Alright."

Zoe left Eva sitting on the wet grass and wondering how it all got out of control. *Well handled, Eva. Well managed.* She looked back at the house and sighed. She would just let Zoe cool down before she went in.

CHAPTER 12

EVA SCOWLED IN THE DARKNESS AS SHE SAT UNDER the tree in their backyard. She braced her back against the tree trunk, trying to figure out how the conversation with Zoe had gone terribly wrong. She hated fighting, hated the feeling that she had lost control, and what was worse, she had started it. She knew that Zoe despised the idea of what she called cover-up boyfriends. She wasn't thrilled with the idea, but she was used to it.

She shook her head. *Used to it. What an ugly thing to get used to. Used to lying. Zoe said I couldn't lie very well, but she's wrong. I do it every day. I'm getting quite good at it.* She sighed in frustration. *Yes, dummy, you tell Zoe that you are used to it. She would really like that.*

How did you manage to really make this even worse than it is? Stupid, Eva. Stupid. You know how she feels about it. Yet you blurt out something so stupid..."

Zoe came out of the living room and walked into the kitchen hoping Eva was there, but she wasn't. "Yeah, well, what do you expect? You yell at her and then you run off. Brilliant work, genius."

She noticed the door to the yard was open and stood at the threshold. She could make out Eva's very distinctive form under the tree.

"I bet I know what she's doing, Ourania," Zoe said to the cat, who had followed her from the living room and was brushing up against her leg. She stepped out on the veranda and down the steps.

"Would you like some company?" She waited for Eva to acknowledge her.

Eva looked up.

"I'm sorry...," they said in unison and stopped when they realized they were both apologizing.

Eva beckoned for Zoe to sit with her. Zoe sat in between Eva's legs and leaned back using Eva as a cushion. She closed her eyes when Eva wrapped her arms around her waist.

"You first," Zoe said and smiled.

"Me first," Eva quipped, earning herself a gentle tap on the leg. "I'm sorry. I'm a stupid woman. I didn't intend to tell you that way."

"Is there a way to tell your wife that she should have a boyfriend?"

"I don't know, but I should have been more sensitive, more aware..."

"I still would have blown up as I did. I'm sorry I did that. I hate fighting."

"Me too."

"I think we should be mad at the idiot people. They are the ones who want me to have a boyfriend."

"I don't know." Eva brushed Zoe's hair away from her

neck and kissed her. "I don't know. All I know is I hate fighting."

"You're not very good at it."

"I'm good at lying."

"What?" Zoe half-turned to see Eva's face and noticed her unshed tears. "What?" She moved completely around and held Eva's hand. "What did you say?"

"I said I've become good at lying."

"Who said that?"

"You did."

"When did I say that?"

"You said that I was convincing in showing people that I loved Earl."

"Yes, to people that don't know you. You are not a very good liar. Your face gives it away."

"How?"

"Your eyebrow twitches," Zoe said. "You have a very expressive face."

"My eyebrow twitches?"

"Yes." Zoe traced the dark eyebrow. They gazed at each other, and Zoe leaned in for a kiss. "You are not a good liar. You have never been a good liar. I have no idea how you could fool anyone who truly knew you."

"Fooled you in Larissa."

"No, you didn't. I saw past that cold bitch routine even back then. Trust me, if I had known what I know now, there is no way you would have fooled me even for a second."

"So I'm a lousy liar but good at convincing people."

"Not even that. Earl does a better job at convincing people you two are together. He's the one that initiates all the touching and the kissing." Eva blinked in surprise, much to Zoe's amusement. "I pay attention. You are just following

Earl's lead. That's what I realized when I was thinking about our fight. You don't initiate. You follow."

"I never thought about it."

"You don't think about *that*. Remember how you told me that you were used to it?"

Eva rolled her eyes. "Yes."

"You are used to it. You are used to the lie you have to live, but that doesn't mean you are good at it. I wouldn't care if I told the world how I feel about you, but I would like to tell the world to go to hell."

"You have told the world to go to hell." Eva smiled. "You rode Mabel because it wasn't a polite thing to do. You enjoyed shocking people like that lady in the department store when you were shopping last Christmas."

Zoe giggled at the memory of when she played with the saleslady. "I did enjoy that."

"There's the difference. I don't do that. You do."

"You tell the world to go to hell by surviving what they did to you," Zoe said, quietly. "Every day you are alive, you tell them to go to hell."

"That's a lot of telling off," Eva joked, which made Zoe smile.

Zoe turned to sit on Eva's lap and rested her head on Eva's shoulder. "Larissa."

"Hm," Eva said and waited.

"There isn't much I can do. I'm here, and they are over there."

"Yes, but you can go over there."

"Really?" Zoe gave Eva a suspicious glance. "How do you think that could happen?"

"It's easy enough to do, love. There are ships," Eva teased.

"Right."

"Zoe, seriously now, you can't let your inheritance just disappear."

"It doesn't matter to me." Zoe shrugged.

"You really don't want to go and claim what's yours?"

"No."

Eva sighed. "Why don't you want to go?"

"I won't go without you."

"Who said you would be going alone?"

"I said it."

"I'll be with you."

"No." Zoe shook her head. "I'm not going to drag you to Greece for some bricks and some dirt."

"You can't drag me," Eva teased, earning herself a very angry look. "Come on now, Zoe…"

Zoe took Eva's hand and held it for a moment before she looked up. "It will tear you apart to go back to that place. It will tear me apart to know that I did that to you."

"It won't tear me apart."

Zoe grunted. "Larissa nearly killed you."

"You were also in the war zone," Eva gently reminded her.

"I lived there."

Eva sat quietly for a moment. "I fell in love and was reborn there. It's not all horrible memories. It's not my favorite place, but I can bear it for a few days."

Zoe frowned. "You would endure it for a few days?"

"Yes. I endured it for three years. I think I can manage three days. I also think falling in love trumps getting shot." Eva kissed Zoe.

Zoe remained stone-faced. "Evy, I don't—"

"Zoe, this is your inheritance. You can't disrespect your

family's memory this way. Not because you can't leave me or you think I can't bear it for a few days. Your family will always be important whether they are alive or dead."

Zoe cupped Eva's face in her hands and gazed at her. "You are my family. They are no longer around, but you are right here."

"They will always be around. Always. Your parents, your brothers; they will always be in your heart and in your mind." Eva sighed. "I'm alive. You see me every day, but they are not. What's left is their gift to you. You can't disrespect their memory. It's not right."

"I saw what Larissa did to you."

"I'll have you beside me," Eva replied before kissing Zoe's hand.

"Do you think family is so important?"

"Yes."

"So if we go to Greece, will we go to Germany?"

Eva sighed.

"You are willing to go back to hell for me," Zoe said as she held Eva's hands in her own. "We will go to Germany. For you. You need to visit your mama's grave."

"I can't argue against it when I've just told you about your family."

"No, you can't. I know you don't want to, but you won't get another chance, as I don't want to stay in Larissa after these property issues are resolved. We don't know if we will ever go back to Europe, so now would be a good time to pay respects to your mama."

"I know." Eva nodded. "Germany...that will mean you will go into hell for me."

"I'll have you beside me." Zoe gazed at Eva in the dim light for several moments. "I'm getting a boyfriend."

"Sounds like we're getting a puppy."

Zoe looked up and smiled. "Boys are like puppies."

"I hear they are house trained."

"So are puppies after a while." Zoe giggled. "Patrick? Earl's Patrick?"

"How many Patricks do we know?" Eva chuckled. "Earl seems to be in love with him. He's a teacher, and he looks alright."

"Mousy-colored hair, grey eyes, good-looking, he's got a scar above his eye, but that's okay," Zoe stopped and noticed Eva's incredulous look. "I'm an artist, so I notice these things. He's a little taller than you."

"So he's good boyfriend material?"

"Earl seems to think so." Zoe laughed at her own joke. "Hey, that's a good one."

"If you say so," Eva chuckled as she cupped Zoe's face. "I'm sorry I was insensitive."

"I'm sorry I blew up," Zoe responded.

Eva slipped her hand behind Zoe's neck and gave her a passionate and sultry kiss. The kiss turned into two, and then three until Zoe moaned at the incredible feel of the tongue teasing her own.

Bam.

Eva broke off the kiss, and Zoe groaned in frustration. They looked in the direction of the noise.

Earl took two steps from his backyard to their yard through the connecting gate. He grinned and sat down cross-legged in front of them. "You were kissing."

"Yes," Zoe growled in frustration.

Earl chuckled. "Hmm, I interrupted."

"You did," Eva replied.

"So how did you like my warning signal?"

"What was that?"

"My cricket bat." Earl chuckled. "Do you often make out under the tree?"

"How long were you there for?" Zoe asked.

"Just saw you kissing."

"We had a fight," Eva responded.

"Oh, so I really interrupted some good kissing." Earl pushed up on his arms to get up. "I'll let you continue your making up."

"Sit down." Zoe pulled Earl's hand. "We can continue the kissing later."

Out of the darkness, Patrick walked up to them with a bottle of wine and some flowers. "Good evening, ladies..." He leaned down for a quick kiss on the cheek to Eva and Zoe, sat down gracefully, and crossed his legs. "So what are we doing tonight?"

"We interrupted their kissing," Earl said.

"You interrupted our kissing," Eva corrected him. "Patrick was more polite."

"Pfft." Earl waved his hand. "When's dinner?"

"Soon," Eva replied as Zoe turned and sat between her legs and leaned back against her chest. "We have something to ask Patrick."

"Now?" Zoe turned slightly and looked up.

"It's a good time."

"Alright."

"Patrick, we have a favor to ask of you."

"Hmm?"

"Zoe is going to need a boyfriend, and you need a girlfriend."

Earl and Patrick exchanged looks and then gazed at Eva.

"We were talking about that before we got here," Earl said.

"I'm getting transferred to Earl's school next week, and you know how those people are about knowing all about your life." Patrick got up and went down on one knee in front of Zoe and took her hand. "Will you be my girlfriend?"

Zoe was stunned into silence and blinked. "Uh..."

"Well, you won't see that every day...Zoe is speechless," Eva said.

"Stop that." Zoe tapped Eva on the knee. "Of course...I guess this works for the both of us."

Patrick kissed Zoe on the cheek. "I'm going steady...hey E, I'm going steady with a girl. My mother would be so proud." He chuckled and sat back down. "I know it's going to be difficult for you and for me."

"We were also discussing that before you two came," Zoe said.

"So was that what the fight was about?" Earl asked. "Can we talk about this at dinner? I'm starving." He signaled his watch.

"Alright, let's go eat, and we can figure this out," Eva said as Zoe got up and held out her hand for her. Eva stood and looked down at Zoe for a moment. "I love you," she whispered and kissed her.

"Ewww, stop that. I'm going to go blind," Earl said as they walked inside the house.

CHAPTER 13

July 5, 1950

Soft moonlight filtered through the lace curtains, and a stiff breeze caused the curtains to flutter as Zoe stirred in bed. The other half of the bed was empty. She yawned and lifted her head to look into the bassinet to make sure little Rebecca was asleep. The bassinet was also empty. It was their first-night babysitting, which allowed the Jacobs to get a good night's rest. *Someone is going to be very sleepy tomorrow. Should I get up? I'd better, and also see if Eva needs help.* She yawned again and stayed where she was for a few more minutes. She threw back the blanket, got out of bed, and put on her slippers.

She heard Eva's voice. She stood still for a moment and then decided to sit on the floor beside the door, which was ajar.

"So little Rebecca, it's just you and me. Aunty Zoe is asleep," Eva said. "Your mutti and papa are also asleep."

Zoe shook her head at Eva's soft voice.

"I hope one day you will be kind and gentle like your mama," Eva said. "I also wish you would be like your Aunty Zoe and be fearless, strong, and just have the gentleness she does. She is my knight in shining armor. The look in her eyes when she sees me, whoo. Burns me right up. You don't know anything about that now, but wait until you grow up. You will find someone who loves you that much. Your papa and mutti love you so much, and one day you will see their love."

Zoe brought her knees up and rested her chin on them, unable to stop herself from listening. *I'm a knight in shining armor?* She knew Eva loved her. There was no doubt about it. But she never saw herself the way Eva did.

"Do you know what I would love to have in the whole wide world?" Eva said, and then stopped, causing Zoe to lean forward in anticipation.

"I want to have a baby, Rebecca. Just like you. I want to hold one of my own and to give them a loving home. It won't happen, little one. My stepfather saw to that. Your papa won't be like that. He's a good man. He won't rip your heart out and shred it into a thousand pieces. I want to give Zoe what she wants too. A little Zoe running around would just about be perfect. Just like you."

Zoe's eyes glistened on hearing Eva's desire, the longing in her voice, and the despair at her stepfather's treatment. Eva's wish would never be realized for herself. It was impossible.

"You know, little one, I think I'd better put you back to bed because if I don't get some sleep, I'm going to be a very cranky Aunty Eva."

Zoe very quietly and quickly got back to bed and lay there, waiting for Eva to return. Eva's heartfelt longing broke her heart. If she could give Eva that wish, she would. She wasn't sure how, but there had to be a way.

The bedroom door opened, and Eva walked in with Rebecca, who was now fast asleep. Eva very quietly put the baby in the bassinet. She removed her robe and slipped under the covers. Just as she closed her eyes, Zoe leaned over and kissed her.

"Oh, I woke you," Eva whispered. "I'm sorry, love, the baby wanted a feed."

"I heard you, Evy." Zoe wrapped herself around Eva. She took her hand and held it. "I want to give you what you want."

"How much did you hear?"

"All of it," Zoe replied as Eva gazed back at her, the moonlight catching the unshed tears in her eyes making Zoe's heart ache that much more.

"I can't ask you to do that. I can't."

"You're not. I want to do it. I want to give you what that bastard stole from you. I want to have a baby with you. I'm not sure how we're going to do that, but there has to be a way."

"Really?" Eva lifted herself up and rested her back against the headrest. She gazed at Zoe in amazement. "You would do that?"

"Yes," Zoe whispered as she put her hand on Eva's scarred lower belly, the constant reminder of her unbearable loss. "I want to be the one to give you what they took away."

"Don't promise me that. I don't think I could bear it if you changed your mind." Eva's voice broke.

Zoe didn't need light to know Eva was crying. She sat with her legs tucked under her, took Eva's hand, and met her gaze. She wiped the tears from Eva's cheek. "I promise I won't change my mind. I give you my word."

Eva swallowed and nodded, and then kissed Zoe tenderly. "You know what this will mean."

"Yes, I know." Zoe nodded. "I may have a solution to that."

"What?"

"I was raised on a farm, Evy. I saw Papa trying to impregnate the animals..."

"Your father was impregnating the animals?" Eva smiled through the tears.

Zoe stopped and blinked in the darkness. She chuckled. "Um, no. I saw Papa do it once."

"You saw your papa doing it once?"

"Stop that." Zoe tapped Eva on the arm, which only made Eva chuckle. "You know what I mean."

"I don't know how we are going to do that, Zo."

"I do. We get a book, and we study up on impregnating animals. I'm sure there is a book on that. Then we follow what they say. Nine months later, we have a baby."

Eva gazed at Zoe for a long moment. "I don't think it's that easy."

"Well, I saw my father do it, and nearly nine months later we had a calf."

"A cow is pregnant for nine months?"

Zoe giggled and nodded. "Actually it's eight months and a half. You didn't know that?"

"I'm not from a farm, and it never occurred to me to ask about cows," Eva responded.

"Well, lucky for you, I was born and raised on a farm, and I know these things."

"Wasn't the pregnancy courtesy of the bull?"

"Sure, when there was a handsome bull around," Zoe replied and grinned on seeing Eva's eyes widen. "Sometimes we couldn't get the bull, but Papa could get bull semen."

"You watched when all of this was going on?"

"Of course. Mama hated it because she said it was no place for a young lady, but I would watch. I was also there when the cow gave birth."

"Let me guess, you named the calf?"

"Yes! You can't go nameless even if you are a cow," Zoe replied.

"So how are we going to do it? There may be a lot of handsome boys, but I don't want them anywhere near you."

"Well, Papa used a long syringe that looked like a turkey baster."

Eva blinked. "A turkey baster? Do you mean like the one we use for turkeys? Really?"

Zoe giggled. "Have you used a turkey baster, Evy? You city girls have a lot to learn about farming. Yes, Papa used a long thing that just pushed the semen into the cow."

Eva screwed up her face, which only made Zoe laugh. "I'm sure we will find a more elegant way."

Zoe gently cupped Eva's cheek and kissed her. "We're going to make a baby, and it won't involve finding the most handsome boy around."

"We're going to make," Eva's voice broke, "a baby." She closed her eyes.

Zoe kissed her and Eva sniffed back tears. Zoe laid the pillows flat, opened her arms, and Eva curled up with her head on Zoe's shoulder.

"I have one condition," Zoe said.

"What's that?" Eva sniffed back the tears.

Zoe gazed at her and smiled. "I want the baby to look like

you. I want her to have dark hair, blue eyes, and a dimpled chin."

"I don't think you can order one like that."

"We will find a way. God owes us." Zoe looked down to find Eva's eyes were closed, her cheeks tear-stained, but Zoe was sure they were happy tears. She drifted off to sleep, dreaming of dark-haired children with blue eyes.

CHAPTER 14

July 12, 1950

A LOT HAD CHANGED since they finally decided to head back to Greece and Germany. It was a whirlwind of activity to get the necessary leave from work to allow them to be in Greece before the government's deadline.

They also decided on the ship and date for going back to Europe. Eva knew the ship's schedule since the latest batch of migrants was in the waiting room. They only had four weeks to make all the necessary arrangements.

Eva walked back into the Interpreter Department with a hot cup of tea and was about to take a sip when she caught sight of Debbie trying to attract her attention without calling out in the middle of a bustling waiting area. It was yet another busy Monday. Migrants speaking in hushed voices crowded into the small waiting area, which was not the most welcoming of places. Hard wooden chairs and dog-eared copies of the Woman's Weekly magazine littered a corner of the room.

"Psst!"

Eva looked around to see if anyone was behind her. She turned back to the now bemused receptionist.

Eva smiled and approached Debbie. "Psst?"

"Where have you been?"

"Morning tea, tea room, over there." Eva pointed towards the Staff Room. "Before that, I went to Personnel."

"I have something for you."

"Every time you tell me that, I'm busy for the rest of the day," Eva grumbled good-naturedly. "How many today?"

"You have four waiting, but that's not it. This is." Debbie handed Eva a flyer. "You're sailing on the Arcadia, aren't you?"

"Yes." Eva took it and read it aloud. "Filmmakers following Returning Refugees Back to Europe."

"That's interesting, isn't it?"

"It is. They usually want interpreters to be on staff permanently." Eva wanted to get back to her office and drink her tea before it got cold.

"Yes, normally that's what they are after, but I spoke to the lady who was giving these flyers out, and she tells me that they are looking for one or two interpreters for this trip to help out with the regular staff. I asked her what type of people they wanted and how much they paid and all of that. I specifically mentioned that you were sailing on the ship."

"You told her about me?"

"Yes, I hope you don't mind. I know you are very private, what with your father being who he is…"

"Yes."

"I thought you wouldn't have a problem. Turns out that

since you are sailing on the ship, if you get the interpreter job, then your cabin will be upgraded to first class. You booked the tickets already, didn't you?"

"Yes." Eva nodded.

"I told Miss Pinfold you can speak four languages and you were traveling on the same ship."

"What did she say?"

"She asked if you were Jewish."

"Ah." Eva sighed.

"She wasn't enthusiastic at first, but when I told her you were German, she was very interested. I told her you were traveling with your friend. She wanted to speak to you if you would be interested. If you accepted the job, then Zoe would be included since you are sharing the same cabin."

Eva pursed her lips in thought. She would have to work, but that meant they would get a first-class cabin and more room. She could give Zoe four weeks of luxury before leaving the ship in Athens. She smiled. "I'll give her a call."

"I took the liberty of making an appointment for you to see her at three pm after your final client." Debbie handed Eva a piece of paper with the woman's name, the office location, and the time.

"Thank you, Debbie." Eva took the paper and, teacup in hand, she proceeded to her office.

She closed the door and gazed down at the paper. *Zoe is going to be so happy.* She smiled.

Eva went to her desk and sat down still smiling. She sipped her tea as her eyes fell on the silver ring on her finger. Her mind went back to another ship and a tiny cabin. She had been quite sick with the flu that was running through the refugees. She spent the day trying to pluck up the courage to ask Zoe about their future together. They were on the same journey, but Eva wasn't sure if at the end of the voyage they would still be together. It was not the best way to ask Zoe to be with her, but it turned out better than she had hoped for.

Eva sighed contentedly as she played with the ring. Yes, that was some journey, and Zoe patiently waited for her to start healing from the damage done to her in Aiden.

"I think a first-class cabin for my girl on this trip is perfect," she said to the empty office.

"Are you serious?"

"Yes, I'm serious," Zoe said as she made a funny face at the baby in her arms and played with the tiny fist. "You are adorable."

"Zoe, focus for a moment." Elena clicked her fingers in front of Zoe's face. "You are going back to Greece?"

"Yes."

"I thought you said you didn't want to."

Zoe looked up and shrugged. "Eva convinced me that my family's inheritance is worth it."

"That doesn't sound right to me."

"Which part?"

"All of it," Elena replied. "You don't care about the inheritance, and you don't want to go back to Greece."

"I know."

"But you are going without Eva?"

Zoe shook her head. "Eva is coming."

"Ah." Elena nodded. "That's why you are going."

"Eva wanted me to go back home and didn't want me to give up my inheritance. I wasn't going to go without her, so she said she was coming with me."

"That's going to be hard."

"I know," Zoe replied as baby Rebecca gurgled in her arms. "It's been only five years."

"It's going to take more than five years for the people to heal."

"I don't think they ever will, El. Can you forgive those bast... er? " Zoe glanced down at the baby. "Sorry Rebecca, Aunty Zoe said a bad word."

Elena grinned. "I don't think she understands you yet."

"Can you forgive the Nazis, El?" Zoe looked up and instantly knew the answer to that question. Elena was a Holocaust survivor, and it was evident she was never going to forgive.

"Eva wasn't a Nazi. She was part of the Resistance."

"She was the enemy. Doesn't matter that she was helping the Resistance. Most of them don't know that. She's the Butcher's daughter. Imagine that, El, her going back to that hell."

"Why are you making her do this?"

"I'm not making her do this," Zoe said defensively. "She practically begged me to go."

"There's another reason. There has to be. You don't give in that easily."

Zoe turned to Elena and smiled. "Sometimes I do."

"No. I've known you for three years now, and in those three years, you have never surrendered or backed down. If I had a wager on whether you would go to Greece, I wouldn't lose it."

"Usually." Zoe smiled down at the baby. She gazed up at Elena. "I surrender what I want when it comes to Eva. Always. You just don't know about it."

Elena blinked. "That's the first time you've said that to me."

"I know. Eva comes first. She always will. She wanted me not to lose my inheritance. We talked about it, and I gave in." Zoe didn't usually talk about her intimate conversations with Eva to anyone, including Elena, but this was different.

"What are you going to do?"

"We will stay in the cabin on Athena's Bluff," Zoe explained. "I want to stay only for a few days, finish up this inheritance problem, and move out of the place. Maybe head to Thessalonica and spend a few days there."

"Then back home?"

Zoe shook her head. "No. We're catching a train to Germany."

Elena stared at her in shock. "You are going to Germany?"

"Yes."

"Oh my." Elena put her hand over her mouth in surprise. "Why?"

"I surrender to Eva." Zoe smiled. "Eva surrenders to me. I asked her. It's probably going to be the last time we will be in Europe, and she can't leave without paying her respects to her mother. It wouldn't be right. It wouldn't be fair. She needs this; her heart needs this." Her voice broke, and she looked away, trying not to let the tears flow. "I'm doing this for her. It's a small price to pay."

"It's not a small price, my friend." Elena sat beside Zoe and put her arm around her shoulders. "It's not a small price. You are going into the heart of the enemy."

"I hear the war has ended," Zoe joked. "I know, El, but this is for Eva. She is going back to her hell for me."

"I'm very proud of you." Elena kissed Zoe on the cheek. "Will you be going to Berlin?"

"Yes, Eva grew up in West Berlin, in a borough called Zehlendorf."

"Zehlendorf? That is a very nice neighborhood. We lived in Berlin-Mitte. That's very close to where we had our shop, and we lived upstairs."

"It is? Maybe we can go by and see if it's still there?"

Elena bumped her shoulder against Zoe. "I would be astonished if that shop is still standing. I don't think it's there anymore."

"How do you know? It might be."

"No, my friend, it's gone. Everything we owned was taken from us, so nothing is left."

They sat quietly for a long moment, baby Rebecca making most of the noise.

Zoe turned to Elena. "I will go to the shop and see if it's still there."

"Zoe..."

"We will go. Just give me the address, and we will go." Zoe smiled and kissed Elena on the cheek.

CHAPTER 15

August 14, 1950

"What?" Zoe scowled at the letter. She was sitting in the Journey Room, having finished off the last of the painting she was to deliver to the studio in the morning. It was well past midnight, and Eva had gone to sleep.

Zoe reread the letter.

My dearest niece, it is with such heartfelt relief that we hear you are well. We couldn't believe it when Father Haralambos informed us that you are safe and well. Your Uncle Dion, myself, and Maria are eagerly looking forward to seeing you after your long journey back home.

Zoe made a face at the cat. "I am home, silly woman." Ourania looked up at her mistress for a moment, stretched, and laid her head down again. "I know, this is boring you as much I'm bored reading it."

Zoe stared at the mural of Athena's Bluff before she went back to the letter.

My dearest niece, we have some great news to share. We are not sure if you remember Kiriakos Vaskos. Kiria Despina, the best matchmaker in all of Greece, assures us this young man is very suitable.

"I don't believe in hell but, if I did, hell would freeze over, and the demons will be ice-skating before that happens. Kyriakos? Ourania, they want to marry me off to some boy. Do you believe that?"

Ourania ignored her.

Zoe turned away from the cat and back to her letter.

We will discuss this when you come home. I'm sure there will be a lot of delicate issues we need to address that can only be discussed in person. Hoping this letter finds you well. Godspeed, your beloved Uncle Dion, Aunt Keramia, and your cousins Maria, Petros, and Magdalena.

Zoe got up from the sofa and crumpled the letter in disgust. "I bet Evy is asleep."

She put away her easel and took off her art smock. She quietly turned off the light and went into their bedroom, which was cast in semi-darkness, the only light coming from a full moon filtering through the lace curtains.

Zoe gazed at Eva, who was fast asleep. The evening was hot, and Eva wore nothing more than a white singlet and underwear. She lay on her back with the white cotton sheet pooled at her feet. Zoe grinned at Eva's pink panties—a funny reminder of Eva's first laundry disasters. It seemed like yesterday they had fled war-torn Larissa and made their way to Egypt to await the refugee ship. Two fragile souls sailing on a ship to a country on the other side of the world, far removed from the war in Europe.

Zoe turned to the open window and lowered it, but left it ajar. Eva always wanted to sleep with the window open, and Zoe wanted it closed. So they found a compromise. Zoe smiled.

They had reached that compromise on the journey to Australia when Zoe found out that Eva felt claustrophobic and needed the porthole open while she slept. Eva didn't tell her, but she woke every night and opened the window, and then went back to sleep. Zoe awoke in the morning to find the fresh breeze blowing into the cabin, and thinking the porthole latch was faulty, reported it to the crew. They played that game for a week until Zoe woke and found Eva opening the porthole. Zoe then patiently extracted the reason why Eva was doing that.

But you didn't tell me it had to do with Aiden. A lot of things have to do with Aiden, that god-awful demonic place, Zoe mused as she watched Eva sleep, her face relaxed and looking much younger than her thirty years.

Zoe took off her clothes and slipped under the covers. She scowled and glanced at Eva. She rolled over and very gently shook Eva.

Eva didn't move.

Zoe leaned over Eva. "Evy?"

Silence.

"Hmm," Zoe muttered and laid her head on Eva's arm. "Evy, wake up."

Eva made a noise.

"Evy, wake up."

"Wha..." Eva mumbled.

"I have to talk to you."

"Hmm."

Zoe waited for a few moments and realized Eva had fallen asleep again. "Evy, I need to talk to you."

Eva grumbled and turned her head towards Zoe. Very sleepy eyes opened and regarded her. "Are you sick?"

"No."

"Hmm." Eva closed her eyes. "Someone dying?"

"No."

Zoe smiled as Eva yawned. "You are so cute in the morning."

"What time?"

Zoe leaned over Eva's body to barely make out the clock on the night table. "Nearly one am."

Eva sighed. "Zoe..."

"I know, I know, but I've been thinking."

"Oh."

"I've been thinking about our trip, and these thoughts keep running around in my head..." Zoe realized Eva had fallen asleep. "God, I love you, but you really need to wake up." She kissed Eva on the cheek. "Evy, I need to speak to you."

After another gentle shake, Eva's eyes popped open, and she gazed at Zoe. "Am I going to sleep tonight?"

"Yes, as soon as we talk about this."

Eva sighed as she hitched herself and rested against the headboard. "Alright, I'm awake."

"Do you want a cup of tea?"

"Are we going to chat til mornin'?"

"It is morning." Zoe grinned when Eva gave her an exasperated look. "Technically it is."

"Zoe."

Zoe cuddled up beside Eva and took her hand. "I received a letter today. Not today but yesterday, but I only found it today."

Eva smiled and closed her eyes. "Uh-huh."

"I have to tell you about my cousin Maria and her family."

"Alright," Eva replied sleepily.

"When I was eight or nine years old, we were celebrating Easter at my uncle Dion's farm," she related, getting more comfortable snuggled up to Eva, who she thought was awake but had closed her eyes. "It was a big gathering with all my uncles and aunties, my grandmother, and all my cousins. The men were outside smoking and doing what men do."

"They often do that," Eva mumbled.

"Me and my cousin Maria—"

"Which Maria was this?"

"My uncle Dion's Maria."

"How many cousins did you have called Maria?" Eva asked.

"Six," Zoe replied.

"What about your aunty Stella?"

"Stella doesn't have children as far as I know..."

"Why were they named Maria? Did they run out of names?"

Zoe shrugged. "Every son in our family wanted to name a child after their mother."

"But not your father?"

"No, Papa didn't want another Maria Lambros in the Lambros clan. I was named after my mother's mother."

"And how many cousins do you have named Zoe?"

"None. There's just one Zoe, and I'm it." Zoe leaned over Eva's body to retrieve Eva's cigarette case and lighter from Eva's bedside table. She lit the cigarette and took a drag before she gave it to Eva. Eva opened her eyes and smiled before she took the cigarette from Zoe's fingers."

"This is going to be a long story, isn't it?"

"Yes, but not too long."

"Alright," Eva mumbled as she took a drag of the cigarette. She blew the smoke and turned to Zoe with a smile. She leaned down and kissed her tenderly on the lips.

"Now this I like," Zoe said before stealing another quick kiss.

"So what happened with Maria?"

"I'm not sure who suggested it, but we wanted to smoke as well. I knew where Uncle Dion kept the papers that he used to roll up his cigarettes, so we snuck into his room and we took a couple." Zoe laughed. "We couldn't find the tobacco he used, so we decided to make our own."

"Uh oh..."

Zoe gave Eva a gentle poke. "I thought tobacco looked like hay, but Maria said that it smelt like cow poop."

Eva burst out laughing and slapped her hand over her mouth. Regaining her composure with difficulty, she said, "Go on."

"Well, Uncle Dion didn't have a cow, but he had horses, and he had hay, so we went into the barn. I got the hay and Maria got the poop."

Eva lost control again and started laughing as Zoe collapsed against her and giggled.

"Um, well." Zoe took a deep breath. "We went behind the barn, and we rolled the hay and the poop into the cigarette paper. I knew how to do it because I had seen Papa do it many times."

"Did you smoke it?"

"Uh-huh. We had a cigarette each, and we took a puff at the same time. Ended up coughing and spluttering so much, Michael came rushing over to see what we were doing."

"Then what happened?"

Zoe grinned. "We explained to Michael what we had done, and he couldn't stop laughing. That brought Thieri and Theo over to see what the commotion was about." She rocked back and looked up at the ceiling. "Papa heard the boys, and next thing we knew, he came over to see what the trouble was."

"Oh, no," Eva squeaked.

"Papa couldn't believe it, and he really tried not to laugh, but I knew he wanted to because his eyes were going crinkly."

"What did he do?"

"He rolled and lit a proper cigarette, gave it to me, and told me to smoke it."

"He didn't! Did he?"

"Yeah. I took it and took one puff, inhaling deeply as he told me to. My eyes watered, my throat burned, and I began coughing." Zoe snickered. "When I could talk, I told him I wasn't going to smoke ever again."

"Smart man, that Papa Lambros," Eva said, grinning.

Zoe nodded in agreement. "Brilliant man. So that's why I didn't smoke before I met you. Now I do, but you're such a good influence on me..."

"Yes, I'm passing on the great habits. Willie got me started on cigarettes... Well, actually it was cigars."

"Cigars?"

"My grandfather used to smoke these great big cigars." Eva smiled. "Willie really wanted to try one, but he was scared he might get caught. So he convinced me to go with him. If we got caught, I would say I was there to see my grandfather."

"Did you get caught?"

Eva looked down at Zoe and smiled. "We got caught with our hand in the cigar box," she said, and then laughed.

"What happened?" Zoe asked.

"Well, my grandfather came in and caught us. We tried to stammer our way out of it. Willie was terrible at lying—"

"And you are good at it?" Zoe smiled.

"Well, I was better at it than Willie."

"Did your grandfather believe you?"

"No."

"So you weren't better than Willie."

"Ha ha." Eva shook her head. "Opa—"

"Opa?"

"Grandpa." Eva translated the German word into Greek. "He gave us a cigar each, and taught us how to smoke it."

"You're joking!"

"No, he said if we were going to smoke, we should do it right."

"Did you enjoy it?"

"Oh, yes." Eva nodded. "I made the mistake of being so excited that I told my grandmother. She was furious with my grandpa!"

"How old were you?" Zoe wondered out loud.

"Fifteen. I miss him," Eva said with a sigh, then took Zoe's hand and kissed it. They fell silent. "So the long route to telling me about the smoking story is about Maria? What happened to Maria?" Eva asked.

"Uncle Dion moved to America just before the war," Zoe replied. "She's probably married to some American boy."

"So you have family in America?"

"Yes, well, I did until they went back to Greece."

Zoe watched Eva attempt to keep her eyes open, but she was losing the battle. A part of her wanted Eva to go back to sleep, but her news was going to outweigh that desire for her partner. "Evy..."

"Hmm? What about Aunty Stella?" Eva replied sleepily.

"No, Evy, pay attention. Aunty Stella was married, but her husband died before I was born. Uncle Dion is my father's brother."

"Right," Eva said. "Stella didn't have children?" She yawned.

"What? No." Zoe gazed at Eva, who had her eyes closed. "Evy, follow me."

"I'm following, love. Smoking cow dung, Maria sent you a letter, and your Uncle Dion and Aunty Stella...something."

Zoe sighed. "Wake up please."

Eva opened her eyes wide before they half-closed. "I am awake and smoking a cigarette in the early hours of the morning talking about cow dung Maria."

"Well, we are talking about Uncle Dion and cow dung Maria, but we were also talking about Aunty Stella."

"Stella isn't dead, right?"

"No, but that's not the problem."

"What is the problem?" Eva asked as she closed her eyes again.

Zoe shook her head. "They want to marry me off." She counted to one before Eva's eyes popped open. "I thought that would get your attention."

"Who wants to marry you off? Aunty Stella?"

"No. Uncle Dion, Maria's father."

"Huh?" Eva stifled a yawn.

"Maria and the family are back in Larissa from America, and they heard that I was coming back." Zoe waved the crumbled letter in front of Eva. "They write that they have found a good boy."

Eva giggled.

"That's not funny."

"No, it's not," Eva replied, amusement in her voice.

"Why do you find that funny?"

"I have this mental image of you hitting this poor boy on the head." Eva dissolved into a fit of giggles. "What's the boy's name?"

"Kyriakos Vaskos."

"Zoe Vaskos... don't like it."

"That is really *not* funny."

"Zoe, my love, there is more chance of you growing two heads than you becoming Mrs. Vaskos."

Zoe tried not to grin. "I'm yours."

"Lover, best friend, wife, partner." Eva brought Zoe closer and kissed her. "Uncle Dion will find out how much of a handful you are, and poor Kyriakos Vaskos will just be out of luck."

"Don't you think that's a problem?"

"For them, yes."

"I don't know what gives them the right to want to marry me off."

"They love you, Zoe."

"I don't love them."

"Yes, you do. They just want you to be happy."

"Where were they during the war? In safe America, that's where. The first sign of trouble with the Italians and Uncle Dion gets scared and runs off to America. The Coward. He didn't stay and fight the Italians, and he didn't come back to fight the Germans," Zoe replied vehemently.

Eva opened her eyes. "I know how you feel about those who didn't stay."

"Cowards." Zoe looked up and found Eva's loving

gaze. "They couldn't stay and defend their home, their countrymen, their way of life. They ran off like scared rabbits, leaving us to defend our town against the invaders. You know how I feel about those miserable cowards. They collaborated with the enemy by running away."

"I know."

"Larissa's soil is stained with the blood of the brave souls who did stay, who fled to the mountains to fight in the Resistance, who resisted in the town. Uncle Dion ran and didn't look back. He's back in Larissa because of the property law. He has the nerve to want to marry me off? Where was he when Mama died? He didn't come rushing to help me then. How dare he?" Zoe said bitterly. "To hell with them."

"They are still your family, love."

"I know, but they have no right to want to meddle in my life."

"I think Uncle Dion is going to find out that he can't tell you what to do."

"And Aunty Stella."

"Apparently she's still alive. She's happy she's not dead and crazy, I suppose." Eva chuckled. "I don't know, love. Let's wait and find out what Crazy Aunty Stella is like."

"Alright."

"Can we go to sleep now?"

Zoe played with the fringe of the blanket. "It's going to be a long day tomorrow."

Eva yawned. "Yes."

"I sent Debbie a note thanking her for giving you that flyer, although I don't like the idea of you working for the four weeks."

Eva smiled. "First class cabin, Zo, with a little lounge. We won't have to travel in a broom closet."

Zoe laughed lightly at the description of their journey to Australia. "It was cozy."

"It was claustrophobic. Two months' wages for a first-class cabin. I don't care that I have to work. It's going to be really comfortable." Eva yawned. "Zoe, I want to sleep." She kissed the top of Zoe's head. "I love you dearly, but I'm tired. Need to sleep."

"Yes." Zoe watched Eva's eyes close. "Evy?"

"Huh?"

"I love you."

Eva smiled. "Yes, love," she said as she stubbed out the cigarette in the ashtray that sat on the bedside table. She wrapped herself around Zoe and dozed off.

"To hell with them, those silly people," Zoe mumbled as sleep overtook her.

CHAPTER 16

THE ARCADIA BOUND FOR GREECE

THE NOONDAY SUN shone brightly and glistened off the blue-green water of the harbor. The vast ocean liner, The Arcadia, sat docked in the international passenger terminal as passengers and crew boarded her for the four-week journey to Europe. Its white hull was a stark contrast to the colorful display of flags aboard the ship that fluttered in the gentle breeze.

Zoe smiled at the ship as Earl's car came to a stop. She didn't believe in signs, but she hoped that it was going to be a trip that would finally put a few demons to rest.

Eva was in a very animated conversation with Earl in the front seat. Zoe smiled at Eva's laugh. Eva's natural beauty made Zoe's heart skip a beat, even after five years of their relationship.

She was a far cry from the teenager that she had been,

with so much hatred in her heart that it was the only thing that kept her alive.

Zoe glanced out the window, and her mind went back to Larissa. It was to be their last day in the Greek village. They left before daybreak as if they were thieves. A donkey, two bags, and enough supplies for a few days. They walked up to Athena's Bluff and away from Larissa.

"Zoe?"

Zoe turned around to find Eva watching her from the front seat.

"Are you alright?" Eva asked. "You looked like you were miles away."

Zoe smiled. "Years away. I will seriously 'heavy like' you no matter what language you speak to me," she whispered in German in Eva's ear and saw the look in Eva's eyes as she remembered that day.

"Our last day in Larissa," Eva said.

The car stopped, and Zoe and Eva got out on the same side. Zoe looked around quickly, finding that no one was really paying attention since they were blocked by a large tree. She turned to Eva and pulled her down for a quick kiss on the lips.

"My, aren't we romantic today." Earl came up from behind them and wrapped his arms around them. "Is that kiss number 4891 today?"

"You're just jealous, and that was kiss number 5482," Eva said.

Earl gave her a quick kiss.

"Hey." Zoe lightly slapped Earl's shoulder in mock outrage.

"You can kiss her later, Stretch," Earl said and walked away towards the nearest crew member.

"So do we find out where we are going to live for the next month, Miss Eva?"

"That would be a good idea, Miss Zoe," Eva replied, tweaking Zoe's nose.

"Will the two of you stop making gooey eyes at each other?" Earl teased, making them laugh.

They caught the attention of a porter who came over with his cart and placed their luggage on it. They walked silently to the ship and stopped at the passenger terminal.

"This is where I leave you, girls, to fend for yourselves." Earl put his arms around them.

"We will write to let you know how everything is going," Eva said. "Keep Henry updated in Melbourne. The poor boy is stuck there for a few more weeks."

"I will let Henry know. I suspect by the time your letter arrives, you will be back here."

"I'll send a telegram." Eva kissed Earl on the cheek. "Look after Ourania, and when Henry gets back, you two can fix the back shed."

"I'm sure the cat and I will be the best of friends if she doesn't scratch me to death. Henry is a big boy, and he can look after himself."

Zoe giggled as she stood on her toes to kiss Earl on the cheek. "Goodbye, Wiggy."

"Farewell, my lovelies."

Earl gave them a final hug and walked away from the line. He turned and waved to them before he left the area.

"Well, it's just the two of us again, love," Eva said.

Zoe looked up at the giant liner. "Just the two of us back on a ship." She looked back at Eva. "Come on, let's go find that super first-class cabin."

Zoe took Eva's hand, and they made their way up the

walkway.

"Hello, can you help us find our cabin?" Zoe asked the first person she saw in what looked like a uniform.

The man greeted her with a huge smile. "Most certainly, Bella." He half bowed. "Alas, I am not ship's crew. I am Dr. Vito Salvatore. I am pleased to meet you, Miss?"

"Zoe Lambros and this is my friend Eva Haralambos."

Dr. Salvatore smiled and kissed Zoe's hand.

"Oh, I'm sorry. I thought you were the purser." Zoe took her hand back and gave Eva a glance.

"No, I'm not, but for this one moment I wish I were," Dr. Salvatore replied, getting a smile from Zoe. "I am a doctor here."

"Are you a crew member?" Eva asked. "I thought you said you were not."

Dr. Salvatore turned and looked up, and Eva smiled.

"I'm Dr. Salvatore." He extended his hand and Eva took it.

"Eva Haralambos," Eva replied.

Dr. Salvatore's eyes never left Zoe. "Your surname is Greek, but you have a German accent?"

Eva tilted her head. "Yes."

"Can you show us the way to a crew member who can help us?" Zoe asked, a little perplexed at Eva's behavior.

"Certainly, just go to that young man over there." Dr. Salvatore pointed to a crewmember. "He'll help you out."

"Thank you." Eva took Zoe's hand, and they walked away.

"Be seeing you again, little one." Dr. Salvatore chuckled.

"He was nice." Zoe bumped Eva as they walked along.

"I don't like him," Eva replied.

"Why?"

"Humph." Eva screwed up her face and shrugged.

A crew member approached them. "Welcome aboard the Arcadia," he greeted with a smile. "Can I have your names, please?"

"Eva Haralambos and Zoe Lambros," Eva responded.

"You are on deck B, cabin 51." The young man showed Eva a chart to find her way.

They followed the porter to their cabin.

"So why were you rude to the doctor?" Zoe asked.

"I wasn't rude," Eva replied under her breath. "Italian men are so..."

"He was nice," Zoe commented, not understanding why Eva disliked the man. It was quite surprising for her partner to pass judgment so quickly.

She glanced up at Eva, who didn't look at all happy.

Their porter stopped in front of a cabin. He opened the door and led them inside.

Zoe looked around at the cabin in astonishment. "This is not a cabin," she said in Greek.

They were standing in a tiny lobby, which led off into two rooms. Zoe walked into the bedroom. "Mary, mother of God, Evy," she called out.

The room was beautifully decorated and spacious, with two single beds in their own nooks with a dressing table and mirror in between. They had enough space for a small round table and a chair.

Zoe leaned over the bed and pulled the curtain to the side to look outside. "Evy, come and have a look at this."

Zoe heard Eva talking to the porter before the door shut.

She heard a gasp and turned to find Eva's face was ashen.

Zoe scrambled down from the bed and rushed to Eva's side just as Eva grabbed the chair and sat herself down.

CHAPTER 17

Zoe fell to her knees in front of Eva, who sat with her head bowed.

"Evy, what's wrong?"

"Give me a moment, love."

Zoe exhaled and sat back on her heels, her eyes riveted to Eva, who was looking better than a few moments ago. She took Eva's hands and waited.

Eva swallowed and shook her head. "I'm sorry."

Zoe rose from the floor and went in search of some water. She found a glass in the small kitchenette and filled it with water, then brought it back, and put it in Eva's hands.

Eva's hands shook as she drank.

Zoe waited. Over the past six years, she had learned to be patient with Eva. Being patient was not in her makeup, but when it came to Eva, she had infinite patience.

Zoe rifled through Eva's handbag and found her cigarettes. She took one out of the case and lit it with Eva's lighter. She gave it to Eva, who accepted it with a wry smile.

"I'm not sure where to start. I'm sorry I scared you." Eva leaned forward.

"I'm still scared," Zoe said quietly.

"Um...it was something I just saw."

"What?" Zoe got up and held out her hand.

Eva took it, and Zoe led her to the bed, took off Eva's shoes, and gently pushed her down. She took Eva's cigarette and held it until she found an ashtray. She then shucked off her own shoes, got into bed, and faced Eva.

She rested her hand on Eva's hip. "Tell me."

"I've had this dream. I've had this dream since Aiden."

"What dream?"

"This is going to sound crazy." Eva took a drag of her cigarette and watched the smoke billow up. "I came into the bedroom, and you were there, and your silhouette...and it was the same, and..." She frowned in confusion. "It's not making any sense, is it?"

"Not much."

"The first time it happened was in Aiden. I had just had my first treatment, and my mind was so fuzzy. I never knew what was real and what wasn't. You could have convinced me I was living with Santa Claus and I would have believed you."

"What happened?"

"I had a vision."

"A vision? Like a ghost vision?" Zoe looked around.

"Not a ghost vision."

"What?"

"I saw the silhouette of a woman with a bright light behind her."

"Wow. How many times did you see this woman?"

"Every time I had a treatment."

"You saw a woman? Are you sure it wasn't all those drugs they gave you?"

"No, it wasn't the drugs, Zo. I'm not on drugs now. I can still remember what she said."

"She talked? What did she sound like?"

"I don't remember. All I remember is what she said and what she looked like."

"Alright. Let's start with what she said."

Eva closed her eyes for a long moment. "Have faith."

"Have faith? What does that mean? Have faith in what? You were being tortured, and she said 'have faith'?"

"That's what she said. Have faith," Eva whispered. "To keep my faith in God that He would see me through it."

"Oh." Zoe was stunned into silence. "But who was she? Was she your guardian angel? She wasn't doing an excellent job if that is what she was."

"It helped Zo. I knew that someone cared about me and knew what was happening to me."

"It's why you have such a strong faith in God."

Eva gazed at Zoe and nodded. "I had to believe that it was from Him. That's what kept me going. I wasn't alone."

"What did she look like?"

"I couldn't see her face. All I could see was the silhouette and the bright light."

"Was she tall or short?"

Eva shook her head. "She was as tall as me with long hair. I don't know the color, but her hair was long."

"You can't remember her voice?"

"No. Just her message and what she looked like."

"What made you think of this today?"

"I saw her again," Eva said.

"When?"

"When you were standing near the window, and when I walked in...she was standing next to you."

"She was standing next to me?"

"Yes."

"Did you see this woman again after Aiden?"

"Yes."

"You did?"

"Yes."

"When?"

Eva blinked. "In Larissa. The day I arrived in Larissa."

"Are you sure?"

"Yes." Eva nodded. "I was in the car with my father as we drove into town. I looked out the window. She was standing out in the fields next to the bodies of three Greek men that had been shot."

"That's the day you drove into town for the first time. The Germans executed three men that they caught."

"Yes. She was standing next to their bodies."

"What did she look like?"

"I don't know. All I could see was her silhouette; the sun was behind her, and I couldn't see her face."

"What was she doing?"

"Nothing. Just standing there as if she was guarding the bodies. I heard her in my mind again."

"What did she say?"

"At last you are here," Eva said.

"What does that mean? Why was it important for you to be in Larissa? Why then? All the times you've seen this woman, you have been in some sort of pain, starting in 1938 and then when you arrived in Larissa in 1942."

"Yes, I thought I had seen her one more time after we arrived."

"When?"

"The day your mama was killed," Eva replied softly as she gazed at Zoe. "I thought I saw her in the crowd, but I'm not sure."

"Did she say anything to you then?"

"No. I never saw her again after that."

"When you got shot, did you see her then?"

"No."

"But you saw her now?"

"Yes."

"Did she say anything?"

Eva's eyes glistened. "You will find the truth."

"The truth of what? What does that mean? You heard her?"

"Yes, in my mind. I heard her voice."

"What did she sound like?"

"I don't know. My own voice."

Zoe blinked. "Your own voice?"

"I'm not going mad, Zoe. I know what I saw and heard."

"I believe you, Evy. I do." Zoe gazed into Eva's eyes, and she indeed believed her. "Great, so now our first-class cabin is haunted," she joked, trying to ease the knot in her stomach.

"I don't know, but something is going to happen on this trip that will tell me about some truth that I should find out."

"Every time this woman has appeared, something good has happened." Zoe cupped Eva's face and smiled. "In Aiden, she helped you. In Larissa, she said 'at last you are here,' and she sounds to be like a protector. What she was doing out on Maragos Field is uncertain, but it doesn't sound like the ghost wants to hurt you. Here she said 'You will find the truth.' It's positive, right?"

"Yes."

"So there is nothing to fear because you saw her, is there?"

"Other than a woman appears in a vision next to my lover? No, there isn't anything to fear," Eva replied and swallowed. "I don't know what this means."

"Normally I would want to go down to the archdiocese and ask for an exorcism, but I really don't think it's the work of the devil."

"You don't?"

"No. You're not going mad either. I think there is a meaning, although I don't know what, every time this woman has appeared, it has been a good omen."

"It wasn't out on Maragos Field."

"The woman appeared to you, not me, Evy," Zoe said. "After my mama died, everything changed. Your life changed, and my life changed."

"Time for another change?"

"Maybe, but I know one thing for certain." Zoe smiled. "I'm with you on this journey, so whatever it is, it has to be good, right?"

"I hope so." Eva kissed Zoe. "I hope so, love."

"Alright, let's get up and go to watch us sail out of Sydney Harbour." Zoe tweaked Eva's chin and rolled out of bed. She held out her hand, and Eva took it as she got up.

They left the cabin holding hands.

CHAPTER 18

It seemed all the passengers were there to watch as the ship left the dock. Streamers and confetti filled the air as they slowly sailed away. Eva leaned against the railing, watching the sunset over the Harbour Bridge. The sunset left the city in a golden glow. It was a city she came to love and call home, more so because of the woman leaning over the railing beside her.

"Do you remember the evening we sailed into Sydney Harbour?" Eva whispered. "Remember what I said?"

Zoe took a deep breath. "Together we build a new life. We have. We have built a new life."

"If only our old lives wouldn't intrude on our new one," Eva replied as she played with a streamer.

Zoe looked up. "One day."

Eva felt a tap on her shoulder. She turned around. "Yes?"

"Excuse me, are you Miss Eva Haralambos?" A young woman asked.

"Yes, I am."

"Thank goodness. I thought it would be difficult to find

you with all these people here," the young woman exclaimed. "My name is Alice Fortane. I'm Mrs. Muldoon's girl Friday."

"Pleased to meet you." Eva stuck out her hand.

Alice ignored her hand and pulled her into a hug.

"Can you come with me? Mrs. Muldoon would like to speak to you." Alice took Eva's hand and started to walk off only to be stopped by an unmovable Eva. "You have to come with me."

"Yes, Eva, you have to go with her." Zoe snickered. "I'll see you when you get back."

Alice took Eva's hand and led her away through the throng of people and down the corridor.

"You are tall," Alice said.

"Yes."

"Does everyone tell you that?"

"Yes."

"You have a German accent."

"Yes."

"But your name is Greek. I found that so interesting."

"Hmm."

"Oh, we're here," Alice announced, much to Eva's relief. Alice put the key in the door and entered. "Mrs. Muldoon should be here soon."

Eva sat on the edge of a seat and waited. The cabin door opened, and Mrs. Della Muldoon entered. Eva had seen her in the newspaper with her husband, who was the owner of Muldoon & Sons, one of the largest iron-ore mining companies in Australia. She carried herself as if she was self-assured and in command. Della Muldoon was an imposing woman—not short or tall, with dark blonde hair and blue eyes. She carried herself as if she was self-assured and in command.

"Miss Haralambos, so pleased to meet you," Mrs. Muldoon greeted her in German. "Can I call you Eva?"

Eva stood and shook Mrs. Muldoon's hand. "Good morning, Mrs. Muldoon. Yes, of course."

"Sit, sit, we have a great deal to discuss. You can call me Della—I prefer that in private. Would you like some tea?"

"I would, thank you." Eva smiled and sat down. She folded her hands on her lap and waited.

"So have you settled into your cabin?"

"Yes, it's very comfortable," Eva responded as Alice brought them cups of tea. Alice then left the room.

Della sat back and took a sip of her tea. She regarded Eva over the top of her steaming teacup with a smile. "In your application, you didn't mention that you had a previous surname to the question, 'Is there anything else you need to tell us?'"

"I didn't think I needed to tell you."

"You didn't think that telling me you are the granddaughter of Beatriz Muller of AEMullerStahl was important?"

Eva regarded her teacup for a moment. "No. I see you know who my grandmother is."

"I met your grandmother before the war. Herbert, my husband, dealt with AEMullerStahl before the war when we were at the British Embassy in Germany. We had dinner with Wilbur Muller and your grandmother. A delightful evening."

"Yes," Eva responded noncommittally.

"Why did you leave that information out?"

"I haven't had any contact with my family for a decade, so I didn't think it was important."

"Hmm." Della nodded as she took a sip of her tea. "Was it because you are a lesbian that there was so little contact?"

"You're a straightforward woman, Della."

"I believe in being direct and honest. You do not?"

"I value my privacy," Eva replied.

"While I admire that, I like the people that work for me to be open with me."

Eva nodded. "I will be honest and open with you when it pertains to my employment."

Mrs. Muldoon gave her a cold look.

Eva mentally sighed. "I *am* a lesbian."

"That took the long way to be revealed. Thank you for being honest even it was after the fact. Tell me about Miss Zoe Lambros. Is she your lover?"

"Zoe is twenty-two years old, and she was born in Larissa."

"That's nice, but is she your lover?"

Eva wanted to tell Mrs. Della Muldoon she didn't want to be a part of her team, but then she thought of Zoe and the first class cabin. Zoe deserved this luxury. Eva reluctantly resigned herself to exposing a part of her life. "Yes, Zoe is my lover."

"Is she Jewish?"

"No, she's Greek Orthodox."

"Is she as tall as you?"

Eva smiled. The notion of a tall Zoe tickled her. "No, she's petite."

"Hmm...Did she have a problem with you being the daughter of a Nazi commander?"

Eva tilted her head, a slight smile playing on her lips. "With all due respect, ma'am, that's none of your business."

"It is my business, Eva. I'm taking a group of Jewish

refugees back to Greece and to Germany, and having the daughter of a Nazi on board is my business."

"If you knew who I was, why did you agree to my employment?"

"It was because of who you are," Mrs. Muldoon replied with a smile. "I find you absolutely fascinating. You are the granddaughter of Beatriz Muller, you are sent into a war zone, you collaborate with the Resistance, and you end up in Australia with a Greek woman."

Eva shrugged. "Yes, that does sound interesting."

"You said you live with Miss Lambros?"

"Yes. We came out on the same ship, and we share a house."

"When I had some background checks on you, I came across this interesting photo." Mrs. Muldoon took a photo out and handed it to Eva.

"Yes, it's an interesting photo." Eva hoped her face wouldn't turn any redder than she knew it was at that moment. The photo was taken from the War Crimes folder, and it was of her and Zoe in Sydney, kissing on the grass. Eva knew who had shot that photo and when it had been taken. She wanted to kill David Harrison, her friend, and a war crimes investigator, for forgetting to remove the picture from the file.

"Actually that's how Greek women show affection," Eva deadpanned.

Mrs. Muldoon gave her an incredulous look before she fell back on her chair and laughed. "But you're German."

"Yes, but I was trying to fit in." Eva shrugged.

"You have a funny sense of humor. While I had your records checked, I found that you were responsible for the

War Crimes investigation office apprehending your father, who was wanted for war crimes a few years ago."

"Yes."

"Let me guess, none of my business?"

"That question wasn't on the application."

"You are right, but my curiosity was piqued. Tell me more about Zoe."

"She's an artist, very gifted, and she was in the Resistance." Eva smiled. "But you already knew that."

"Yes, I did. I would like to meet her. Your language skills are impressive, but you are also a photographer?"

"I am an amateur photographer."

"You may have solved one of my most pressing problems. The photographer I hired had to pull out of this trip, so can you step in?"

"I can do that but what about my—"

"I would prefer it if you stepped into the role of photographer. We have several interpreters, but we don't have a photographer. One can't document a journey without photographs. Is that alright with you?"

"Yes, of course, but my final journey is Larissa rather than Thessalonica."

"Marvelous. I'm sure we will find a photographer in Thessalonica, but until then you are now the official photographer. That's one less thing I have to worry about on this trip. I'm not sure if you brought your camera along, so I will get Alice to give you the camera we have. So tell me. Why did you work with the Resistance? You are a Muller and the last person I would expect to do that."

"Not all of us were Nazis," Eva replied defensively.

"Didn't say you were. You were involved in the Resistance in Larissa?"

"No. I didn't have a lot to do with the Resistance. I was helping the village priest with forged papers to allow the Jews to escape."

"But you weren't working with them?"

"No."

"But you were working against the Germans?"

"I was working against the Nazis rather than Germany. I would never betray the Fatherland."

"Isn't that hair-splitting?" Della reasoned. "Germany was ruled by the Nazis, so that would mean if you worked against the Nazis, you were working against Germany."

Eva stared at her now cold tea for a moment. "I was working against the notion that my life is worth more because I'm a Catholic and their lives were worthless because they were Jewish."

"I've never heard it expressed that way before. So you love your birthplace."

"I was born in Vienna, Austria, but I grew up in Germany. I love my country even the Nazis committed heinous crimes. It is not the country but the men at the head."

"Fascinating. Did you know that Larissa had the highest concentration of Jews in Greece before the war?"

"Yes, my father told me."

"Major Muller told you?"

Eva mentally rolled her eyes. "No, the village priest told me."

Mrs. Muldoon cryptically smiled. "I was wondering how you were going to explain that."

Eva sighed. "I don't need to explain who my parents are. If you know the answers to the questions, why are we playing this game?"

"I've been curious to see how you would answer."

Eva stared at her for a moment. "Have I lived up to your expectations?"

"No," Mrs. Muldoon replied. "You've exceeded them. It would have been wonderful to have some Jews from Larissa on the journey with us, but we don't. The Greeks on board are going to Thessalonica. I think it would have been interesting for them to meet the woman who helped them escape."

"I never thought about that before."

"It would have been a good way for them to meet their savior. I have arranged for a darkroom for the duration of this trip so you can work there." She gave Eva a key. "Don't forget to let Miss Lambros know I would like to meet her."

"I will."

Mrs. Muldoon rose and stuck out her hand. Eva took it and smiled warmly. "I'm looking forward to working with you, Eva."

Eva walked quickly out of the cabin, feeling a little unsettled. It was not what she had expected. Something niggled at her, but she wasn't sure what it was. The person she needed to speak to was waiting for her in her cabin. Zoe was going to find the latest developments exciting. She stopped and looked back at the door before she resumed her journey back to their cabin.

CHAPTER 19

STEAM ROSE FROM THE BATHTUB AS ZOE RELAXED into the water. Her head rested on the rim, and she had her eyes closed as she hummed. She heard the cabin door open. "I'm in here, Evy."

"That tub is small even for you," Eva said as she walked into the bathroom, grabbed the stool nearby, and sat on it. She held a rose in her hand.

"I saw it, and I don't think we can both fit in this."

"*You* can't fit into it. That's going to make bath time boring." Eva chuckled. "Look what I found outside our door."

"Is it from you?"

"Not from me. The rose is yours, and you did get a note." Eva handed the note to Zoe.

"'Greek roses are quite beautiful,'" Zoe read aloud.

"Argh," Eva muttered, and then made a noise halfway between a snort and gagging sound. Zoe wasn't sure which one.

"How do you know it's not for you?"

"Which one of us is Greek?"

"Well, I'm fully Greek, and you're partly Greek," Zoe replied smugly.

Eva sighed. "Which one of us sounds Greek?"

"Me."

"We can safely assume that it's for you."

"Tsk tsk." Zoe tweaked Eva's chin. "Do I have to warn my admirer that my wife is going to throw him overboard?"

A smile spread across Eva's face.

"Eva Theresa Haralambos." Zoe chuckled. "He is just nice."

"I'm a jealous shrew," Eva joked.

"No, you're human," Zoe replied. "You've got nothing to fear. Now how did the meeting with Mrs. Muldoon go?"

Eva shook her head. "Remember when you said you wanted to throw David out the window for taking that photo of us kissing?"

"I like that photo." Zoe smiled. "It didn't belong in a war crimes investigator's file, but it was a nice photo."

"David didn't remove it."

Zoe stopped smiling. "How do you know?"

"I was given the photograph by my new boss."

Zoe groaned and slid under the water as her feet stuck out. Eva laughed. Zoe came back up and looked at Eva, who was still chuckling. "So what did Mrs. Muldoon say?"

"Interesting photo," Eva responded. "I told her that that's how Greek women show affection."

Zoe stared at her open-mouthed. "You did?" She giggled. "That's my girl."

"I'm also not working as an interpreter."

"Why? Because you're Greek?"

Eva looked at Zoe for a moment. "That's funny, Zo."

"I know." Zoe giggled.

"Their photographer couldn't make it, so I'm the photographer. She's going to give me a new camera."

"Oh, that's exciting. When are you getting that?"

"I don't know. Alice is going to bring it over."

"And give you a nice hug as well." Zoe snickered.

"Now who is being jealous?"

"I'm not jealous," Zoe replied smugly. "She's not your type. You are jealous of my not-so-secret admirer." She pointed to the rose.

Eva got up, left the rose on the floor, and knelt at Zoe's head. "I know I have nothing to fear." She put her arms around Zoe's neck.

"If there is nothing to fear, why the jealous streak, my little sugarplum?"

"Little sugarplum?" Eva looked down with a crooked grin.

"Big sugarplum?" Zoe giggled. "So tell me what's wrong."

"How do you know something is wrong?"

"I just know." Zoe smiled.

"I don't know. Something is niggling me, and I don't know what it is. There is something about Mrs. Muldoon."

"You don't like her?"

Eva paused for a moment. "I do like her, but I just can't put my finger on the 'why' I'm feeling the way I am. Maybe I'm just feeling a little apprehensive about this trip, my strange vision, and Mrs. Muldoon."

"Or a mixture of the trip, this new job, and my new admirer," Zoe teased. "We will find out what is bothering you."

"Hm, yes." Eva rested her hands on Zoe's shoulders. "Would you like a massage?"

"Are you offering?" Zoe looked up into Eva's smiling face. "I'll have you know that I used to be an excellent bathing attendant in my younger years, so I know all about that."

"Really?"

"Of course. When I was fifteen, I got this job with this gorgeous woman, and I helped her bathe, you know."

"Hmm, were you any good?" Eva asked as Zoe reached up and held her hands.

"I was so good," Zoe looked into Eva's eyes, "that that gorgeous woman couldn't bear to be without her bathing attendant."

"Hmm." Eva cupped Zoe's face and kissed her. "Smart woman."

Eva gently massaged Zoe's shoulders, which were knotted and a little tense, as Zoe let her head fall forward. She moaned when Eva increased the pressure. Eva scooped water onto Zoe's hair before applying shampoo. She massaged Zoe's head, eliciting a very happy moan.

"Lean forward, love," Eva bathed Zoe's back with gentle strokes. She rinsed her back and washed her face.

Zoe opened her eyes and gave Eva a crooked smile.

Eva kissed her. "After we are done scrubbing you clean, we are going to find the cabin Mrs. Muldoon wants to turn into a darkroom. She also wants to meet you."

"She wants to meet me?"

"Yes. Not sure if she's ready."

Zoe stopped and looked up at Eva. "Why?"

"Not sure if Mrs. Muldoon is ready for Zoe Lambros." Eva giggled and then laughed harder as Zoe scooped the warm water and splashed Eva's face, hair, and blouse.

They laughed, and Eva picked up a towel. "Rise, Miss Lambros."

Zoe rose, the water falling from her slender frame. She smiled as Eva wrapped the towel around her body. Eva put her arms around her, and they walked out of the bathroom and headed back into the bedroom.

"This is small," Eva said as she turned slowly around the small room. The cabin, if you could call it that, was a converted broom closet. She wondered if it was similar to the one they had stayed in on their journey to Australia.

"It's not similar to the first one," Zoe mumbled.

Eva turned to her, startled. "Are you reading my mind now?"

"Nope." Zoe took Eva's hand and led her to a blacked-out portal. "You see that?" She pointed to the unpainted part of the wall where a bunk used to be.

Eva bent down to try and see what Zoe was pointing at. "What am I looking for?"

"Zoe Loves Eva." Zoe giggled and wrapped herself around Eva.

Eva grinned. "Did you write that in the old cabin?"

"Yes," Zoe replied with a smile. "When we boarded."

"So I took two months longer than I should have?"

"Well, better late than never," Zoe teased as she put her arms around Eva's waist.

The door opened, and Zoe jumped back.

The door opened a little more, revealing Dr. Salvatore. Eva frowned.

"Oh! Hello, I was wondering who was in here," the doctor said. He saw Zoe, and his smile grew.

"Dr. Salvatore." Eva smiled weakly.

"Miss Haralambos, how are you this evening? I heard voices coming from the cabin, and I knew it wasn't occupied, so I thought I would investigate." Dr. Salvatore took a seat on the only stool in the room.

Eva scowled as she leaned against the wall.

"This is Eva's darkroom," Zoe added.

"Ah yes, Mrs. Muldoon told me you were our new photographer."

"Just temporarily," Eva supplied.

"Eva has a good eye," Zoe continued.

"What will you be doing while Eva is playing photographer?"

Eva glanced at him, unsure if she should say anything.

"I'm not sure," Zoe replied.

"Will I see you around?" he asked.

Zoe giggled. "I'm not leaving the ship any time soon."

Dr. Salvatore chuckled. "Yes, so very true. Oh well, I have a few bones to set..." They gave him confused looks. "Sorry. Small chiropractor joke."

Zoe's face split into a huge smile. "That's funny."

"Yes," Dr. Salvatore replied. "I have been learning a new technique."

"What's that?" Zoe asked

"Are you interested? I call it the Salvatore Technique."

"Very original," Eva muttered in Greek.

"Absolutely," Zoe answered, giving Eva an irritated look. "What's the technique?"

"It is a holistic system of soft tissue manipulation. It was developed by me, and it's excellent," Dr. Salvatore replied happily.

"I've never heard of it," Eva commented.

Dr. Salvatore nodded. "Do you need a chiropractor?"

"No," Eva answered as Zoe answered "Yes" at the same time.

Dr. Salvatore gave them a baffled look. "Yes?"

"Yes," Zoe answered, giving Eva a mock scowl. "We've never heard of the Salvatore Technique."

"I'm not surprised they haven't told you. It's a holistic approach to back pain."

"I don't like doctors," Eva muttered in German.

Salvatore looked at Eva and then back to Zoe with a questioning look.

"You have to excuse my friend. She doesn't like homeopathy treatments. We've had a few that didn't work that well," Zoe said.

"Oh, well, this technique isn't like that," Dr. Salvatore said. "It actually works. Would you like me to try...?"

"No," Eva replied.

"But..."

"I'm not interested," Eva persisted.

"I am," Zoe said.

Dr. Salvatore smiled at her.

"Would you teach me?"

"Zoe..." Eva said.

"What harm will it do? If it doesn't work on you, then it doesn't work," Zoe reasoned.

Eva gave her a frustrated look. "Alright, do what you want."

"When you have some time tomorrow, I would be more than happy to show you," Dr. Salvatore said. "It's ten easy lessons."

"How much would that be?" Eva asked.

Dr. Salvatore smiled. "For you, tell you what, you take a photo of me with Zoe, and it will be free."

"That's not a bad price, Eva." Zoe chuckled.

"Well, I'll see you tomorrow," Dr. Salvatore said and closed the door as he left.

"My camera might break," Eva mumbled.

"Hey, what's wrong with you?" Zoe turned Eva around to face her. "Ever since we came on board, you've been really jealous. This isn't like you."

Eva shook her head. "I just don't like him."

Zoe frowned. "He hasn't done anything."

"Not yet," Eva replied, putting her arms around Zoe. "He's after something I have."

"What?"

"You," Eva replied.

Zoe looked up incredulously. "You can't be serious. He just offered to show me a technique that might help you."

Eva sighed. "Zoe, I love you, but sometimes you are too blind."

"Am not," Zoe replied.

"He was flirting with you." Despite her annoyance with the doctor, Eva found it endearing that Zoe couldn't see how much of an effect she'd had on him. "He's interested in you."

Zoe snorted. "You are the one seeing things."

Eva shook her head. "Our baker flirts with you, and our milkman—"

Zoe laughed. "Eva."

"I'm not jealous," Eva muttered. "It's a fact."

"They don't flirt with me. The baker is interested in you." Zoe giggled.

"Is that why he leaves crumpets?" Eva replied as she turned off the light, and they left the cabin. "I don't like crumpets. All I ask is you be careful of him."

"Who? The baker?" Zoe teased.

Eva sighed as they walked back to the cabin together. They passed a few couples in the corridor holding hands, which annoyed her even more.

They got to their cabin, and Eva pouted a little as she removed her clothes and got into bed.

Zoe returned from the bathroom and looked at Eva, who was staring at the ceiling with her hands behind her head.

"I thought you were sleeping on the other bed?" Zoe whispered.

Eva rolled her eyes and tapped the empty side of the bunk. Zoe grinned, put on her pajamas, and joined Eva.

Eva scooped her into her embrace.

"You are not squished there, are you?" Zoe asked.

"No, I'm fine," Eva replied.

"Evy?"

"Hmm."

"He wasn't flirting with me."

Eva blew a strand of hair from Zoe's eyes and grinned. "Remember Jessica?"

Zoe groaned. "Jessica, who always wanted to hug you or touch your arm at work? Yes, I remember her. She just couldn't keep her hands to herself."

"She wasn't flirting with me." Eva cuddled Zoe to her.

Zoe emitted a derisive snort, precisely what Eva was expecting, and she quietly chuckled.

"Dr. Salvatore is not Jessica," Zoe said.

"Given half the chance, the good Dr. Salvatore would love to do that with you," Eva reasoned.

"I really think we should get your eyes checked," Zoe teased.

"Ha ha." Eva shook her head.

Zoe put her arm around Eva and rested her head on her shoulder. "You are wrong."

"What if I'm not?"

Zoe turned and hitched herself up on her elbow. "You know you have nothing to fear, don't you? I have been repeating this to you all day."

Eva nodded.

"So what's the problem?"

"He's going to touch you."

"Yes, to show me the Salvatore technique. We've gone to chiropractors that had you half-naked on their tables. You didn't see me getting jealous."

Eva chuckled. "Oh, how easy we forget."

"Huh?"

"Dr. Patakas."

Zoe snorted in disgust. "He touched your breasts."

"By accident," Eva said. Zoe had taken an instant dislike to the man after only one visit. They never went back again.

"That wasn't an accident," Zoe replied. "I think it would be good to learn this Salvatore technique and see if it works."

"Yes, dear," Eva said, earning herself a gentle tap on the leg. She sighed and closed her eyes. She opened them again when she felt a soft kiss on the lips.

"I love you, Evy," Zoe whispered. "You've got nothing to fear."

Eva smiled. "I'm not afraid of that. That's one thing I'm quite certain of."

"You have such a jealous streak." Zoe giggled.

"You are mine," Eva sleepily replied, and drowsed in Zoe's arms.

"Evy."

"Hmm."

"Is this cabin haunted?"

Eva popped her eyes open and regarded Zoe for a moment. "No. What I saw was real. It's not a ghost."

"How do you know?"

"I don't know. I just feel that it's not something to fear."

"I hope not. The last thing I need is a jealous wife and an angry ghost." Zoe giggled, causing Eva to laugh.

CHAPTER 20

Zoe stood in Mrs. Muldoon's cabin, waiting for her to arrive. Instead of sitting down and being patient, she got up and looked at the various artwork hanging on the walls. The cabin was unlike any of the others. It was larger and quite luxurious.

One piece of artwork caught her attention, and she tilted her head and gazed at it intently.

"Miss Lambros, this is Mrs. Della Muldoon," Alice said.

Zoe turned and stepped forward to shake Mrs. Muldoon's hand. She

thought Mrs. Muldoon looked as imposing as she did in the newspapers.

"Please, sit down," Mrs. Muldoon said.

Zoe was surprised at Mrs. Muldoon's accent. She had always thought

she was English. She sat down, mesmerized by her voice. She was sure

she was German since she knew that accent very well.

"You are Zoe Lambros?"

"Ye...yes," Zoe stammered.

"How old are you, Miss Lambros?" Mrs. Muldoon asked as she sat near the window. She looked directly at Zoe and smiled.

"I'm twenty-two."

"Did you like the artwork you were looking at?"

Zoe gave the artwork a quick glance. "No."

Della leaned forward and smiled. "Why is that?"

"The colors are all wrong, the composition is quirky, and there is something not quite right with it. I'm sure if I stare at it a bit more I'll find the reason."

"Is that right?"

"Yes."

After a beat, Mrs. Muldoon leaned back in her chair. "That's my artwork."

"Well, there's something wrong with it," Zoe replied. "The colors are just...washed out."

Mrs. Muldoon laughed lightly. "How would you fix it?"

"Burn it and restart," Zoe replied. The artist in her took an interest in how Mrs. Muldoon was framed against the window, how the sun hit her hair, and created a halo. She snapped out of her artistic trance, hoping she hadn't noticed the lapse.

"What were you thinking just now?" Mrs. Muldoon asked as she took off her gloves.

"Um, I was thinking of how beautiful you looked framed against the window and the light," Zoe admitted. "The sun was hitting your hair, creating a halo." She totally forgot her nervousness. "The lighting and how you were sitting were perfect."

Mrs. Muldoon leaned back in her chair and smiled. "If

you were painting my portrait, would you have me in that pose?"

Zoe blinked. "Um, no," she stammered and found herself wishing she would stop acting like a star-struck teenager.

"Tell me, how would you paint me?"

Zoe took a deep breath to steady her nerves. She looked up at the ceiling deep in thought for a few moments and then returned her gaze to Mrs. Muldoon, who was looking at her. "You are a woman that likes to surround herself with beautiful art...Um, I would paint you as the central figure surrounded by beautiful art as far as the eye could see." She smiled.

Mrs. Muldoon leaned forward in her chair and smiled. "That is one of the most interesting concepts I've heard in a long time. It's fascinating."

"Thank you." Zoe sat back, feeling a little less overwhelmed.

"Can I call you Zoe?"

"Yes, ma'am." Zoe nodded.

"You have a quick artistic mind. How long have you been an artist?"

"All my life. For as long as I can remember, I've liked to draw."

"Are you the only artist in your family?"

"No, ma'am." Zoe shook her head. "My mother was an artist, a very well-known artist in Greece. Her paintings were even bought by the Prime Minister and, although I didn't see her, his wife came to Larissa, and while she was there she bought one of my mother's paintings..." Zoe stopped when she realized she was rambling. She felt a little bit silly. She often wished she had Eva's poise and confidence when dealing with influential people.

"So you come from an artistic family. That's excellent to know."

"Yes, ma'am," Zoe mumbled.

"I was talking to your roommate..."

"My wife," Zoe corrected and waited for Mrs. Muldoon's reaction.

Mrs. Muldoon sat back. Zoe couldn't see any shock or, more to the point, revulsion. Her expression was neutral. "I guess one should expect an artist to be...different," she finally said after what seemed like an eternity.

"Well, that's me. I'm different," Zoe quipped before she could censor herself.

"I have a secret to tell you, Zoe."

"You're a lesbian?" Zoe regretted the words as soon as she spoke them but kept a neutral expression or the best one she could muster. *One of these days, you are going to get yourself into deep trouble. Wait until Eva hears about this one.*

Mrs. Muldoon laughed.

It wasn't that funny. Zoe gave Mrs. Muldoon a half-smile. She was more than a little confused about how the conversation was going.

"No, no, that's not the secret, although Herbert would be most surprised if this were true." Mrs. Muldoon chuckled. "No, that's not the secret."

"Oh." Zoe nodded and tried to look relaxed and less annoyed.

"I know all about you, Zoe Lambros."

Zoe pursed her lips and waited.

"You're not going to ask me what that means?"

"I could, but I don't have to since you know all about me."

Mrs. Muldoon crossed her legs and sat back in the seat with a cryptic smile that Zoe was finding very annoying. "You're annoyed with me."

"You could say I don't find being interrogated all that nice."

"I like you, Zoe."

"I like me as well." Zoe rolled her eyes at her own silliness.

"It was a pleasure meeting Eva. What do you call her?"

"I call her Eva," Zoe replied.

"Yes, that's her name, but what do you call her?"

"She answers to Eva. Actually, it's Eva Theresa Haralambos, but it was Eva Theresa Muller—"

"You know what I'm asking, don't you?"

"Oh, sure. What do you want from me, Mrs. Muldoon?" Zoe asked, having reached the end of her minimal patience. She didn't care if Mrs. Muldoon was the queen herself.

"You are a forthright young woman." Mrs. Muldoon grinned. "I like that in my assistant."

"Pardon?" Zoe looked around the cabin.

"I want you to work for me."

"Why?"

"I want someone who knows their art, I want someone honest, and I like your feistiness."

"Uh...what?" Zoe just couldn't make any sense of what Mrs. Muldoon was talking about. "You know famous artists, and honest ones at that."

"Yes, I do know a lot of artists."

"And some of them are different like me if that's what

you were after," Zoe said before once again wishing she would shut up and not say another word.

Mrs. Muldoon laughed.

Zoe scratched her head in total befuddlement.

"Zoe, as much as I think you are an attractive young woman, that's not what I am looking for."

"Oh, good, Eva wouldn't be at all pleased," Zoe said.

Mrs. Muldoon smiled. "I want an assistant for my art collection back home. I visited the Art's Council recently."

"Yes, I know. I was there."

"Indeed. I saw your work on some restored art that the Arts Council had on display, and I wanted to meet the artist."

"Do you always do background checks on the artists you like?"

"No, just those I want to hire."

"I have a job."

"Indeed, but I have a better job for you. Don't you want a better job with more money than what you are getting now?"

Zoe was intrigued. "But I have the job I wanted and other than the money, what will you offer me that's better?

"It's not every day you get the offer of working and meeting talented artists, learning from them, and helping me set up a scholarship for young artists to excel. What Australia needs is culture. Every society needs art and literature and for the young to embrace these as well as cricket and football."

"Uh-huh."

"Is that all you can say?"

"I don't know why you want me."

"I like you," Mrs. Muldoon replied with a sincere smile that reached her blue eyes. "I need an assistant that has the same passion for art that I do. You're an artist and a passionate one. You are also not very diplomatic, and I like that as well."

"How do you know that?"

"Your diplomacy is non-existent, but I've seen your art, and your passion runs through it. You know, you are making this a very tough sell. I didn't think it would be this hard to convince you."

"Did you think I would just come in here and you would magically say the right words and I would fall into line?" Zoe asked and got up. She wasn't sure where she wanted to go, but she stood up and circled the chair. "You have totally confused me."

"Actually I thought you would say yes right away. I underestimated you," Mrs. Muldoon replied with a little wave of her hand. "I need someone like you. Of course, I didn't know what you were like before. It was only when I read Eva's application and did some checking that I realized who you were."

"Uh-huh."

"So what do you say? Would you like to work for me?"

Zoe took a deep breath and remembered what she had said to her mother eight years previously. *I want to draw, to be a great artist...I want to see what's over there. I want to know what's out there beyond Mount Ossa.*

She bowed her head in thought. "I want to speak to Eva before I say yes."

Mrs. Muldoon cocked her head and smiled. "Why?"

"Don't you speak to Mr. Muldoon about the decisions you make?"

"Yes."

"Why should I be any different? I share my life with her."

"I understand. I am aware of the nature of your relationship."

"When do you need to know my answer?"

"Yesterday," Mrs. Muldoon replied with a smile. She got up and extended her hand to Zoe. "I hope we can work together, Zoe."

Zoe took the offered hand and watched as Mrs. Muldoon put on her gloves and hat and walked out, leaving Zoe alone in the cabin.

"Well, that was interesting," Zoe said before she got up and walked out of the cabin.

CHAPTER 21

Zoe ambled to her cabin. Her thoughts swirled around the extraordinary meeting with Mrs. Muldoon. She let herself into the room. Eva was not inside since she had gone to acquaint herself with her new darkroom and her new camera, and to meet with the returning refugee coordinator.

Zoe sat down on the chair and pursed her lips.

"Something...something."

Zoe got up, picked up her sketchbook, and left the cabin. She went outside on the deck. She scanned the area and found a sweet spot in the sunshine.

She sat in a vacant lounge chair. She brought her knees up and used them to rest her sketchbook. She smiled when she caught sight of Eva talking with the refugee coordinator.

"Don't slouch," Zoe muttered. Eva was indeed slouching to avoid making herself appear taller. "It doesn't work. You still look tall because you are tall."

"Hello, Miss Lambros."

Zoe quickly turned her head and mentally rolled her

eyes. Alice. "Hello." Zoe turned back to watch Eva. "How can I help you, Alice?"

"Mrs. Muldoon wanted to give you this." Alice handed Zoe a folder. "It's just some of her ideas about what you discussed. She forgot to give this to you at your meeting."

"Hmm." Zoe took it, gave a brief look inside, and put it aside. "Thank you."

"Um, is there anything I need to pass on for Mrs. Muldoon?"

Zoe paused then turned to Alice. "How long has Mrs. Muldoon been an artist?"

"Mrs. Muldoon isn't an artist." Alice chuckled. "She loves art, but she's not an artist. She just appreciates great art and has a sizeable collection."

"Oh." Zoe pursed her lips. "Are you sure?"

"Oh, yes."

"Hm." Zoe nodded. "Thank you for the folder. There isn't anything you need to tell her from me."

Alice smiled and walked off.

Zoe started to draw Eva standing near the railing; her hair was being whipped up by the breeze, and she had a camera around her neck and a concentrated look on her face. "You are just too gorgeous," Zoe mumbled as her hand flew across the page.

EVA LOOKED up at the sound of children yelling and laughing at a clown on deck. She wondered what kind of person smiled and joked for a living. She knew she wouldn't be able to do the job. Photography afforded her the perfect way to let her creativity shine, and she was very proud of her work. It also allowed her to be at peace with herself.

Eva leaned against the railing. She spotted Zoe sitting on the lounge chair and, while her head was down, she took a photo. *I bet she's drawing another one of me. Well, I'm going to shoot a few more of her.* She chuckled to herself and fired off a few more shots before Zoe lifted her head, and their eyes met. Zoe turned her sketchbook around and laughed. She gestured to Eva to take photographs of other people instead.

Eva reluctantly took off her sunglasses and trained her camera on the clown. Decked out in blue trousers, with yellow hair and a big red nose, she was enough to set the children all giggling.

Eva was busy taking photographs of the children with the clown but spied Dr. Salvatore as he made his way to Zoe. He talked to Zoe, gave her a smile, and then took her hand and kissed it.

Eva grunted and turned away. She trusted Zoe would tell the doctor about their relationship as they had discussed. She turned her attention to her camera equipment on the deck.

She was feeling more than a little jealous as she packed her equipment. She was startled when someone touched her. She turned around quickly to find Zoe staring down at her.

"I'm sorry, Evy, for startling you. I called you several times." Zoe knelt down. "Can you pack that up pretty quickly?"

"Huh?" Eva was puzzled. "Why?"

"I need you," Zoe replied.

"Um, Zoe, I'm working."

"I know that." Zoe packed the camera in the bag. "This is important."

Eva scratched her head and got up. Zoe hefted the camera bag, took Eva's hand, and led her off the deck.

"Zoe, I don't think..."

"Trust me," Zoe quietly said.

Eva shrugged and followed Zoe. She realized they were headed in the direction of Dr. Salvatore's room. "What are you up to?"

"Me? Nothing." Zoe giggled.

They arrived at the cabin and walked in.

Eva looked around the cabin, which was laid out the same as theirs. A single examination table covered with a white sheet stood in the back, a desk and chair nearby. Nothing remarkable about the place.

"Zoe, is that you?" Dr. Salvatore's voice drifted out from another room.

"Yep," Zoe replied.

"Okay, if you could get your shirt off and lie on the examination table, I'll be out shortly. Just sing out when you're ready."

Zoe smiled up at Eva. "Sure thing." She began to unbutton Eva's shirt.

"Zoe!" Eva hissed.

"Yes?" Zoe continued to unbutton the shirt while Eva buttoned it up.

"I don't think..."

Zoe sighed. "I'm not about to go through a charade with this man so I can learn this technique. I'm not going to do it, and that's that."

"But..."

"Dr. Salvatore needs to know that I'm not interested in

him but for what he can teach me," Zoe said. "It aggravates you to the point where you sneer every time the man is near me."

"I don't sneer."

Zoe snorted. "You sneered when he spoke to me up on deck."

"How do you know that?"

Zoe raised her eyebrow and resumed unbuttoning Eva's shirt.

Eva chuckled and removed her shirt and bra.

"I'm going to learn how to do this, and you're going to benefit from a good massage," Zoe said. "That makes sense to me."

"Yes, dear," Eva replied.

Zoe gave her a playful pat on the backside as Eva walked past and chuckled.

Eva stretched out on the table. Zoe unfurled the folded sheet and placed it over Eva's backside.

"I'm ready, Doctor!" Zoe said and gave Eva a quick kiss.

"Oh, good." Dr. Salvatore entered and stopped short when he saw Zoe standing near his desk. "I thought..." He looked at the table.

"I owe you an explanation," Zoe said and leaned against his desk.

"Yes, that would be good." Dr. Salvatore crossed his arms and waited.

"I want to learn this technique."

"That's good." Dr. Salvatore nodded.

Zoe glanced at Eva, who rested her head on her arms. "This is Eva."

"Yes, I know that."

"She's my lover," Zoe said.

Dr. Salvatore closed his eyes for a moment. "You are lesbians?"

"Yes," Zoe replied.

"Mamma Mia." Dr. Salvatore smacked himself on the side of the head. "Had you told me you were lovers I would not have been so forward. Apologies, but I am not a mind reader. I thought since you wanted lessons, it's not the usual response I get when I tell people my profession, yes?"

Eva sighed. "We don't tell people, Dr. Salvatore."

"Yes, yes, I understand."

"It can be difficult.

"Do you really have a back problem?"

"Yes." Eva nodded. "Yes, I do."

"At least that was the truth," he said. "And you really wanted to learn about my technique?"

"Yes," Zoe replied.

Dr. Salvatore again smacked his hand against his head. "I am sorry. I misunderstood, and I thought you were interested...you are so friendly."

"I'm friendly with people, Dr. Salvatore," Zoe said. "I didn't think you would take my friendliness to mean...I mean...Not that I wouldn't find you an interesting man. You are, but I'm...umm..."

Eva hid her face and chortled.

"If I had known you were...ah lovers...I wouldn't have been so forward. Forgive me." Dr. Salvatore bowed. He reached out to take Zoe's hand and stopped himself. "Okay now." He went over to Eva. "Does your back hurt now?"

"No." Eva shook her head.

"I figured that if you showed me the technique on Eva, then I would learn how to do it," Zoe explained.

"Yes, that is an excellent idea," Dr. Salvatore said as he

lowered the sheet down to Eva's waist. "How long have you had the scarring?"

"A bomb blast in Paris during the war did the major damage."

"Hmm," Dr. Salvatore said, and scratched his ear. "Was it a long time before you saw anyone for your back?"

Eva twisted around a little to face the doctor and covered her chest with the sheet. "A few weeks."

"I'm not surprised you have a bad back," Dr. Salvatore muttered. "Who did this to you?"

"The French Resistance bombed the house my father was in, and I was in the room where the bomb went off."

"Ah. No, there is more damage here than just a bomb going off. You were in a concentration camp, yes?" Eva shook her head. "No..."

"Yes," Zoe said from where she sat on a stool.

Dr. Salvatore looked at Zoe and then at Eva. "Yes or no?"

"Not like Auschwitz," Eva mumbled and settled back down. "It was..."

"Someplace equally as bad," Dr. Salvatore said. "I've seen survivors, Miss Haralambos..."

"Call me Eva," Eva said.

"Thank you, Eva. People carry many scars both here." He gently touched her back. "And here." He touched the side of Eva's head. He washed his hands at the nearby basin. "Zoe, are you ready to learn?"

Zoe nodded. Eva was relaxed enough, which was most unusual. Her relationships with chiropractors were always short-lived.

The doctor touched Eva's lower back and began his instruction for his new pupil.

CHAPTER 22

Zoe opened her eyes and smiled. Eva's dark head was resting on her shoulder. She usually used Eva as a pillow. She tenderly stroked Eva's head and knew the reason she was curled up against her. The morning's massage so relaxed her that she fell asleep on the examination table, much to Zoe's amusement. She ran her hand through the dark locks hoping Eva would wake up.

"What have we got here," Zoe mumbled as she poked at a white hair. She plucked the offending hair.

"Ow," Eva mumbled and rubbed her head. She gazed up at Zoe. "That hurt."

"Oh, you poor baby," Zoe cooed and kissed the top of Eva's head. "That white hair was all lonely, so I plucked it."

"It's like a hydra," Eva mumbled as she pulled the blanket up to her shoulders.

"Really?"

"Yeah, you pluck one and two grow back," Eva replied.

Zoe laughed.

"Why'd you wake me?"

"It's a big day tonight," Zoe said.

"Tonight wouldn't be the day."

Zoe made a face and then smiled. "Your jokes are really, really terrible."

"No, they're not. Made you smile." Eva chuckled.

"Tonight is special."

"Really?" Eva yawned as she played with Zoe's buttons. "I have to photograph tonight's group meeting and a scramble game. Yep, that's special."

"You've forgotten, haven't you?"

"What? I'm getting old. Remind me," Eva said.

"Oh yeah. You're old all right." Zoe giggled.

Eva reversed their positions, and Zoe was staring up into light blue eyes that reminded her of a summer day.

"Very old," Zoe said.

"Uh-huh." Eva traced a finger down Zoe's cheek. "How do I love thee? Let me count the ways. I love thee to the depth and breadth and height my soul can reach when feeling out of sight For the ends of Being and ideal Grace."

Eva recited her favorite poem each anniversary of their special day, when she had proposed, and some days just because she felt like it. She was a true romantic in every sense of the word.

"I love thee to the level of every day's most quiet need, by sun and candlelight. I love thee freely, as men strive for Right; I love thee purely, as they turn from Praise." Zoe smiled at the beautiful woman who loved her more than life itself.

"I love thee with the passion put to use In my old griefs, and with my childhood's faith. I love thee with a love I seemed to lose With my lost saints I love thee with the breath, Smiles, tears, of all my life! and, if God chooses, I shall but love thee better after death." Eva kissed Zoe. "I love you, Zoe."

Zoe sighed. "I love you so much. Happy anniversary."

"I can't promise you the mountains today," Eva said.

Zoe grinned devilishly and very slowly unbuttoned Eva's sleep shirt. "Oh, I don't know." She traced the tip of her finger over Eva's exposed breast. "I can guarantee you that I'll be doing some climbing." She giggled.

Eva laughed and shook her head.

A knock on the door startled them.

Zoe glanced at the clock. "Are you expecting anyone?" She rolled over Eva.

"That was nice," Eva mumbled as Zoe rose from the bed. "Want to try it again?"

"Hold that thought." Zoe tweaked Eva's chin. She put on a robe and went to the door. Eva got out of bed and messed up the other bed. She indicated to Zoe to go ahead and open the door. Very casually, Eva leaned against the doorjamb.

Zoe opened the door. No one. She looked down and found a dozen roses resting against the doorjamb with a note. "Oh, I thought we cleared that up already," she muttered as she brought the roses inside.

"Obviously not," Eva mumbled and scowled.

"Well, I'm going to take them back." Zoe removed her robe to change.

"Shouldn't you read the card first to make sure it's from Dr. Salvatore?"

Zoe gave her a look. She plucked the card from the roses. She read it and looked up into Eva's smiling face. "Five down, Eternity To Follow - ETH," she whispered. She put her arms around Eva.

"I've got something for you," Zoe said.

"Oh? You're going to find more white hair and pluck them?"

Zoe laughed and went into the tiny bathroom. She grabbed a cloth-covered canvas and went back into the bedroom.

"Oh, I like the cloth, very festive," Eva joked as Zoe set up the painting against a chair. "You shouldn't have gone to all that trouble of finding such beautiful material."

"Unveil it." Zoe stepped back.

Eva took the edge of the cloth and pulled it away. Her jaw dropped. In the center of the canvas was a large tree. Eva rested against it, with Zoe in between her legs leaning back against her. Surrounding them were images of their lives, places they had been.

"Do you like it?"

"I love it." Eva put her arm around Zoe and kissed her tenderly. "This is gorgeous."

"I had the artwork sent here, so I didn't have to carry it."

"It's just so beautiful." Eva kissed her again. "So, are you going to tell me what's been on your mind since you came back from the meeting with Mrs. Muldoon?"

"How did you know that? Now, who is reading my mind?" Zoe asked as Eva led her to the sofa. "Never mind, don't answer that. You always know."

"Like you know when I'm thinking about something."

"Ah." Zoe nodded. "Yes. I have been thinking about my meeting with Mrs. Muldoon."

"What tipped you off about her?" Eva smiled.

"You were right. There was something there."

"Yes. I was suspicious the minute she gave me the photo."

"What about it?"

"I know you know this, but describe what we are wearing in David's photo," Eva said.

"What we are wearing? Um...you were wearing a light blue blouse with those cute monkeys on them, pleated dark blue pants, and you wore your hair short because it was when we were living in the apartment. I was wearing a bright pink shirt with embroidery around the collar and a black pleated skirt. It was a sunny day." Zoe opened her eyes and smiled.

"Are you sure it was sunny?"

"Yes."

"Was a ship docked at the international terminal?"

"I don't know because we weren't overlooking the terminal. We were close to the heads than inside the harbor. Is that all?"

"We both had long hair in the photo that Mrs. Muldoon showed me. But what made me wary, and I just couldn't put my finger on it, was that, other than the long hair, there was the healing cut above your eye."

"The cut above my eye? Right after the accident?"

"Yes. Remember it was the first weekend that you got out of bed and we went out?"

"Yes, I remember that."

"It was a cloudy day, love. It wasn't sunny at all. I remember because I took photos of the harbor and kept hoping the cloud cover would clear so I could take a wonderful photo of the ship that had just sailed in."

"Are you sure?"

"The ship was in the photo," Eva said. "There was no ship in David's photo. We were sitting in a spot that had a good view of the international terminal in this photo, but not in David's photo."

"You were looking a little perplexed this morning," Zoe added. "You had this weird look on your face when you spotted Mrs. Muldoon at breakfast."

"It all clicked this morning."

"Wow. That's good detective work, Miss Holmes. She spied on us."

"That photo was taken before we even thought about going to Europe." Eva put her arm around Zoe. "She was spying on us."

"Do you think she caused my accident?"

"No." Eva shook her head. "I thought of that but dismissed it. There was no way of knowing which route you were going to take that day. Half the time you don't even know."

Zoe grinned. "I like changing the route."

Eva returned Zoe's smile. "You drove me crazy because the Legacy Road route is longer and you like to speed on it. What happened to you was an accident."

"She isn't responsible for my accident but she has gone to a lot of trouble to keep a close watch on us. I don't remember her from Egypt or anywhere else. Do you know her?"

"No."

"She wasn't one of Muller's mistresses, was she?"

"No, that's not it either."

"Maybe she's Nazi?"

Eva put her arm around Zoe and kissed her on the cheek. "No, love, not another Nazi, but I may have some idea of who she is working for. She may be working for Frau Beatriz Muller."

"What? Why would you think Mrs. Muldoon is working for your grandmother?"

"She told me she knew of my grandmother."

"Doesn't mean she is working for her, just that she knows about her."

"Do you really think she would come and tell us that she's working for her?"

"For someone that doesn't love you, she wants to know a lot about you."

"It's not about love, Zoe, it's about control. My grandmother doesn't like to lose control. She never has, and I doubt she has changed much."

"I do not like your grandmother, even though I've never met her. That photo of her from Larissa tells me everything I need to know. Cold. Your grandfather I liked a great deal. He had nice, kind eyes, but not her. So you think Grandmother Muller wants to keep an eye on you?"

"Yes."

"So she knows where you are but hasn't made any contact."

Eva sighed. "She has made contact. Now, with Mrs. Muldoon."

"Such a loving thing to do," Zoe replied sarcastically. "Why doesn't she just leave you alone. She disowned you."

"You are not capable of discerning what goes on in her head; she is the matriarch of the family and has always wanted to know what everyone was doing. If she disagreed with it, she made sure the person knew it and would 'correct' their ways."

"Awful woman."

"How did your meeting go with our spy?"

"She said all the things a young artist would like to hear." Zoe shrugged. "Tickled my ears and all of that."

"But?"

"She made a mistake. If you showed me a photo, you have taken and asked me what I thought of it—"

"As I have many times."

"Yes. If I didn't like it, what would you say?"

"I would want to know why and what was in that photo that I could do better."

Zoe smiled. "That's the reaction an artist has. You and I are artists. You create your art through your photos, and I create my art through painting and drawing. I saw her artwork. Truly hideous colors. Mrs. Muldoon asked me if I liked it. I said no."

"Not that you tickle anyone's ears with fake praise but that was too blunt, wasn't it?"

"There was something in the way she looked at me and asked my opinion that didn't seem genuine. She told me it was her artwork and then said nothing to defend it. Every artist I know would defend his or her work. She didn't."

"That made you suspicious?"

"It made me curious, but when I went up to the deck where you were taking photographs with the clown, Alice was there to deliver some paperwork from Mrs. M. I asked her if Mrs. M was an artist."

"Was she worth all that trouble?"

"Of course. Alice told me that she wasn't an artist. Did you see the artwork when you met with her?"

"No, there wasn't any art on the walls, but it could be because they had just moved in and didn't have time to hang any. Was her signature on it?"

"I don't remember seeing it."

"So it was just that she didn't defend her art?"

"Yes. It's not normal for an artist not to defend their work. You know how much I hate liars." Zoe shook her head as she got comfortable and leaned back into Eva's body. "As much I like to think I'm a good artist and you think I'm the next Berthe Morisot, you are biased."

"I don't think you're the next Berthe Morisot." Eva kissed the top of Zoe's head. "I think you are better than Berthe."

"I love you, but you are so blinkered." Zoe giggled. "Anyway, Mrs. M paid too much attention to my work. Work that she described as seeing when she came to visit the Gallery."

"How do you know she didn't?"

Zoe looked up at Eva. "The artwork was sitting on my desk and nowhere near where she was. I'm a young artist, and she's the patron of the Arts Council. Not in my wildest dreams would I dream that this woman would even know my name."

"Unless you were Eva Muller's lover."

"Exactly. She doesn't behave like a woman that found out about us only a few weeks ago when you submitted your application."

"So we reached the same conclusion."

"Yes."

"The question now is..." Eva took Zoe's hand and kissed it. "What do we do about this?"

"Do you want to stop working for her?"

"I like taking photographs, and I like this cabin," Eva admitted. "The issue of her working for my grandmother won't disappear. We don't know how long she has been working for her and how long she has been spying on us."

"So we play along?"

"I don't see any benefit in telling her we know. You agree

to work for her, but don't do anything to arouse her suspicions."

"This is like an Agatha Christie novel."

"Yes. Hopefully, we won't find out that the butler did it in the parlor," Eva said.

Zoe shook her head.

"What? That's funny."

"No, that's awful. Agatha wound never write something so awful." Zoe chuckled. "Alright then. I'm Mrs. Muldoon's new art assistant. A fancy name for a job I'm never going to have. Do you think Dr. Salvatore is real?"

"Oh, yes." Eva nodded. "That man has great hands."

"Oh, yes. How could I forget? The one and only time you have ever fallen asleep during a massage."

"It was very soothing."

"Is that right?" Zoe straddled Eva's legs. She gently cupped Eva's face in her hands. She looked into Eva's beautiful eyes and tenderly kissed her.

CHAPTER 23

September 15, 1950

Eva yawned for the second time as she put away her camera. The dark room had become her own for the last few weeks, and she was not going to be sorry to see the back of it. It was cramped and made her feel slightly claustrophobic. With a sigh, she turned and surveyed the drying pictures. She had taken so many photos she wasn't sure which ones were going to go into the magazine. She would have to come back in the morning and finalize everything before they docked in Athens.

Eva smiled at a photo of Zoe hanging over the rail. The wind had tousled her long red hair, giving her an impish look. She couldn't believe Zoe was twenty-two years old. It seemed like yesterday when she had met the young, fresh-faced teenager. Now she was going back to where it all began. Not the happiest of places, but the whole trip was one huge step down the emotional pain that was part of her past life.

"Just a few weeks and you will be rid of it. Just endure for a few more weeks," Eva said and turned off the light.

She shut the cabin door and pulled her jacket around her. The weather had taken an unseasonably cool feel and the warm nights outside on the deck were long past. Rain and cold weather, she smiled, just what she liked.

It was late in the evening, and she had promised Zoe she would be back to their cabin before midnight. She had spent the last few days trying to get all the photos developed. That required spending long hours in the dark room. She glanced at her watch, which read eleven-thirty, and smiled. She was rather pleased with herself that she had managed to finish everything before midnight.

Dr. Salvatore leaned against the railing.

"Are you trying to catch a cold?" Eva asked as she came up beside him.

Dr. Salvatore laughed and shook his head. "Guten Nacht."

"Buona sera," Eva replied in Italian.

They had developed a rapport while Dr. Salvatore taught Zoe his technique on her throughout the last few weeks. He was supportive and trained with great skill and patience. One of the most delightful side benefits was the massages Zoe gave her.

"No, not trying to catch a cold." He turned to Eva. "And how is Miss Haralambos tonight?"

"Very tired," Eva replied. "I want to go to sleep."

Dr. Salvatore nodded. "You've been working long hours."

"I've been trying to finish up." Eva rubbed the back of her neck.

"How's your back?"

Eva grinned. "I haven't had any problems thanks to you."

"Ah." Dr. Salvatore chuckled. "Thanks to Zoe. She's been giving you the massages. She is a good student. So where to from here?"

"Athens, Larissa, and then Berlin," Eva replied. "Are you staying in Athens?"

"Yes. I have some things I need to do," Dr. Salvatore said with a pensive expression.

"Something wrong?" Eva asked.

"No, not really. I have some friends I need to meet and then go to Genova. I have an apartment I need to sell and then go back to Australia," Dr. Salvatore replied. "Lots of memories."

"Good memories?"

Dr. Salvatore smiled sadly. "Do you have a certain date in your life when you say, from here it's good memories, and from here it's bad memories?"

"Yes," Eva replied.

"I see you know what I mean." Dr. Salvatore sighed. "Before the war, I was married."

"Oh? You have never mentioned Mrs. Salvatore."

"No." He shook his head sadly. "My Katarina was killed during the war."

"Oh." Eva looked down at her feet, not knowing what to say. So many lives had been shattered during the war that she doubted there was anyone alive who hadn't felt the sting of death in their family. "How old was she?"

"Katarina was seventeen years old, a young girl. I was twenty-five years old and a medic in the Italian army.

Katarina was Jewish, and I foolishly believed that she was not going to suffer the fate of other Jews. Not my Katarina. I was an officer in the army. I am a stupid fool to have believed that. I've never seen her since. I tried to find out where she was but she was sent to a concentration camp. I don't know which one." He glanced at Eva.

"People have survived the camps..."

"Yes. I told myself that for many years. I went to Poland and Germany looking for her. I haven't found her. I tried to convince myself that she was in a hospital and didn't know her name or some other thing. Last year I tracked down some Auschwitz survivors from Genova."

"Did they remember Katarina?"

"Hmm." Dr. Salvatore looked out into the heavens. "The last they saw of her was when they were on the trains."

Eva shivered and closed her eyes.

"Do you know why there are so many stars in heaven?" Dr. Salvatore asked.

"God created them?"

Dr. Salvatore turned to her and smiled. "There's an old myth that says that when someone dies, they are reborn as stars."

Eva looked up into the myriads of stars in the heavens. "There's a lot of them."

"Yes. It's a nice little story, but I used to sit outside in my apartment in Genova and see this bright star up in heaven and talk to my Katarina," he said wistfully. "Do you think that's strange?"

Eva shook her head. "No, not strange at all."

"Hmm." Dr. Salvatore nodded. "I would have been in big trouble if Katarina had responded." He chuckled. "I would make up stories in my head. She was just stuck in some refugee place, and she would find a way to get to me. I would find her. I would scold her for being so tardy in returning back to me, and we would be fine."

"We all want to believe."

"Yes, I want to believe, but with each day that passes, another summer, another autumn, another winter, and spring, it is obvious she is not coming back."

Eva put her hand on his shoulder. "How long were you married for?"

Dr. Salvatore looked down at his hand and the ring on his finger. "Three months. Three very short months."

"I'm sorry, Vito. Are you going to sell up and go back to Australia?"

"Yes. I don't have any family in Genova." He glanced at Eva. "I have to apologize to you."

"What for?"

"For trying to woo Zoe," he replied.

Eva smiled. "I can't say I was overjoyed by your attention on her. She is a beautiful woman."

Dr. Salvatore laughed. "If I had been paying attention at the time, I think I'm lucky I wasn't thrown overboard."

Eva chuckled. "Alright, I was a little jealous."

Dr. Salvatore laughed even more. "Just a little, but I have a good reason for trying to woo Zoe."

"Apart from the fact that she's a gorgeous woman?" Eva smiled. She surprised herself by how relaxed she was with him.

"That she is," Dr. Salvatore said and looked up. "But there is another reason." He took out a photo from his top pocket. He looked at it for a moment and gave it to Eva.

The photo was lined in the middle, and the edges were tattered. The young man in the picture wore a uniform and was smiling broadly, his arm around a young woman. Eva looked at Dr. Salvatore with an upraised eyebrow. The young woman was slightly shorter than Zoe but with the same smile, and although the photograph was damaged, the woman's coloring did, in fact, resemble Zoe.

"Katarina had chestnut-colored hair, like Zoe, and those green eyes." Dr. Salvatore closed his eyes and smiled. "She was the most beautiful woman I had ever met."

"She does look like Zoe," Eva said and looked at the photo again.

"Yes, I saw Zoe, and my heart nearly stopped. I thought, at last, I had found my Katarina." He looked away, his voice breaking a little. He cleared his throat and turned back to Eva. "I thought my search was over and here she was, but she is not my Katarina."

"When did you last see her?"

"On the day I was being shipped to Greece in 1940." He took out his handkerchief, wiped his eyes, and put the handkerchief back in his pocket. "Excuse me. I don't usually talk about my Katarina. I'm a sentimental fool some days." He sighed. "Where did you two meet?"

"Larissa," Eva replied, giving the photo back to him. "Zoe saved my life."

"The bullet scar on your shoulder?" Dr. Salvatore asked.

"Nothing slips by you, does it?" Eva gently teased. "Yes, I got that just before the war ended for both of us."

"Hmm. God was looking out for you."

Eva looked up into the heavens and contemplated how true that statement was. "Do you believe in guardian angels?"

"I used to believe in God and guardian angels, but not

anymore. There is no God, and there are no guardian angels. This God took my Katarina. Why should I believe in Him?"

"I used to think that too, but He sent me a guardian angel when I thought He wasn't there."

"You are lucky. Few people heard from God, and His angels were not working."

"The angels were doing overtime during the war," Eva said quietly.

"Too many stars in the sky, too many stars," Dr. Salvatore said as he gazed up into the heavens.

They watched the stars for a while.

Eva glanced at her watch. "I have to go because my guardian angel will be most upset if I'm later than I already am."

"Yes, it's good to have someone to go home to." Dr. Salvatore clasped Eva on the shoulder. He gazed at her and then gave her a hug. They parted, and he kissed her on the cheek. "Take good care of her, Eva."

"I always do, Vito," Eva replied. "May I suggest you close the door or you're going to get a cold?"

"Yes, yes, Mama," he replied as Eva shook her head.

"Good night, Vito." Eva smiled and walked off the deck and down the corridor. "Good night, my darling Katarina," Dr. Salvatore said quietly as the door closed from the deck.

Eva stopped and smiled.

Eva quietly opened the door, hoping not to wake Zoe, as it was well past midnight. She smiled on seeing Zoe sleeping sitting up on a chair, the book she was reading on her lap. She watched her for a few moments as the light from the nightstand cast Zoe in shadows.

She put down her bag and went quietly to Zoe's side. "Zoe," she whispered.

Zoe stirred, opened her eyes, and smiled. "Hi." She rubbed her eyes.

"Were you waiting for me?"

"Uh-huh. I thought I would read a bit, but I must have dozed off." Zoe got out of the chair. "You look tired. Did you get all of them printed?"

Eva nodded and put her arms around Zoe's waist. "Yes. I'll take them down tomorrow." She couldn't help a yawn from escaping.

Zoe smiled. "I think it's time for bed, huh? You are a bit late."

"Yes," Eva replied. "I found Vito outside gazing at the stars."

"Out in this cold?"

"I don't think he was feeling the cold. He was saying goodnight to his Katarina."

"Who?"

"His wife," Eva replied and went into the bathroom. "He lost her during the war."

"Oh, that's sad," Zoe said as she leaned against the door.

"Hmm, he apologized to me," Eva mumbled as she brushed her teeth and gave Zoe a smile.

"Why?"

Eva rinsed her mouth out. "For going after you."

"Oh gosh, Evy, you didn't—"

"No, of course, I didn't say anything. He did. It seems you have a twin or had a twin."

"Huh?"

"Katarina looked like you so much that he thought it was

you when he first saw you. The red hair, the green eyes, the smile." Eva smiled. "My kind of woman."

Zoe laughed. "I have a thing about tall, dark-haired, blue-eyed women."

"Women?" Eva raised her eyebrow.

"Woman. Just one." Zoe pulled Eva out of the bathroom and wrapped herself around her. "Absolutely just one."

"Oh, good." Eva kissed her. "So are you going to keep me?"

"Hmm." Zoe tapped her finger against her chin and looked up into Eva's eyes. "Oh, absolutely. I don't have the time to break in a new wife."

Eva yawned again, and Zoe giggled as she tried to stifle her own yawn. "You're tired; let's go to bed. I've been thinking, Evy..."

"Am I in trouble?" Eva asked.

"Have you done anything to be in trouble?"

"No, I've been good," Eva replied. She stopped before removing her shirt. She smiled as Zoe started on the first button. "I like it when you do that."

"You do, huh?" Zoe looked up and caressed Eva's cheek. "I like undressing you."

"I know." Eva chuckled as Zoe removed her shirt and slacks. She leaned against the top bunk while Zoe folded her shirt and set it aside.

Zoe put her arm around Eva's waist as they snuggled together in the bunk.

Eva drifted off but then remembered what Zoe had said. "What were you thinking about?"

"EHZL Studios," Zoe mumbled.

"EHZL Studios? What kind of name is that? Sounds like a disease."

"That's our new photography studio and art gallery, Eva Haralambos Zoe Lambros." Zoe grinned. "It doesn't sound like a disease."

"Want another name."

"When we get back, I think it would be a good idea to open one, and we'll find a good name."

"We don't have time to manage a studio. I'll still be working at the Immigration Department."

"No, you won't be."

"What?" Eva asked, trying to keep her eyes open.

"I've listened to so many stories from the returning refugees. I've spent time with them, and they all talk about what if and what should have been," Zoe explained. "We both know life is so very short, and we don't know what will come."

"We have always known that, love."

"I know, but I've seen you these last four weeks, and you have been so happy. You have been in love with what you do. That makes me happy too. I want you to be this happy every day."

"I am."

"No, you are not. You come home from that place, and some days you hardly say two words because of all those stories you hear. They are sad, and they make you sad."

"What do you want me to do?"

"I want you to do what makes you happy. Photography makes you happy."

"Zoe, we have a mortgage and—"

"I know, but I'm going to sell all the properties I own in Larissa. Yes, it is my inheritance, but I know Mama and Papa would want me to be happy."

"But—"

"Bricks, wood, mortar, and dirt won't make me happy. I can never forget my family, and I don't need buildings or fields to remind me."

"Okay," Eva sleepily replied.

"The money would give us some good capital." Zoe looked up. "I've had this dream that you owned your own studio, and I had the art gallery. It's something we both want."

"What about Mrs. Muldoon's job offer?"

"You really want me to work for a woman that has spied on us?"

"No." Eva yawned and tightened her arms around Zoe.

"So do you think it's a good idea?"

"If it will make you happy, my guardian angel, then yes, it's a good idea."

"Your guardian angel?"

"Hmm, lots of stars in the heavens and my guardian angel," Eva mumbled as she closed her eyes and drifted off.

"Oh, you have that so wrong, my love. You are my guardian angel." Zoe looked at Eva, the moonlight casting shadows across her face. She pushed herself up and kissed her tenderly on the lips before snuggling back down to sleep.

CHAPTER 24

ATHENS, GREECE

THE ARCADIA SAILED QUIETLY into the seaport of Piraeus, devoid of the fanfare that started her voyage in Sydney. It was a solemn occasion for many of the passengers, who stood quietly—the first time many had returned home since the war.

Eva stood at the railing, looking out at the sleepy port. It was early in the morning, and fishing boats slipped in and out of the harbor at a leisurely pace—a different scene from 1942. The Italians had been defeated on the Albanian border, but that didn't stop the German war machine, which crushed the Greek army and occupied Athens and the rest of Greece.

Against this backdrop, Eva remembered the last time she had sailed into the port, standing at a railing and looking out at the docked ships. She felt a cold chill run up her spine as she recalled the mad scramble to get out of Greece.

"Very different from when we were here last time," Zoe whispered to her.

Eva turned to find Zoe looking up at her. "How did you know what I was thinking?"

"I just know," Zoe replied as she looked out at the harbor. "We have two days here before we leave for Larissa, so I think it would be a good idea to go to the Acropolis and see the pile of rocks."

"You do?" Eva smiled at Zoe's attempt to distract her from the memories. "They are not a pile of rocks, love."

"I know, but that's what Michael called them." Zoe smiled. "He said his favorite place was where Saint Paul preached to the Athenians. We have to go there. Michael said that if I take the Bible and sit on the steps, I can hear Saint Paul telling them about the one true God."

Eva put her arm around Zoe's shoulders. "I love how you want to distract me. Love you," she whispered in her ear.

"I will distract you in other more enjoyable ways as well," Zoe whispered back. "So, it's a date. We will go up to the Acropolis." She bumped Eva with her hip.

"We will, but Mrs. Muldoon wants me to interpret for some of the refugees later today since they don't speak Greek, and they want to—"

"Let her find someone else."

"Zoe, you know it's part of my job."

"*Was* part of your job. You were rehired as a photographer, not as an interpreter."

"Well, she is paying the bills, love, so that means I'm back to being an interpreter."

"The sooner we get rid of Mrs. Muldoon the better."

"She won't be disappearing for a while. She will be on

the same train to Larissa with the rest of the refugees going back to Thessalonica."

Zoe shook her head. "Why do we have to travel with her?"

"Because you booked it for that time." Eva smiled and turned away, not wanting to laugh at Zoe's very sour look.

"Just my luck we would have Mata Hari on the same trip. Can't we change the train tickets?"

"We can try, but Father is expecting us, and if we delay it longer than necessary, you're going to miss Thanasi's wedding."

"Don't you mean *we* will miss Thanasi's wedding?"

"They don't want me there. They are just courteous to invite me."

"Fine," Zoe replied.

Eva shook her head. Zoe's 'fine' meant that it wasn't fine at all. She was well aware that Zoe's easy capitulation meant she was going to have a battle on her hands. It was a lost battle, but that wouldn't stop her from trying to get out of going to the wedding.

CHAPTER 25

THE PORTER OPENED THEIR DOOR AND ENTERED with their suitcases. Zoe glanced around the room, which was quite spacious and airy. Against the wall were two single beds and two small bed stands with a lamp on each.

The two beds could quickly be moved together, Zoe mused. The mattresses on the ship were just wide enough, which allowed them to sleep together, but the single beds in the hotel room were very narrow. *Good thing it's only two days.* There was a desk with a reading light near the window and a comfortable-looking recliner next to it.

She poked her head into the bathroom and grinned at the tub. It wasn't as big as the one back home, but she thought Eva could stretch out in it. She would pamper Eva tonight and let her get some sleep.

Eva had been working long days and slept fitfully. Zoe was pretty sure it wasn't the workload but the impending arrival to Larissa. As the days turned into weeks and the ship neared Greece, Eva's mood had also changed. She had become quieter, which wasn't unusual, but she stayed up till the early hours of the morning and only slept for a few hours.

Zoe answered a light knock on the door.

The young man who had assisted her to their room smiled at her. "The housekeeper said you would like some more towels."

"Ah, thank you, Emmanuel." Zoe smiled.

"For a pretty lady like yourself, it's my pleasure," Emmanuel replied. He was a little taller than Zoe with mousy brown hair and twinkling brown eyes. "You're not with Mrs. Muldoon's group, are you?"

"No, I'm with my friend Eva."

Emmanuel gave her a blank look.

"The tall, dark-haired woman. You can't miss her."

"Oh! Yes, she's very tall. Has nice eyes." Emmanuel grinned.

"Yes, she does." Zoe nodded.

"And you have beautiful green eyes." Emmanuel looked around and smiled. He quickly turned back to Zoe. "If you have some free time, would you like to see the sights with me?"

"That's very sweet of you, but Eva and I will be going out. We only have two days here in Athens."

"Let me know if you need a guide." Emmanuel flashed her a quick smile and strode past Eva in the corridor.

Zoe took Eva's hand, pulled her into the room, and closed the door.

"I think you've won another one, Zo," Eva joked as Zoe put her arms around her waist. "Not that I blame him."

"You see things that are not there." Zoe snuggled up in Eva's embrace and sighed, then looked up into tired blue eyes. "Emmanuel brought up some towels. Here's the plan.

Let's take a bath." She undid Eva's shirt buttons, pulled the shirt off her shoulders, and let it fall. "Then I'm going to give you a nice soothing massage, and you are going to sleep because you haven't been sleeping." She put her arms around Eva, unclasped her bra, and let it fall to the floor.

"Yes, I have."

"Three hours of sleep isn't sleeping. It's snoozing."

"That's sleeping," Eva protested as she removed the rest of her clothes.

Zoe brought her down for a kiss, her hands entangled in Eva's dark hair. She let out a contented little moan and broke off the kiss.

"Time for some pampering."

"You, me, bath. I like that idea," Eva replied, getting another kiss.

"Oh, yes. Come with me, Miss. H." Zoe took Eva's hand and walked into the bathroom.

Zoe leaned against the window, gazing at the view of Athens stretched out before them. In the distance, she could see the famed Mount Olympus—the home of the gods. She smiled when she thought of her childhood and the stories her brother used to read to her about Zeus and the rest of the pantheon. It was a lifetime ago. The child that believed in mythological gods and their deeds was long gone.

She gazed back at the bed and smiled. Eva was sleeping soundly, her dark hair framing a face that looked very tired. She was asleep on her stomach and wearing only a singlet and her underpants despite Zoe's urging to wear pajamas in case they needed to get out of the hotel in a hurry. Eva merely laughed and ignored the pajamas.

They'd had a bath in between kissing and cuddling. They were both too exhausted to go further, and Zoe was anxious to get Eva out of the tub and into the bed so she could give her a massage. It didn't take long for Eva to fall asleep while Zoe massaged her back.

Zoe had pulled up the blankets and watched her sleep. She was tired but too excited about where she was to get any sleep. She turned back to the window and watched the sky turn dark, and the stars begin to twinkle.

"Zo?"

Zoe turned and met sleepy blue eyes. "Why aren't you asleep?"

Eva blinked a few times. "Come to bed."

"That single bed won't fit the both of us."

Eva went to the very edge and patted the side for Zoe to come to her. Zoe took off her robe and spooned against Eva.

Eva curled around her. "Much better," she mumbled.

"Yeah, I think so too," Zoe replied. "You didn't sleep much."

"I can't turn my brain off."

"That's why you've been working long hours in the darkroom," Zoe said.

"It didn't help."

"We won't be in Larissa too long. I think maybe four days, and then we are out of there for good."

Zoe could feel Eva's breath on her neck, and for a moment thought she had finally gone back to sleep.

"No. We'll stay for as long you need to be there."

"It won't take me long to sign the papers, Evy."

"You have a wedding to go to."

"I don't care about the wedding. We're not staying in Larissa but at Athena's Bluff. It's still too close, but we will be there for only a few days."

"Okay," Eva said quietly. "I just don't...you must think I'm a coward."

Zoe turned in Eva's arms and looked at her. "I don't think you are a coward. That's the last thing I would ever think about you. I know it's hard for you to go willingly into that place again. It was the reason I didn't want to come back."

"I thought it wouldn't be such a problem." Eva brushed a strand of hair out of Zoe's eyes. She cupped her cheek. "Sometimes I fool myself into thinking that I can do this and it won't hurt, but it will."

"I know, but you do it anyway."

"I just can't let it go."

"One day you will. One day it will be just like a horrible ache, but it won't be so bad."

"Is that how you feel?"

"Yes." Zoe nodded. "There's an ache that doesn't go away. It's there all the time, but I just have to look at you, and it's not so bad. I think of the cabin and when I nearly lost you, I get the overwhelming urge to scream, but I didn't lose you."

"That's because you were the one that saved my life. You were my guardian angel, Zoe. If you hadn't brought Henry and the Resistance with you, it would have been over."

"I had no intention of letting some German loser take something that belonged to me," Zoe said, trying to lighten the conversation.

"A little possessive, aren't we?"

"Me? Possessive? Absolutely." Zoe grinned. "I'm now changing the subject because it will get us both crying. I want to show you the farm. It's outside of Larissa in Farsala, and it's beautiful."

"Really pretty?"

"Yes. Fields surround the farmhouse. Papa grew cotton. I want to show you the happiest place I knew even though I always wanted to leave."

"You always wanted to see what was past Mount Ossa." Eva smiled.

"You were past Mount Ossa." Zoe tweaked Eva's chin. "Isn't life strange some days?"

"It is. God was listening, and instead of you going to find me, I found you."

"Fate brought you to me."

"If you say so," Eva replied sleepily. "What do you want at the farm?"

"A book." Zoe smiled. "Theo gave me a copy of *Oliver Twist*, and I left it in the chicken coop. Hope it's still there."

Eva smiled. "*Oliver Twist* in the chicken coop?"

"Yes. It's one of my favorite books, and I want it back."

"Why is it in the chicken coop?"

"Not exactly in the coop but under it. That's where I left it the last time I was there." Zoe closed her eyes for a moment. She felt Eva's lips on her own, and she opened her eyes to find Eva's eyes just inches from hers.

"Then we shall go to the farm and get it."

"Can you do me a favor?"

"What's that?"

"Go to sleep. Please."

"I will try." Eva nodded and closed her eyes.

Zoe turned and smiled as Eva pulled her body towards her and held her in her arms. Having Eva's arms around her was the most comforting feeling. She brushed the tear that tracked down her face. Larissa had nightmares for both of them, and they were going to face them together.

The incessant ringing of the alarm woke Zoe, and she lifted up her head to scowl at the clock that was on Eva's side of the single bed. She wasn't complaining, but the alarm bell was going to wake Eva, and that was the last thing she wanted to happen.

Before Zoe could get out of bed, a long arm snaked out from under the blanket and smothered the alarm clock. Eva turned, her hair messed up in a way Zoe found totally adorable.

Eva smiled at Zoe. "I couldn't throw it on the floor. It's not ours."

Zoe grinned. Quite a few alarm clocks had been broken over the years, usually by Eva flinging them on the floor or throwing them out the door.

"You are so adorable in the morning," Zoe said and kissed her soundly. "How are you feeling?" She snuggled up.

Eva pursed her lips. "Better. I think the sleep helped. I know talking about it helped, and I know your hands on my body helped."

"I don't have a bad back, and your hands on my body help me a great deal," Zoe whispered, nuzzling Eva's long neck and giving her a gentle nip.

"If you keep that up, I don't think I'm going to make my eight-thirty meeting," Eva said, a trifle breathlessly as Zoe slipped her hand under her singlet, cupped a firm breast, and gave it a gentle squeeze. She let out a small gasp.

"What meeting?" Zoe whispered.

"The one Mrs. Muldoon arranged...oh dear..."

Zoe's other hand stroked her inner thigh.

"Huh...Zoe, please stop."

Zoe gave her an evil grin. "You sure?"

Eva lay back and groaned. "Huh, no. Yes."

Zoe slid the singlet off Eva's shoulders and kissed the now bare shoulder. "Are you sure?" She grinned as she placed gentle feather-light kisses on Eva's stomach and then worked her way downwards.

Eva looked down at her and groaned.

Zoe took pity on her and stopped her gentle teasing. "Tell Mrs. M to schedule meetings at a more reasonable hour."

Eva sighed. "And if she asks me why?"

Zoe looked up into the now alert twinkling blue eyes. She tweaked Eva's dimpled chin. "Tell her the truth—because your wife wants to make love to you."

"I don't think she would understand." Eva eyed the clock and sighed. She pushed back the cover and climbed out of bed. She looked back down at Zoe and sat down.

She crooked her finger, and Zoe crawled closer and rested her head against Eva's thigh. Eva gave her a long and sensual kiss. "Good morning." She kissed her again before releasing her.

"Good morning." Zoe watched Eva remove her panties. "I think you've lost some weight. I should check, you know."

"You just want an excuse to come and put your arms around me," Eva replied, picking up a towel.

Zoe grinned. "I don't need an excuse." She got out of bed and wrapped herself around Eva.

Eva disengaged herself from Zoe. "I need to go and have a bath."

"Want some help with it? I'm a good back scrubber."

Eva snorted. "You are wicked," she muttered as she headed for the bathroom.

Zoe chuckled. "And you are incredibly sexy."

Eva turned around and gave her a dazzling smile before closing the bathroom door.

Zoe heard the click of the key locking and wondered if there was a spare key lying around.

There was a gentle knock on the door.

Zoe put on her robe and opened the door to discover a middle-aged woman with a fresh set of sheets in her hand.

"*Kalimera.* I'm Evthokia." She smiled.

Zoe smiled back and opened the door. "Uh, my friend is in the bath."

"I just came to change the sheets and ask if you had any laundry you would like to have done." Evthokia stripped the bed Zoe, and Eva had shared and remade it. She noticed the other bed was already made up. "You didn't need to make the bed. Leaving it is okay. I will take care of it."

Zoe nodded while Evthokia stripped back the bed and replaced the sheets. "Um, what time do you normally come around?"

Evthokia looked at her. "Every morning at seven-thirty."

Zoe rolled her eyes and sat down slowly on the seat as Evthokia went about her chores.

CHAPTER 26

"Aphrodite."

"No."

"Persephone."

"No."

"Athena?"

"Absolutely not."

Zoe smiled as they walked up the walkway to the famed Acropolis. Other like-minded tourists, eager to see the Greek monument, surrounded them. Their morning's banter about names for their not-conceived child had taken on an Ancient Greek feel to it when Eva started rattling off names.

"You're named after your maternal grandmother, right?"

"Yes. Grandma Eva Mitsos."

"What if we call her Daphne?"

"Do you want our daughter to go to school and be called Daphne?"

"What's wrong with that?"

"Ever heard of Daffy Duck? Daffy Lambros?"

"Not Lambros."

"Yes, she will have your name, Zoe. She will be your child."

Zoe stopped walking. "She will be *our* child. I don't want to hear that from you again."

"Our child," Eva corrected. "Well, our child won't be burdened with a silly name like Daphne."

"That's your mother's name!"

"Yes, and I don't like this Greek naming ritual. See how silly it is that you have several thousand cousins called Maria."

"Several thousand?" Zoe giggled.

"It has to be unique; it has to be hers."

"Who else's would it be?"

"The name has to mean something. It has to mean something to both of us."

"Oh. I think we need to think about that." Zoe took Eva's hand and held it. "Oh look! Athena's Monument!"

"You like Athena?"

"Theo told me tales of the wise goddess Athena and of the monument in her honor. For a while, I called myself Athena because it was richer sounding than plain Zoe was."

Eva gazed at Zoe. "You don't look like an Athena."

"Why? Was she taller?"

"I don't think she was half as beautiful as you are," Eva whispered, earning herself a kiss on the cheek.

The child in Zoe was in awe that she'd finally arrived at the site of one of her many long-held dreams. The sun shone brightly on the marble columns of the ancient monument. Zoe fingered the hand-knit light sweater she had been coerced into buying by one of the gypsy vendors on the way up to the monument. It was the ugliest thing she had ever seen, but the gypsy was so insistent that Zoe gave in.

"I still can't believe you didn't haggle with the gypsy. You are the Queen of Haglers."

"She ambushed me." Zoe chuckled. "I think it's too big for me, but it would look perfect on you." She pulled the sweater out and grimaced. The multi-colored pattern made her eyes hurt. Zoe doubted Eva would ever wear it. She'd paid twenty drachmas for it, and she had no idea why she had done it.

"I hope you don't mind me saying this, but that thing is *ugly*." Eva made a face.

Zoe looked up. "Sure is. Want it?"

Eva shook his head. "I wouldn't ever want to be seen wearing that."

"You're no help," Zoe muttered good-naturedly and stuffed the sweater back in her knapsack.

They went a few more meters down the walkway and then Zoe stopped, took out a pad and a pencil, and began to sketch.

Eva wandered around for a moment. She took out her camera from her bag to shoot some photographs.

A young man near Zoe glanced her way. "Excuse me, are you an artist?"

"Yes," Zoe replied as she sketched.

"I love this place. It's so full of history," he said, gazing at Zoe. "What's your name, pretty lady?"

"Zoe," Zoe answered, her attention focused on the Acropolis and Eva, who had walked into her line of sight carrying her camera.

"My name is Cosmas. Where are you from?"

"Farsala. Why do you want to know that?"

"I like to know if I'm going to chat up a communist. I despise communists."

Zoe mentally sighed and stopped sketching. She looked over at Cosmas.

Cosmas chuckled and took out his packet of cigarettes from his shirt pocket. "How old are you?" He asked and offered a cigarette to Zoe who declined.

"Your mother raised an idiot."

"Ouch," Cosmas put his hand over his heart and fell back against the stone steps. "You wound me, *koukla*."

Zoe stared at the young man whose lopsided smile made her angry for reasons she didn't understand.

"You're feisty, I like feisty."

"Go away, Cosmas. I don't have time for dumb boys."

"Oh, come now Zoe. You would like me if you knew me. Are you heading back to Farsala?"

Zoe went back to her sketching and ignored Cosmas until he grabbed her pencil. Zoe looked up and wished she had her gun with her. "You are a lucky fellow."

"Oh? Are you warming up to me?"

"You're lucky I don't have my gun."

Cosmas chuckled and gave the pencil back to Zoe. "Ah, Zoe, I don't mean to be rude to you. So, where are you headed after this?"

Zoe stopped drawing and put her sketchbook away. With a shake of her head, she got up and went to look at the ruins more closely, leaving Cosmas begging her to come back.

Eva joined Zoe and whispered. "It's not worth the effort."

"You heard that silly boy? Boys are so stupid."

Eva smiled. "Some are. Why don't we go over there and we can forget about silly boys?" Eva took Zoe's hand as they stopped outside the Church of the Twelve Apostles to admire the architecture.

"I think it's rather funny to have a church here." Zoe put her hand out and touched the stones.

"Why?"

"Well, we've just passed the Altar of the Twelve Gods, the Temple of Zeus, the Temple of Ares, the Temple of Apollo, and then here we come to the church where the Christian God is real and not a mythical being," Zoe explained. "Don't you find it odd?"

"Odd, yes, but the Greeks have never been a logical people." Eva teased. "I don't think it would have served any purpose to demolish the old temples and obliterate the past to make way for the new."

"Hmm, true," Zoe agreed. She looked around the area known as *the Agora*. It was an ancient marketplace where the Greeks would trade and worship. The ancient site fascinated her.

They wandered onto Areopagus Hill and climbed the steps, which were a little slippery from the overnight rain. Reaching the top, Eva put her arm around Zoe's shoulders and pointed to the view of the Agora.

Zoe looked around her in awe and then looked at Eva with a huge smile.

"What's funny?" Eva asked.

"Michael told me the story about how Ares was tried here for the murder of Halirrhothios. I just found it funny that the others would accept his word."

Eva nodded. "Ares, the god of war and deceit. The old myths served a purpose, you know."

"They did? How?"

"Well, when Saint Paul finally made it to Greece, he

preached right here, and he spoke to the Athenians about an unknown God." Eva looked around the area and tried to imagine the courage necessary to speak to the Greeks about a God they didn't know. "He stood down there," she pointed to the square down below, "and he preached about Jesus and about God. Imagine, Zoe, this place was filled with Greeks all wanting to hear this Roman preach to them."

Zoe took a deep breath and closed her eyes, letting the images form in her mind. "He was a braver man than I would have been," she quietly said as she opened her eyes again.

"I don't agree; you are the bravest person I have ever met. He only did what he was commissioned to do, love. I'm sure if you were given the job he was, you would do it magnificently." Eva squeezed Zoe's hand. "You put your heart and soul into everything, and I don't doubt it for a minute that you could do what Saint Paul did."

"I think the job would be easier if I had you by my side," Zoe said. "With you, I can do anything."

"I think I'm biased when I say this, but you have more bravery than Saint Paul."

"You're right—you are biased." Zoe laughed. "Do you know all this exercise gets me in the mood?"

"In the mood for what?" Eva asked. "Do you want some ice cream?"

"No."

"Cake?"

"No. Something far sweeter and delicious."

"Oh, I get it now. You want some baklava." Eva took Zoe's hand, and they walked down the steps, stopping every couple of steps when Zoe was on the top step and leaned down to whisper in her ear, causing Eva to laugh.

Eva lay back on the rumpled sheets and let out a contented sigh. She loved the feel of Zoe's naked body against her own. Zoe was burrowed against her side, letting her fingers lazily trace Eva's belly button. Eva played with Zoe's unruly red hair and put her arms around her.

"Oh, that was *so* good," Zoe mumbled and kissed Eva's shoulder.

"Hmm, I enjoyed myself." Eva got a little slap on the thigh. "Hey, stop hitting me!"

"Oh, my poor baby," Zoe cooed. She leaned on her elbow. "Did I hurt you?"

Eva made a show of examining her thigh and looked into Zoe's eyes. "You are a brute."

Zoe chuckled. "You are such a wallflower, aren't you?"

"That's why I have you to defend me...unless you're the one hitting me!" Eva teased. "I think we may have to explain why there is damage to the wall."

"Huh?"

"You hit the wall with your bag when we came in. Hard. You were so angry with that silly boy." Eva grinned as Zoe scrambled up to look for any damage to the wall beside the bed.

"Did not." Zoe scowled.

Eva chuckled. "Did too. I was scared for the wall."

Zoe smirked. "You are *so* bad." She tickled Eva, who yelped and tried without much success to grab Zoe's hands. Eva fell off the bed with a thud and landed on the carpet laughing. Zoe hung over the bed and grinned down at her.

"Oh Evy, are you alright?"

"Yes, although it's a little less comfortable."

"Are you going to explain *that* to the manager as well?" Zoe smirked and made room for Eva to climb back into bed.

"Oh, let's see. 'Mr. Danalis, Zoe threw her bag on our wall.' Yeah, that sounds good. What do you think?" Eva grabbed Zoe's arms before she could be tickled again.

"If I give you a kiss, will you let go of my hands?" Eva nodded, and Zoe rewarded her with a quick kiss. "You are so easy." Zoe snuggled up against Eva and rested her hand on Eva's bare waist. "So, tomorrow we head for Larissa."

"Train leaves in the evening, and we'll be there the next morning."

"I don't remember the train taking that long when my brother Theo made the trip."

"We have to change trains for some reason. Mrs. Muldoon told me as we were leaving for the Acropolis. We have to get off and wait for a few hours for the other train to arrive. I think we are stopping far too much. Why was your brother in Athens?"

"He had a girl down here." Zoe grinned. "Every so often he would come down from Larissa with flowers and sweets."

"What happened? Did they get married?"

"They were going to, but she met someone else and married him instead."

Eva gave Zoe a tender kiss, and they both fell silent. "Are you nervous about going home?" Eva asked.

"I am a bit. I haven't been back to the farm since Mama died." Zoe sighed. "I sometimes wonder what I would have done if I hadn't fallen in love with you and what my life would have been like."

"There would be one less happy soul in the world," Eva whispered.

"Oh, no. We were destined to meet and fall in love. I think that whatever happened, I would be with you."

"You think so?"

"Absolutely. I think we are born on this earth for a reason, and I think Fate said, 'Zoe, my girl, you see that tall, gorgeous woman coming up that street? She's yours.' So you were mine from the moment you were born."

"Is that so?" Eva smiled.

"You bet. It just took me eight years to figure out it was time to get myself born, that's all." Zoe settled back down. "Remember how you surprised me at the beach by taking your shirt off?"

Eva frowned. She didn't know where Zoe was headed with her line of thought. She couldn't make the connection between Zoe going home and her decision to let go of one of her fears by allowing others to see her scarred back. "I'm confused."

"Well, you made the decision to not let Muller dictate to you and to stop being afraid."

"Hmm, but what—"

"I'm afraid to go back to the farm," Zoe admitted quietly.

"Why?"

Zoe didn't answer for a short while and then looked back up into Eva's eyes. "On the day Mama was killed, I had an argument with her. I said things to my mama that were hurtful," she whispered.

"What did you say?"

"I told her that I wanted to leave and see what was beyond Mount Ossa."

"That's not so bad. At least you didn't lie to your mama,"

Eva said, remembering she lied regarding her whereabouts on the night her own mother was killed.

"I hurt her, Evy. I told her I hated the place, which meant I hated to be with her. Then she was dead. I didn't have a chance to apologize for my stupidity."

Eva sighed. "You told me you went to your mama's grave and spoke to her. Didn't you apologize?"

"I did."

"The dead can hear our thoughts, love," Eva said. She kissed the top of Zoe's head and held on to her. "Your mama would be very proud of you."

"You think so?"

"Oh, I know it. Look at the woman you have become. I think she would be very proud of how beautiful and compassionate you are."

"You say the nicest things."

"Just the truth, my love."

Zoe sighed and snuggled closer to Eva.

CHAPTER 27

On The Train To Larissa

THE RHYTHMIC BEAT of the train lulled Eva to sleep. A short while later she suddenly woke with a start. It was not one of her recurring nightmares, but she knew something was wrong. She shifted in her bunk and concentrated on the sounds around her. She then heard the sniffle coming from the bottom bunk. Usually, the train from Athens to Larissa wasn't an overnight train, but the original train had broken down, and it was replaced with an overnighter which suited Eva just fine. The train was taking an extraordinary amount of time to traverse the 217 miles between Athens and Larissa. It frequently stopped for hours at a time. The usually four-hour journey was becoming a long-drawn-out affair.

Eva rolled, braced her hands on the bunk, edged out, and looked down. She was surprised to find Zoe staring back at her. Without another word, she sat up and jumped the short distance, forgoing the bunk ladder and landing with a gentle thump.

"Hey." Eva brushed her fingers against Zoe's tear-stained cheek. "Are you having a bad dream?"

Zoe shook her head. "No. You have to be asleep to have one of those."

Eva couldn't help but smile at Zoe's response. "Scoot," she said. She quickly maneuvered herself onto the bunk and lay next to Zoe, who made room for her. As soon as Eva got comfortable, she found Zoe's arms around her waist and her head nestled against her shoulder.

"I've got you; you can go to sleep..."

"No."

"No?" Eva looked down at Zoe with a slight frown. "Zoe, you know you will be grumpy if you don't sleep."

"I can't. I've got too many things going on in my head."

"I know, but you need to rest."

"I know," Zoe replied and nestled closer to Eva's body.

Eva kissed Zoe on top of her head and waited. She knew Zoe would start to talk. Maybe this time she would open up entirely instead of brushing it aside. They were both guilty of that, but Eva always worried about Zoe's response to it. Eva was the quiet one, while Zoe could talk under wet concrete, as their friend Earl was fond of saying.

"Do you want to talk about it?" Eva gently prodded.

Eva felt Zoe's body shudder for a moment. She remained silent, letting Zoe take her time.

"My mind keeps going to when Reinhardt took you to the cabin."

"Ah."

"I've never been so terrified in all my life. Even when Mama died, I didn't have time to be scared. It happened so quickly, but I felt like my heart was going to explode." Zoe fell silent for a long moment. "I heard you, you know."

"You heard me?"

"In the cabin with Reinhardt. You were goading him."

Eva wanted to let out a frustrated sigh but held back. Of all the memories from the war that Zoe was reluctant to talk about, it was the cabin. Other than saying she killed Reinhardt to save Eva, Zoe had remained quiet about her thoughts. Eva always suspected one of Zoe's nightmares centered on that event.

"I was goading him," Eva whispered. "I wanted him to kill me."

"Why?" Zoe shifted and looked up at Eva. "Why did you want to die when we had just found each other?"

"Because we had found each other." Eva sighed deeply. "He was going to kill you."

"I know..."

"Do you remember what they did to that poor girl with the bad leg? I forgot her name..."

"Androniki?"

"Was that her name? With the long hair that reached her bottom, and the lisp?"

"No, that was her sister, Stavroula. She died in a gunfight."

Eva sighed. "It was just after we came to Larissa. She didn't die in a gunfight."

"What happened to her?"

Eva swallowed the lump in her throat. "She was tortured to death."

"Why?"

"I don't know, love, but I do remember overhearing orders to kill her."

Zoe swore and crossed herself before she settled down against Eva. "I wonder if that was when Father Haralambos told me not to go outside."

"Might have been...Reinhardt was the one who did that, and he promised he was going to do the same to you."

"Oh."

"I couldn't let him do that...so I goaded him."

"I could hear you from outside," Zoe mumbled. "You would say something and then there would silence for a minute before...I hated the sound. I couldn't do anything because I was waiting for Henry to get rid of your guard."

Eva nodded. It wasn't one of her pleasant memories, but she did it for the right reason. Getting Reinhardt angry enough to kill her was the only option.

"Every time I said something, I could see the anger building until he exploded."

"It didn't take him long."

Eva scowled. "No, he had a very short fuse. I remember the first blow made me woozy...good thing I was sitting down." She could feel Zoe's body shift.

Zoe looked up at her with a scowl. "That's not funny."

"It wasn't funny, but I wanted him to be mad. He didn't disappoint me. I could hardly breathe after he punched me...It wasn't pleasant. He realized what I was up to and stopped. That's when he was told that the Americans were coming."

"Was he really going to do those awful things?"

"Yes. He told me what he had planned when he took me from the house. He told me in great detail."

"Oh."

"When I saw his gun I thought I had won." Eva smiled.

"You hadn't arrived yet, so I said a prayer and thanked God I had met you."

"I remember that like it was yesterday." Zoe shuddered, and her voice broke. She slipped her hand under Eva's pajama top. "You looked so broken. Every time I think about that, I can still see you on the floor bleeding."

"Do you know what I remember from that? I saw your legs and heard your voice, and that was it. I couldn't keep my eyes open, but I could hear you say something to Reinhardt and then nothing."

"He looked so startled to see me that he didn't have a chance to shoot. I was so enraged by what he had done to you, by what the pigs had done to me and everyone else, that all I could think about was killing the bastard."

"You did the right thing. You didn't kill out of revenge—you killed to save me."

"I killed out of hatred. I killed him in a blinding rage."

Eva finally understood what Zoe had just revealed. It had taken Zoe six years to voice her thoughts on a moment in her life that had changed who she was. "What were you going to do when you stormed that cabin?" Eva reasoned. "Try and talk him into letting us go?"

"No. I wanted to stop him, and I fully intended to kill him."

"This was more personal."

"Something like that."

"I know you told me that you shot the bastard, but what happened afterward?" Eva took Zoe's hand and brought it up to her lips and kissed it. "I love you so much."

Eva felt Zoe's tears as they hit her bare shoulder and she held her in her arms. "You have held that inside you for so long, love. You didn't have to."

"I know." Zoe sniffed back her tears. "I realized that day how much I cared about you...I shot Reinhardt, and then Thanasi came racing in thinking that Reinhardt had shot me. Henry had been shot and was down, so everything was going crazy."

"Thanasi to the rescue." Eva's joke got a tearful chuckle from Zoe.

"I remember dropping the gun and running to where you were...You were barely conscious, bleeding so badly, and I was trying to see where he had shot you, so I tore your shirt to stop the blood."

"I don't remember that."

"Klimis came into the cabin and couldn't believe what he was seeing."

"Which one was Klimis?"

"He was a medic...or he would have been if the war hadn't started. He was a medical student before the war. He told me that you were going to die."

"Nice bedside manner." Eva gently joked.

"He wasn't a bad fellow but..."

"I was the enemy."

"He didn't know. He wasn't very gentle with you until Thanasi told him that you were part of the Resistance. All hell was breaking loose with the Germans retreating..."

"Then what?"

Zoe closed her eyes and remained silent for a long time. Eva thought she had fallen asleep.

"He was the only medic, so he had to leave. Thanasi took you to my house and called Despina to look after us. We waited for the Americans."

"I don't remember that either."

"I do. I didn't know what to do other than to hold you. I

tried to stay awake, but I drifted off to sleep. Next thing I know, this big black American was shaking me awake."

"The Americans had arrived."

"Yes...Not sure how long it was. I was so tired."

"Do you know the first thing I remember when I woke up? I could barely see out of my swollen eyes, but I saw you...You looked so beautiful, even with a dirty face. I tried to speak, but nothing came out."

"I remember that." Zoe nodded. "You drifted off again. Those were difficult days."

"We got through them, love." Eva kissed the top of Zoe's head, and they both fell silent. "I have a name for our studio."

"Really?"

"Hmm." Eva smiled. "Lambros Designs."

"I don't like it."

"I do."

"It doesn't have your name in it."

"It does."

"The last time I checked your name wasn't Eva Theresa Designs."

Eva smiled. "I've been thinking."

"You need to think some more. That is not a good name for our studio."

"It will be when my last name is Lambros." Eva looked down to see Zoe's very startled face looking up at her.

"What?"

"I want to change my name."

"You already have, to Haralambos."

"I know, but this is final."

"Evy, how many times are you going to change your name?"

"Until I get it right," Eva responded making Zoe groan. "Seriously, love. I want to permanently change it to Lambros."

"Why? What's wrong with Haralambos?"

"You don't want me to be a Lambros?"

"It's not that. It's just that you chose Haralambos to reflect your love for Father Haralambos and that he is your father."

"Hmm," Eva said, and attempted to get comfortable in the tiny bunk. "I have a better reason."

"Oh?"

"I want our babies to have the same last name as both their mothers."

"Oh!" Zoe smiled. "I like that reason."

"Thought you might. It's not just that." Eva took Zoe's hand and held it against her chest. "Names mean something, love. I chose Haralambos because it made sense to me, but there isn't a connection there other than Father Haralambos."

"Did you choose it because it wasn't Muller?"

"I don't know, maybe. It seemed like a good idea. When I changed it, I didn't know where our relationship was going to go."

"You didn't?"

"Honestly, no, I didn't. I hoped that I had found someone to spend the rest of my life with, but I wasn't sure."

"You really didn't believe that you deserved this, did you?"

"No," Eva admitted, her voice barely a whisper. "I didn't. I thought you would get tired of me and that would be that."

"I would have to be totally insane to walk away from you," Zoe replied. "Especially since I went to so much trouble to save you." She looked up into Eva's face. "So you want to be Eva Lambros?"

"Yes. When our babies come, I want us to be a family."

"We are a family. The name doesn't change that."

"It means a great deal to me."

"There isn't anything to really discuss. It's what you want, and I want to give you everything you want."

Eva kissed Zoe gently on the lips. "Thank you."

"Always. Now babies? How many do you want?"

"A dozen." Eva chuckled. "I'm an only child, Zoe, so more than one."

"Having three brothers was sometimes fun, sometimes exasperating, and always loving." Zoe smiled. "I want that for our babies."

"I want that too."

"When do you want to do it?"

"Right after we get home. So what do you say, Miss Lambros, do you want to share your last name with me?" Eva asked.

"I think I love that idea." Zoe nodded. "Eva Lambros. That really does sound nice."

"Good. Now can you go to sleep? Larissa is going to make us both crazy for a few days."

Eva's hand gently rubbed Zoe's back until she heard her gentle snoring. Eva smiled but then realized she was stuck in the bunk. She didn't want to wake Zoe now that she had finally fallen asleep. While trying to figure out how she was going to get comfortable in that tight space, she felt Zoe shift.

"Your back is going to kill you in this bunk."

Eva smiled. "Do you look after me even when you're asleep?"

"Yes, it's my job." Zoe's sleepy response made Eva chuckle. Zoe let go of her and allowed her to get back up on the top bunk, where she did have more room. Eva took Zoe's hand and held it as she leaned against the bunk. Zoe opened her eyes and met Eva's gaze. "I promised God, even though I don't trust Him, that I would look after you and love you for the rest of my life if he would just save you."

"You did?"

"I did."

Eva watched Zoe's eyes drift down. She pulled the blanket over Zoe and watched her sleep. "I will always love you," she whispered and leaned in for a gentle kiss on the cheek. She swallowed the lump in her throat. "I promised Him as well," she added and kissed Zoe again before she climbed back up.

CHAPTER 28

"You crazy goat!"

Eva leaned out of the carriage to see one of the train conductors chasing a goat across the hill embankment near the trail tracks. She smiled. "Now that's something you won't see in Sydney."

It was dawn, and they were two hours away from Larissa, or more if the goats had anything to do with it. A light breeze had picked up, causing the tall grasses on either side of the rail line to sway ever so gently. Eva leaned against the doorway and took out her cigarette case. She lit one, lost in thought on the impending visit to Zoe's hometown.

Larissa. She despised the town. The only two good things to happen to her there were finding who her real father was and, more importantly, falling in love with Zoe. Other than that, it was more hell for her, following on from Aiden.

"Good morning."

Eva turned to find Mrs. Muldoon. "Couldn't sleep?"

"Oh, no, I'm a morning person," Mrs. Muldoon replied and looked out of the doorway. "Why are we stopped?"

"Goats."

"Goats?"

"There're some goats on the tracks, and they are trying to get them off before we run over them."

"Oh...goats, well, that's a new one."

"Not around here, it's not," Eva said as she took a drag of her cigarette. "We've been stopped for quite a few hours before the goats showed up."

"So you're up early, I see."

"I'm an early riser."

"Ah, and Zoe?"

"Still fast asleep. Zoe won't get up for another," Eva checked her watch, "two hours or so."

"I've meant to tell you that I saw the photographs you took. They are amazing. You have a good eye."

"Thank you." Eva smiled.

"Is Zoe feeling nervous about going home?"

"Nervous? No," Eva lied.

"How about you?"

Eva shook her head. "No, it's fine." She turned when a goat made another attempt at escape from the conductor. "My money is on the goat."

"Well, I hope he makes it. Would you like to have some breakfast with me?"

"Sure." Eva pushed herself away from the doorway and followed Mrs. Muldoon into the nearly empty buffet cart. They took a booth near the windows. The waiter approached them, and they ordered some tea.

"I've never been to Larissa. What's it like?"

"It's a small farming community—quite nice."

"Not that you were paying attention to the scenery in 1942? Right?"

Eva shook her head. "It wasn't pleasant."

"So you're not nervous?"

"No," Eva replied, realizing Mrs. Muldoon had asked that question earlier.

"You must be a little anxious."

"Why do you want to know?"

"Well, you were there as part of the enemy. I'm going to guess that not all of the residents will be thrilled to see you back."

"I don't really care." Eva shrugged. "Hopefully, they won't want to stone me to death," she added quietly. "I don't know. I'm sure they won't be too thrilled to have the daughter of their enemy come to visit."

"But your father is the local priest."

"That's where it gets complicated," Eva replied as the waiter delivered their tea. She waited for the waiter to pour their tea before she continued. "My father is loved by the town."

"Your life is never easy, is it?"

Eva took a sip of her tea. She put the cup down and shook her head. "It's interesting."

"I find it extraordinary that in the midst of all of that, you and Zoe got together. I'm quite sure you don't want to go into it again, but I find you and Zoe are so fascinating."

"You have a gift."

"I do?"

"Yes. I don't feel like you are interrogating me."

"I'm not trying to interrogate you. I'm just nosey, as my husband would say."

"Zoe would ask a million questions and remember what you had said years afterward."

"I have discovered that." Mrs. Muldoon smiled. "She is a fascinating woman. You, on the other hand, are a closed book—you seldom talk about yourself. You are so different in every way to Zoe."

"Am I? I like being a closed book."

"You also don't make it easy for someone to warm to you."

"Depends on what that person wants."

"What do you think I want from you?"

"I don't know," Eva replied honestly. "It has something to do with my grandmother, so it must be related to that," Eva observed Mrs. Muldoon. Mrs. Muldoon's lips twitched, and Eva knew she had been right. She chose to leave the matter of their collusion alone for now. "How you treat me is irrelevant to me, but how you treat Zoe is totally different. Offering her something she has dreamt about doing and then crushing those dreams is just cruel."

"I wasn't going to renege on my offer, Eva. That was genuine."

"What is your stake in this? What has my grandmother given you to go to such lengths?"

"Your grandmother is not the evil woman you think she is."

"No, she's not evil." Eva leaned back in her chair and looked out at the tall grasses surrounding the stationary train. "She wants to control everything and everyone, including me."

"She does care."

Eva shook her head. "I don't think we will disagree that she cares. She wouldn't have sent you to create this elaborate scheme if she didn't care. She must have offered you some inducement for you to do this."

"Your grandmother didn't offer me anything. I was doing her a favor."

"Oh?"

"My sister worked for your grandmother as her assistant. Her name is Jana, and you have met her many times."

Eva was about to put the cigarette in her mouth when she stopped. She stared at Mrs. Muldoon for a long moment. "Jana Broder? Jana is your sister?"

"Yes." Mrs. Muldoon nodded with a knowing smile. "Jana survived Kristallnacht when your Uncle Wilbur saved her from the Brownshirts that entered his factory."

"What happened to Jana after that night?"

"Your grandmother eventually got her out of the country. You may have a different opinion of your grandmother, and it may be valid, but for me, she saved my sister's life, and I owe her."

"I'm happy she did that for Jana."

"So am I. I got word before we boarded the ship that Jana's husband, Percy Hester, has been appointed as Minister for External Affairs."

Eva caught sight of Zoe coming towards them and smiled. "Hey, sleepyhead."

Zoe stuck out her tongue and scooted next to Eva on the seat. "I woke up, and you weren't there," she said quickly before addressing Mrs. Muldoon. "Hello, Mrs. Muldoon."

"How many times do I have to say this, Zoe? When we are in private, please call me Della."

"Ah..uh.." Zoe stammered. "Della."

"You need to get over that problem," Mrs. Muldoon

replied gently and tapped Zoe's hand. "Did you see if they caught all the goats?"

"No, they were still rounding them up. I offered to milk one of them," she said and turned to Eva. "Have you had breakfast?"

"No, just some tea."

"And cigarettes, I see." Zoe pointed to the four butts in the ashtray.

Eva rolled her eyes melodramatically and stubbed out the fifth cigarette. "Zoe..."

"Don't Zoe me, you have to eat something," she gently scolded. "You promised you would."

Eva sighed. "Alright."

"So what were you discussing?"

"My grandmother and Mrs. Muldoon."

"Oh." Zoe shot a quick look at Eva before she turned her attention to Mrs. Muldoon. "An interesting topic."

Mrs. Muldoon stood up from the table. "Please, excuse me. I'm sure the two of you have much to discuss." Without another word, she left Eva and Zoe at the table.

CHAPTER 29

EVA LEANED AGAINST THE HALF-OPEN WINDOW OF the train cabin. The goats were still running around and she could see the engineer remonstrating with a train guard and another man. Eva caught snippets of conversation that didn't bode well for the train leaving the area soon.

"So what is going on out there?"

"There is something wrong with either the tracks or the train. I don't believe this. We are two hours away from Larissa and the rate we are going, or not going, this trip could take another day!" Eva grumbled. She was exasperated, angry with herself, and tired. "Greeks!"

"Hey, your wife is Greek," Zoe teased.

Eva gave Zoe a shake of the head. "Why is it every time I'm in this country, it all goes to shit?"

"The Larissa Curse." Zoe put her arms around Eva's waist.

"Don't start."

"I know, but you are in a bad mood, Mrs. Muldoon's

made you even angrier, and you think you acted inappropriately, although I don't think so."

"I made such a mess of it." Eva pursed her lips. "I want to know what my grandmother told her. She basically didn't say anything."

"Other than the story about Jana."

"Yes." Eva nodded. "Not sure I believe that one."

Zoe had a dubious look on her face. "Why would she make that up?"

"I don't know."

"Maybe it's the truth."

"What if it is?"

"Are you listening to yourself? If someone didn't know you, they would think you were a heartless soul."

"Zoe..."

"It's true, love. They would. Mrs. Muldoon just told you that your Uncle Wilbur saved her sister's life and you were just indifferent. She might as well have told you that the sky is blue."

"Not exactly."

"Eva!" Zoe admonished.

"I know," Eva said quietly. "I was wrong."

"You don't lead with your heart; you lead with your head." Zoe tipped Eva's chin gently with her fingers and tilted her head. "You're stealing my thunder," she joked and leaned in for a gentle kiss.

"Don't want to steal your thunder." Eva flashed Zoe a lopsided grin. "I need to apologize."

"Yes."

"But she lied."

"Still doesn't make you right. Mrs. Muldoon has been lying to you for four weeks, and now you find you want to confront her? You were curious, and you wanted to see what she knew about your grandmother."

"Yes."

"So. What are you going to do about it?"

"The train isn't going anywhere anytime soon, so taking a walk outside would help clear my mind?"

Zoe shook her head. "No, I don't think so."

"I'm not going to apologize for speaking my mind."

"That's not why you are apologizing for."

"I know," Eva said in a resigned voice. "Do you want to come with me?"

"Of course." Zoe got up from her seat and took Eva's hand. They looked at each other for a moment. "It's funny."

"What is?"

"Usually I'm the one who gets into a mess when my heart rules my head."

"You're rubbing off on me," Eva quipped as she exited. She smiled when Zoe tapped her on the behind. The corridor was narrow, and they passed other passengers in a single file.

They arrived at Mrs. Muldoon's cabin and knocked on the door. She opened the door, smiled at them, and beckoned them inside. The cabin was slightly larger than their own. Mrs. Muldoon sat down near the window.

Eva glanced at Zoe before she turned her attention to Mrs. Muldoon. "I want to apologize."

"All right, but what for?"

"I'm sorry for being insensitive," Eva admitted as she looked directly at Mrs. Muldoon. "I let my personal feelings about my grandmother negate what she did for you."

"Apology accepted. Sit down, Eva." Eva took up her offer and sat opposite her.

"Can I just say that my offer to Zoe was not a lie? That offer still stands." Mrs. Muldoon glanced at Zoe before she turned her attention back to Eva. "Your work is amazing, and the refugees genuinely liked you once they got over their prejudices. I did not lie to you; I just omitted the truth."

"Not John, but Johnny." Eva used one of Zoe's often-repeated sayings.

"I'm not sure what that means, but not telling you the full truth is not a good way to do business. Would you have come to work for me if I had told you?"

"No."

"Yet you found me out at the start of this journey and said nothing. Isn't that the same thing that I did?"

"Not exactly, but I can see the similarities," Eva admitted, giving Zoe a quick look.

"Your grandmother is not the evil woman you think she is. Someone that evil wouldn't spend the time to make sure her granddaughter was well looked after."

Eva remained silent as she pondered these words. "I paid for my cabin by working for you."

"You did, and you did an excellent job. I was very impressed with your work. You are a talented photographer, and you speak several languages."

"Why is that advantageous to you?"

"It is because you have done an outstanding job. I didn't know anything about you other than what your grandmother had told me."

"What was that?"

Mrs. Muldoon's eyebrows furrowed, and her lips pressed together. "That would be betraying a confidence."

"I guess we have nothing to discuss then. I came here to

offer you my apology. That has been done." Eva stood up and did an about-turn to leave.

"She said that you were kind-hearted and loving. She is a very proud grandmother."

Eva sighed deeply and closed her eyes. "I'm afraid we have a different view."

"You are wrong about her. Jana would vehemently disagree with you. As I told you at breakfast, it was your Uncle Wilbur who saved my sister's life, but it was your grandmother that allowed her to escape the Nazis and took her out of the country. She took the risk."

"Yes, it would appear she took the risk because of her political affiliations, and she saved your sister's life." Eva conceded gracefully.

"I hope you get the chance to talk to your grandmother. Now, as our paths will not join up again until we meet back in Australia, I just want you to know that I would like to offer Zoe that job."

"Zoe Lambros! Zoe Lambros, has anyone seen Zoe Lambros?"

Zoe cocked her head at the voice and scowled. "What..."

Eva looked at Zoe and shrugged.

Zoe went to the window, and Eva promptly joined her. Eva didn't see anything except a few passengers, and she was about to turn back to Mrs. Muldoon when Zoe's voice made her stop.

"No..."

"What's wrong, love?"

"Oh, my god..." Zoe ran to the cabin door. In her hurry to open the door, she locked it. She screamed in frustration as she twisted the door handle. When the door finally opened, her knee struck its side, tearing a gash in her knee.

Followed closely by Eva, Zoe ran out into the corridor, crowded with people and their luggage.

"Sweet Mary, Mother of God, now you all get up!" Zoe yelled as she pushed past people.

"Zoe!" Eva yelled just as Zoe was flinging another door open to get to the other carriage. Zoe didn't turn but disappeared through the door as Eva raced right after her.

CHAPTER 30

Zoe flung the door open to the adjoining car and slammed headfirst into someone's body. She looked up to yell at him to move aside when she was struck dumb.

"Theo?" she asked, not quite believing her eyes.

"ZoZo!"

Theodore Lambros was a tall, burly man with short dark red hair and deep-set green eyes. Green eyes were crinkling in delight. He quickly picked Zoe up in his thickset arms as she buried herself in her brother's embrace.

"Theo! You're alive!"

"I am." Theo laughed before tenderly kissing Zoe on the cheek. "Promised you I would be back, didn't I?"

"*Malarka*," Zoe swore and struck his chest with her fist. The ineffectual punch caused Theo to laugh heartily.

"Ow, Zo! You hit like a girl!" Theo cupped Zoe's face and looked into her eyes. "Hello, *koukla*," he said softly as tears rolled down his face. Theo's affectionate baby doll nickname rendered Zoe speechless. She tried to talk, but the words just wouldn't come forth. She gave up and sobbed against his chest.

"You're bleeding on me." Theo pointed at Zoe's bleeding knee.

The door was flung open, and Eva and Mrs. Muldoon raced out and then stopped dead still.

"Zoe." Eva came forward and put her hand on Zoe's back. "You're bleeding."

"Evy, this is Theo. Theo, this is Eva Haralambos."

"Yes, Father Haralambos' daughter," Theo said as he picked up and cradled Zoe in his arms. Eva held the door open, and they went back to their cabin.

Eva took a jug of water and a clean towel. She sat down on the floor with her legs tucked under and applied pressure to stop the bleeding on Zoe's knee.

"Ow." Zoe grimaced.

"It's not too deep. Mrs. Muldoon has gone to find a doctor." Eva washed the knee and applied a makeshift bandage using a towel.

Eva smiled at Zoe and then looked at Theo sitting comfortably on the seat, watching them. She put the jug and the bloodstained towel aside and sat down next to Zoe.

Theo stood, took Eva's hand, and brought her back up. "My mama did not raise a rude boy." He hugged Eva. "Welcome to the family, sister, what's left of it," he said quietly as they pulled apart from each other.

"Ow," Zoe said, causing Theo and Eva to look back at her with matching puzzled expressions. "It's not my leg. I just pinched myself to see if I had a dream. I can't believe you're alive, and why didn't you contact me, why didn't you come back to Larissa, why-"

Theo put his hand over Zoe's mouth. "Stop. You're

going to run out of questions, and then what will we do? Let's wait for the doctor to get here and fix your leg, and then we'll talk. All right?"

Zoe rolled her eyes and nodded. "Yes, but can I ask one question?"

"Yes, just one."

"How did you get to the train?"

"I rode your favorite motorcycle." Theo grinned. "I wasn't going to wait for this bucket to start moving. We got word that it was delayed, and I just couldn't wait another hour to see my sister." He chuckled.

A knock on the door heralded Mrs. Muldoon and a gentleman who identified himself as a doctor. He quickly and efficiently assessed Zoe's knee and bandaged the wound.

"I'm going to give you something for the pain because that will hurt for a while, and it will make you a little sleepy," the doctor said. He took out a needle, and Zoe winced when he injected it into her arm.

Just as quickly, Mrs. Muldoon and the doctor left.

"Right, let me look at you." Theo took Zoe's hand, and she stood. "My God, you look so much like Mama. A little skinny, but just as beautiful."

"You're looking good for a dead man." Zoe gently slapped his bicep as she sat down again. "Explain yourself."

"I will." Theo ruffled Zoe's hair. He turned to Eva and was about to speak when Zoe slapped his leg.

"Theodore!"

"Alright." Theo sat down next to Zoe. "We were at the Albanian border, and we were fighting together."

"Are Michael and Thieri still alive?" Zoe asked expectantly. "Are they waiting in Larissa for us? Why didn't they come with you? I know Michael hates the bike but Thieri—"

Theo put his hand on Zoe's knee. "Michael and Thieri are not there. Our brothers are gone."

"How do you know? They may have survived just like you did."

"I know they are gone."

"How do you know?"

"Zoe, trust me when I say this—they are gone."

"Tell me, how do you know?"

Theo took a deep breath. He glanced at Eva for a moment before he turned his attention back to Zoe. "Michael died in my arms. He was shot in the chest, and he died on the first day of fighting." He reached out and tenderly wiped the tears from Zoe's cheek. "Thieri died the next day."

"Oh. Did you bury them? Did you say a prayer for them? Not that prayer does anyone, but Michael and Thieri believed."

"I did. They are buried on the Albanian border with their other brothers who died defending our country. They died heroes."

Zoe leaned against her brother and sat in silence for a moment. "Where have you been all this time?"

"We won the battle with the Italians, but I was captured and got sent to a POW camp. I don't know what happened, but Papa must have got word that we had all died."

"That was a horrible day, Theo. I had never seen Papa cry before, but when the news came through, he did."

Theo put his arm around Zoe and kissed the top of her head. "I know. I heard Papa died a hero as well."

"Papa was a true hero, and he died fighting the pigs. Imagine our gentle papa fighting those barbarians."

"He was a heroic man who loved his family and his country. He died defending Greece and defending you and Mama." Theo lovingly cupped Zoe's cheek. "So was it only you and Mama to fight against the Germans?"

"No. We had Stavros as well. Then Mama was murdered. I lost Stavros soon after because we had a collaborator in our group..."

"Father Haralambos told me about Stavros and Vassili. He also told me how you bravely fought with the Resistance."

"I did what I had to do."

"You also helped save people with forged identity papers." Theo smiled. "Did you forget that little thing?"

"The person most responsible for that is Eva. She was the one that forged the signatures," Zoe proudly said as she put her hand on Eva's thigh. "Eva is the one that allowed Father Haralambos and me to make that happen."

"Yes, I've heard a lot about Eva, but for the moment I want to talk about you."

"I did what Papa always told us to do. He said we had to stand and fight for what we believed in, and I did. He told me to be brave just like Laskarina Bouboulina. He did it, Mama did it, Stavros did it, and you all did it. When it was my turn, I did it. It's the Lambros way."

"It is the Lambros way," Theo said as he hugged Zoe tightly. "Vassili-"

"No, I don't want to discuss that traitor. He ceased to be family when he collaborated with the pigs."

"He is-"

"No, Theo. I took care of him myself, and I'm not sorry I did."

"I know you did, but you should not have been the one to do it. You should have left it to the men to execute the bastard."

Zoe gazed up at Theo and shook her head. "No. It was my job. Can we not discuss that traitor? I want to know how you survived. We can talk about me later." She waggled her finger at Theo. "So, talk."

"My war ended on the Albanian border in 1941. I was taken as a POW and spent the next four years in a camp. When we were released, I met up with some boys from Larissa, and they told me that there wasn't anyone left. Papa was killed fighting the Germans, you and mama died. It was just me. I had nothing to go back to so I joined up to fight in the Civil War."

Zoe knew there was more to that story than the very cut and dried way her brother stated. "More death and destruction."

"Ah yes, but this time we did it the Greek way," Theo said bitterly. "I was fighting with some boys from Larissa and Thessalonica."

"How did you find out that I was still alive?"

Theo grinned, his smile splitting his handsome bearded face. "Ah, that is an interesting story. I got wounded and was sent to a field hospital, and guess who I found there."

"I have no idea."

"Aunty Stella!"

"Crazy Aunty Stella?"

"The one and only Aunty Stella! Yes, it was zany, crazy, wild Aunty Stella."

"Is Stella a nurse?" Eva asked.

"No, she's a doctor," Theo replied. "I think we were both shocked to see each other, and after she got over that, she told me off for not being dead." Theo chuckled. "I have been staying with her since then."

"But how did you find out?"

"Zoe, my darling sister, you have the patience of a flea."

Eva chuckled. "Oh goodness, Theodore..."

Theo smiled at Eva. "I see you already know about my sister's legendary patience." He kissed Zoe's head and chuckled. "Now back to my story. I was living in Thessalonica with Aunt Stella, and I bumped into Dimitri. We went to the taverna, and we were just talking about a mutual friend, and then he mentioned you. He told me all about your exploits in the war. That boy has always been sweet on you. He was talking about you like you were alive."

"Good ol' loudmouth, Dimitri, bless him."

"I said you were dead, and he was wrong, but he told me to go to Larissa and talk to Father Haralambos. So I went home, I told Aunty Stella that you weren't dead and I was going to find you. I took the train down the next day. I went to the church, and there was Father Haralambos. He was shocked to see me, and once we got over hugging each other, he told me."

"I'm sure he was stunned since he performed a service for you and you were supposed to be dead."

"Yes, I heard that." Theo laughed. "I asked him where you were. He said it was a long story and we should have dinner-you know how he gets with those long stories. All I wanted was to find out where you were, but he wanted to draw it out. So later that night I went to his little apartment, and I heard the most extraordinary story."

"How much did he tell you?"

"Everything," Theo said quietly. "He told me about your courage when Mama died, how you became the woman that you are. My chest puffed out with pride because you are a Lambros and we never ever give up. I was proud of you."

"No, we don't."

"We never give up, and we never cower. You have the heart of a lioness, Zoe, and I was so proud of you I wanted to shout it from the rooftops. I asked him where you were and he said Australia."

"When was this?"

"About five weeks ago. He gave me your address, and I sent a telegram, but I didn't hear anything back."

"We were on a ship sailing to Greece."

"That would explain why I didn't hear from you." Theo scratched his bearded chin.

"Is that all?"

"Isn't that enough?"

Zoe sighed. "Did Father Haralambos tell you anything else about me other than what I did in the war?"

Theo gazed at Zoe for a long moment. "Father Haralambos told me about you and your friend Eva." He looked squarely at Eva, who returned his gaze. "He told me that he put the two of you to work together in getting the identity papers even though you hated each other."

"Is that all he told you?"

Theo put his arm around Zoe's shoulders and stared into her eyes. "He told me your hatred for her turned to friendship."

"And?"

"And what? That's what he said."

"Theodore, is that all Father H said to you about my relationship with Eva?"

"No. That's not all."

"What do you think?"

"She's pretty, doesn't look German with that dark hair, nice blue eyes, and—" Zoe slapped his shoulder in frustration.

"Ow. She's not pretty with nice blue eyes?" Theo ducked when Zoe looked about ready to repeat the dose.

"*Malarka.*"

"I come back from the dead and you call me names!" Theo planted a kiss on Zoe's cheek. "What do you want me to say?"

"Is that all Father Haralambos told you about Eva and me?"

"Zoe, maybe now is not..." Eva gently admonished and stopped when Zoe shook her head.

"Now is a perfect time, Evy."

"Father Haralambos told me you and Eva were very close friends."

"You mean he told you I was a lesbian and I was in love with Eva?" Zoe persisted with her questioning. She noted Theo's eyes never left hers.

"He told me you were a lesbian, yes."

"How do you feel about me being a lesbian?"

"I don't know, Zo. I want to talk about it later, not now."

"I want to talk about it now."

Theo sighed deeply. "This isn't the time to discuss something like this. Not now."

"Theo, I love you, but I also love Eva, and this is important to me."

"You love her just like Mama loved Papa?"

"Yes." Zoe quickly looked at Eva, who had her head down and was looking at the floor intently.

"Are you sure this isn't-"

"Theodore, tell me what Father H told you!"

"He told me you loved Eva and that this is what you wanted. I don't know what you want me to say or ask you. Is she looking after you?"

"Is she looking after me?"

"Does she work? Is she afraid of a little hard work?" Theo explained. "It's what I would have asked if you were going to marry a boy. So is she all of that?"

"We both work, so we provide for each other. We have a good life in Australia."

"You work?" Theo scowled at Eva. "What do you do?"

"I'm an artist like Mama. Before we left, I worked at the Art Council restoring art. I went to university, Theo. Do you believe that!"

"You did? How?"

"Eva worked in a factory so I could go to university. I would say that's a good provider."

"I know you are an artist-I saw some of your art, and that didn't surprise me. You were always good at drawing."

"When? How?"

Theo felt the back of his pants pocket and pulled out a creased piece of paper. "I was going through the cupboards in Michae's house, and I came across this." He smoothed out the paper. "I was wondering who drew it until I saw your mark."

Zoe leaned over to look. When she saw the artwork, she gasped. "Oh, my god." She tried to grab the paper, but Theo pulled it out of her reach. "Theo!"

"Ah!" Theo chuckled and gave the artwork to Eva.

Eva took it, and her eyes widened in surprise. "Ah...when was this?"

Zoe sighed. "Just before Father Haralambos got me to go work for you."

Eva gazed at a younger version of herself. The artwork was good, with the exception that she had horns sticking out of her head and fangs. "You drew horns and fangs on me, love," she said, surprising Zoe by not censoring herself.

"I thought you were evil at the time." Zoe defended her artwork. "I wasn't accurate, but it looks great without the horns and fangs."

"It's a beautiful picture," Theo added.

"Theo, you're not answering my question on how you feel about me being a lesbian."

"Do you have to use *that* word?"

"Yes, that's what I am. So how do you feel about it?"

"You are my sister, and I love you dearly. It should probably concern me that you are a lesbian, but I don't care. You are my only sister and to hell with the church and what everyone else thinks." Theo got up from his seat and grabbed the pillow and blanket. "Why don't you just rest a little so I can go find out when this stupid train is leaving?"

"You really don't—"

"When have I ever lied to you? I never have. I love you." Theo kissed Zoe on the forehead.

"Thank you, Theodore," Eva said.

"Theodore? Only my mother called me Theodore, and only when she was angry with me. My sister calls me Theo, or *malarka* when she's truly angry with me. Since you are now my sister, you are not allowed to call me Theodore."

"Alright, Theo."

"What does my zany sister call you?"

Eva glanced at Zoe and smiled. "Well, she calls me Evy, and Eva Theresa Haralambos when she's annoyed with me."

"Do you mind if I call you Evy?"

"I don't mind." Eva shook her head.

"Good, well, let's leave my rampaging sister here to have a bit of sleep and we can go and find out about this train," Theo said and walked out leaving Eva and Zoe alone.

Eva knelt down in front of Zoe. "I love you," she said and kissed her tenderly.

"Evy?"

"Yes?"

"This isn't a dream, is it?"

"No, love." Eva shook her head. "This is very real."

CHAPTER 31

Theo and Eva walked silently until they got to the train doors. He hopped down and offered his hand to Eva, who took it and effortlessly got off the train. Eva pulled her black cloak around her and lifted the hood against the early morning brisk wind that stirred the sandbank near the tracks..

"Skevos!" Theo yelled out as he approached the train engineer.

"Oh no, not you again. Did you find your Zoe Lambros?" Skevos asked. "Are you Zoe?" he asked Eva, who shook her head.

"No, that's not Zoe, but I did find her."

"Bravo. Now, what do you want?"

"How long will this take? I want to get back to Larissa."

Skevos put his hand on Theo's shoulder. "Son, you are not a paying passenger on this train."

"I can be." Theo took out his wallet and gave the engineer a wad of notes. They exchanged smiles and Skevos pocketed the money. "I'll also get a ticket. I'm not riding back on a motorcycle with two women and their luggage."

"I think it's going to take another two hours."

Theo lightly slapped the man's back. "Thank you, Skevos, I'll go pay my fare to the conductor and bring my motorcycle on the train."

"Yes, yes, now leave me alone so I can fix my train."

Theo chuckled, and he and Eva walked around the train to the other side, where he had left his motorcycle.

"Zoe is going to go crazy with joy when she sees this motorcycle," Eva said.

"This is Athena." Theo laughed and patted the seat.

"Let me guess, did Zoe name her?"

"Yes, how did you know?" Theo mounted the motorcycle to move her onto the train.

"Zoe names everything." Eva chuckled when she found the name emblazoned on the gas tank.

"She still does that? She used to name the cows, the goats, and the chickens. I wasn't sure how she remembered each name for the chickens, but she did."

"Zoe has her own motorcycle, or had one."

"What kind?"

"It has a sidecar but I don't know much about motorcycles," Eva replied as she watched Theo get off the bike and maneuver it towards the train.

"Did Zoe paint it red?"

Eva smiled. "No, it's painted green and gold."

"I'm surprised it wasn't red. Everything had to be red." Theo took the motorcycle and lifted it inside the train and secured it with the help of the conductor. He took out several drachmas and paid for his ticket.

"Alright now, Zoe is going to be asleep for a bit. Why don't we go for some coffee?" he suggested.

Theo held the door open, and Eva walked through into the now jam-packed dining car. They found an empty table and sat down opposite each other. The waiter appeared, took their order, and left just as quickly. Theo took out a cigarette pack from his pocket and offered it to Eva, who took one. He lit her cigarette and did the same for his own.

"I've heard a lot about you." Theo leaned back in his chair. "Father Haralambos couldn't stop talking about you once he told me about you and my sister."

"Fathers tend to do that."

"It was a surprise to find out our Father Haralambos had been a wild boy in his youth." Theo watched Eva intently. "I would have never guessed."

"It was a surprise to me as well." Eva took a drag of her cigarette. "Larissa was a revelation."

"Father H said you arrived in 1942?"

"Yes, with my stepfather, Hans Muller."

"Ah, yes, the notorious Muller, I've heard a lot about him. Your stepfather killed my mother."

The force of the statement caused Eva to feel as if she had been slapped. Whether Theo intended for his words to have that effect on her, she wasn't sure. She took a deep breath and tried to calm her rising anxiety.

"Yes, my stepfather killed your mother and many others."

"Father Haralambos said you saw it all."

"I was. He took me out with him to witness his brutality."

"What did you do?"

Eva stared down at her hands and fell silent for a long

moment. "I did nothing. I couldn't do anything to save her or anyone else that day, Theo."

"That is a bizarre thing to do—to bring you out into a war zone with him," Theo said as the waiter came back with his coffee and Eva's tea. He poured the tea for Eva before he picked up his coffee and took a sip.

"He was very controlling, and that was his way of keeping me where he could keep an eye on me."

"It's too bad you didn't know who your real father was."

"Yes."

"How did you meet my sister?"

"The first time I saw Zoe she was sitting outside and she made a passing comment about my inability to walk properly," Eva replied as she picked up her cup and stared into it.

"A passing comment? That's a polite way of saying my sister told you exactly what she thought."

Eva couldn't help but smile at how accurate Theo was in his description of Zoe. "She called me a cripple."

"Why couldn't you walk properly?"

"I had been caught up in a bombing in Paris when I was there with my stepfather. It damaged my back. It took me some time to recover." Eva left out the reason for the bombing and her part in the French Resistance. It wasn't something she wanted to share with him.

"Why was Zoe watching you?"

"Zoe was in the Resistance, and she used to monitor who and what was going on with the German command house, where I lived with Muller."

"Was this after my mother was killed?"

Eva shook her head. "No. Zoe was involved in the Resistance long before your mother was murdered." She watched Theo's reaction. "She is a courageous woman. I don't need to tell you how young she was when the war came to Larissa. She lost your father first, then your mother and Stavros."

"Yes, Father Haralambos told me how brave she was. It hurts me to know she was alone after Mama died."

"She wasn't alone. She had Stavros looking out for her until he was hanged. She suffered a great deal, but she has such a strong character that, even though your mother's death nearly drove her to the edge. It made her stronger if you know what I mean." Eva glanced outside at one of the conductors, who was talking animatedly with an engineer. "If it weren't for your sister, I wouldn't be here."

"How did that happen?"

"Father Haralambos introduced us saying that it would be easier for me to get the identity papers to him via Zoe. It would arouse suspicions if I kept going to the church far too often. Zoe was going to be my maid."

"That makes sense. You gave Zoe the identity papers, and she gave them to Father Haralambos."

"Yes."

"When I heard from Father Haralambos that she was in Australia with you, I wondered why she would leave Larissa and go to another country with a German."

Eva picked up her cigarette and flicked the ashes in the ashtray. "You were wondering if I had used Zoe to get out of Greece."

"The thought crossed my mind," Theo replied honestly. "The British had just arrived, and you were wounded. Your stepfather was dead, and you were stuck here. Didn't the British think you were the enemy?"

"No. Zoe had told the Resistance about my involvement,

and they told the British that I was working with them." Eva stopped for a moment. "We thought Father Haralambos had been killed when he was put on the same train as the Jews and troops heading to Thessalonica and then heard that the train had been blown up."

"If Zoe wanted you dead, that would have been the perfect time to exact vengeance, but she didn't because she had feelings for you."

"You think I convinced Zoe she was a lesbian and that's why she saved my life?"

They gazed at each other for a long moment before Theo spoke. "I don't know. Maybe."

"Have you thought that Zoe used me to get out of Larissa?" Eva asked. "She did want to leave Larissa; there was nothing here for her."

"I don't know."

"I do. I fell in love with Zoe knowing that if Muller found out, I would be dead. He did find out, and he was going to kill me. Zoe was not in love with me, I knew that. Zoe called it a heavy like, which meant a deep friendship to me."

Theo grinned. "That's one of Michael's sayings..."

"There are three stages to a relationship: Like Heavy Like and Deep Love. I'm in the second stage. Heavy Like. When I get to stage three you can shoot me because I'll be useless," Eva quoted Theo's older brother. "Zoe was in heavy like, and that's all it was."

"She wasn't in love with you?"

"No. Zoe didn't know what she was feeling, other than she was attracted to me. For some time I thought she had talked herself into liking me as a way to accomplish her goal."

"To kill you."

"Zoe saw her mother brutally murdered, and that hatred had to be channeled somewhere or else she would have gone insane with grief."

"Why did she want to kill you if it wasn't you who killed our mother?"

"When your mother lay dying, Zoe heard a woman laugh."

"It wasn't you, or else you would be dead by now. Zoe would never give up if she thought you were responsible for doing that."

Eva shook her head. "No. It wasn't me. It was my nurse, who was behind me. Zoe exacted justice at the right time."

"That sounds like my sister and something I would have done as well. Why didn't Zoe go after Muller?"

"Killing Muller would not have achieved Zoe's goal," Eva explained. "Zoe wanted to inflict pain on him as he had done to her. She could inflict this pain on him by killing his daughter." She stopped talking when the waiter approached the table next to them and waited for him to leave before she continued.

"Zoe spent her time thinking of ways to kill me. Her cousin spent his time trying to figure out how to stop her from doing it because it would have brought death to more of the villagers."

"Ah yes, Stavros. He was a gentle man and never thought he would survive but war shows you who you really are."

"Yes." Eva nodded. "He was killed, which left Zoe with nothing to lose."

"If Zoe wanted to do something, she would have done it. My sister just doesn't give up. Surely she didn't have feelings for you before she met you?"

Eva looked around the now mostly empty carriage for a

moment. "Father Haralambos told her I was his daughter and we were working together."

"That stopped Zoe? She would have found another way."

"You're right. She didn't give up," Eva replied. "Zoe was determined to kill me even though I was working with the Resistance. She was just going to do it another way. She tried very hard to still hate me and would bait me every chance she got."

"Zoe has always been a determined girl."

"It was mentally and physically exhausting." Eva took a drag of her cigarette and exhaled. She watched the smoke rise for a moment. "I thought Zoe would kill me. I didn't know how or when, but she would do it."

"Instead she fell in heavy like with you."

Eva smiled. "Some things are just beyond explanation."

"Muller was a deranged man."

"My stepfather found out about us, and he ordered his second in command to kill me." Eva took a deep breath. "Instead of him taking me to a field and shooting me as Muller wanted, he decided he was going to have some fun."

"Oh."

"He took me to the cabin on Athena's Bluff."

"Thieri's cabin? Zoe loved that cabin, although I don't see the attraction, it being up a mountain."

"Yes. He told the housekeeper to tell Zoe where we were."

"He wanted her there?"

"He was going to... he had plans." Eva shuddered at the memory. "I figured that if I got him angry enough, he would kill me first."

"So his attack on Zoe wouldn't happen."

"That was my plan."

"But you said you weren't even sure if Zoe loved you at that point?"

"No, she didn't love me, but I loved her, and I didn't want her to die because of me," Eva replied. "I made Reinhardt angry, and he did what I thought he would do."

"You loved Zoe so much that you didn't care what they did to you?"

"Yes, I loved your sister that much, and I love her even more now. My problem was that Reinhardt stopped when he realized what I was doing." Eva shrugged. "Can't say it was brilliant of me, but I didn't know any other way to stop him."

"So did Zoe get the message?"

"She did. His plan was thwarted because the Americans were coming and the Germans were retreating. He decided he wasn't going to wait for Zoe to arrive and shot me anyway."

"Where was Zoe?"

"What I didn't know at the time was that Zoe was talking the Resistance leader into coming to save me."

Theo shook his head. "The place is exploding, the Germans are retreating, the British are coming, and Zoe wants the Resistance to stop doing what they were doing so they come to help a German?"

"Yes. Makes perfect sense, doesn't it?" Eva asked with a smile. "It made perfect sense to Zoe. He listened and sent a few men to help Zoe and one of my guards, Henry, who was also helping the Resistance."

"This is an extraordinary story; I think Father H left some bits out of this storytelling. How did the Resistance stop Reinhardt?"

"The Resistance didn't stop him. He was about to finish the job when Zoe came bursting in." Eva smiled. "I don't remember much of it because I was just trying to stay alive, but I do remember seeing the door fling open and hearing Zoe's voice."

"Unbelievable. First, she wanted to kill you, and now she's saving your life!"

"Your sister is courageous, Theo. I know she shot Reinhardt in the face from what she told me, but it was my guard Henry who told me he didn't recognize Reinhardt after he saw the body. She emptied the entire clip into his face." Eva continued to play with the gold lighter in an attempt to steady her hands, which had started to tremble on remembering the fear and pain as she lay on the floor of the cabin.

"You have both been through quite a lot."

"We all have. It's war."

"So whose idea was to leave Larissa for Australia?"

"It was Zoe's idea. I just didn't care where I was going to go or what I was going to do, but it was Zoe who convinced me to leave Europe. When the war came to Larissa, your father helped two Australian soldiers to try to get back to their unit. Those soldiers told Zoe about Australia, and she wanted to go there."

"What made you so sure that she didn't want to finish the job by killing you?"

Eva looked out the train window contemplating the question before she turned back to Theo, who was waiting patiently for her answer. "I thought about that," she said honestly. "She could have let Reinhardt kill me. She didn't, and here we are, both of us alive and well."

"That is some story. I'm glad you made it to Egypt..."

"We nearly didn't. We made it to Athens but then the battle between the government, the communists and the British had started heating up. Zoe wanted to leave before everything exploded. The only way we could escape was to follow some resistance members to Crete. That's a story that will take longer than I have to tell you."

Theo ran his hand through his hair and shook his head. "There is a lot I don't know about and I want to hear it."

Eva looked at Theo, who appeared to be lost in thought before she spoke again. "Must have come as a shock to find out Zoe was still alive."

"I was shocked, relieved, worried, and grateful to God that she was still alive when so many had died."

"Did it come as a shock to you to find out your sister is a lesbian?" Eva asked, taking a leaf out of Zoe's direct approach. She wanted to see Theo's reaction to the blunt statement because his opinion mattered. This was Zoe's brother; the man Zoe idolized while she was growing up. Eva never doubted Zoe's love, but she was painfully aware of the trouble Theo could cause if he wanted.

Theo stared down at his now empty coffee cup. "Not really."

"No?"

"No." Theo shook his head. "Zoe was young, and she had lost everyone. All the men were gone, either dead or fighting. Zoe was at that stage of a young girl's life when changes happen." He looked a little embarrassed. "Only women were around, and Zoe was young..."

Eva resisted the urge to laugh at Theo's absurd reasoning. "So you think Zoe turned to me because there were no men around? So her feelings for me are not real?"

"I don't know, maybe. I'm told that it might be a phase

she is going through, but Father Haralambos said it's real. I've been around...um...ah...it's real," Theo stammered to a stop. "Father Haralambos tells me it's real, and he's a priest, so he must know."

"You really don't understand any of it, do you?"

"Yes...I mean no." Theo shook his head. "Doesn't mean just because I don't understand it that I can stop Zoe from how she feels."

"You love your sister, and I understand that. She's your flesh and blood. I know you are trying to understand."

"Is your brother supportive of your...um...way?"

"I'm an only child," Eva replied. She mentally shook her head at how similar Theo was to Zoe—very direct, and there was nothing hidden. *Must be a Lambros trait.*

"I don't want to make her choose. My father told me that I should never ask a woman to choose because I would lose. The person that asks, well, they don't win that argument."

"Even if your sister is a lesbian?"

Theo leaned back in his chair. "I have a choice. I could accept Zoe for the choice she has made, or I could lose my sister and what is left of my family. I don't want to lose her again. Father Haralambos told me about you and how much you love Zoe. Far worse things have happened to my baby sister than for her to be branded a deviant by the village. She's alive, she seems happy, and that's all I care about. I want Zoe to be happy. My father would want me to protect her..."

"From me?"

"No, from all the evil in the world. She has gone through so much, and I don't want to have her hurt. I wasn't here to protect her or my mother back then, but I'm here now. That

I can do. That means I accept her and accept you in my family."

"Thank you, Theo. You share your sister's forthright nature and honesty."

"What would you have done if I had said I didn't approve?"

"I don't want to talk about something that won't ever happen now." Eva couldn't even think of the nightmare that would engulf them if Theo had decided to oppose her love for Zoe.

"Alright. Has Zoe told you about our family?"

"Zoe talks about the family all the time. I've heard so many stories about you and your brothers. It's like I know you already."

"I have this photo that you might like to see." Theo removed his wallet from his back pocket, took out a creased photo, and gave it to Eva.

Eva took the photo and smiled on seeing a very familiar face looking back at her. It was a photograph of a very young Zoe being held aloft on the shoulders of the tallest of the three brothers. "This is just beautiful."

"I found it in the box where Father Haralambos had put all the photos from the farm. He wanted them kept safe."

"Zoe didn't go back to the farm after your mother was killed."

"Father Haralambos told me. She doesn't know about all our possessions. I have them at my brother's house."

"Your house is the one in town, right?"

"Yes, do you know it?"

Eva nodded. "Yes, the German command house was right across the road. I lived there. That's where I first saw Zoe."

"Ah, yes, the bombed house. That's still there. It's not completely destroyed."

"They haven't demolished it?"

"No. I don't think anyone had the time, and with the civil war breaking out, it wasn't a priority."

"There's something in there that I want." Eva leaned forward. "I hope it's still there, but I don't know if it survived the bombing."

"What is it?"

"It's a photograph of my mother," Eva said softly. "I don't have any photographs of her, and I had it in a desk. There's also a painting that your mother did, and it was also in my rooms."

Theo nodded. "Once I get the two of you settled in Thieri's cabin, I will go and look."

"How do you know we were staying there?"

"Father Haralambos told me." Theo smiled. "I wondered what you looked like since your father is Father H. You don't look like him."

"I look like my mother—dark hair, blue eyes, and tall." Eva smiled. "I'm named after my maternal grandmother, Eva Mitsos."

"Mitsos? Petros Mitsos, the war hero?"

"Yes, my grandfather Petros, his wife Eva, my mother Daphne, and her sister Theresa. You know of the family?"

"I have heard of them. Father talked about him all the time," Theo replied. "The Mitsos family was well respected in Larissa, even though we don't have any of the family left there. Your grandparents passed away before the war. There has been a lot of sorrow in that family."

"Sorrow?"

"You don't know about the Mitsos curse?"

Eva sat back in her seat and regarded Theo for a long moment. "Was the curse brought on by an unmarried mother?"

Theo shook his head. "No, that was terrible, but not worthy of a curse. This was real. I'm surprised you don't know about it."

"No, I don't know anything about a curse. I don't know a lot about my mother's family."

"Hm." Theo took the cigarette from the ashtray and brought it to his lips. He took a drag and exhaled. "I remember my grandmother talked about your grandfather a great deal. She loved him like a brother. There was something wrong with the family. All the women were..." Theo stopped for a moment. "All the women had something wrong with them."

"Well, that's putting it delicately."

"I sound like a gossiping old woman, but when Father H told me he had fallen in love with a Mitsos girl I thought..."

"There wasn't anything wrong with my mother," Eva said defensively. "I don't know about the rest of the family as I didn't meet my Aunt Theresa but..."

"It wasn't your mother. My grandmother told me about Theresa."

"I was told she died in a fire."

"Yes, in an insane asylum."

Eva stared at him and wasn't sure how to react to that news. "That's not the story I was told."

"It's true. Ask Father H when we get to Larissa. He remembers Theresa. She was stricken by the evil eye."

Eva smiled despite the serious nature of the conversation. "I don't believe in the evil eye."

"Mock it all you like, but the evil eye exists."

"Uh-huh, and to avoid it, I have to wear a blue eye on me?"

Theo's bearded face creased into a smile. "You don't because you have beautiful blue eyes already."

"That's a relief," Eva quipped and had a quiet chuckle. "There was something wrong with my aunt, and she was in a hospital. There was a fire, and she died. I don't think it has anything to do with evil eyes or demons or anything like that."

"If you say so. My grandmother knew your great aunt Erika, and like Theresa, she was in an insane asylum as well. Then again you know how old women gossip, so it may not be the evil eye."

"Or you just realized you called your sister's..." Eva stopped and wasn't sure what to call herself, but decided she wasn't going to hide her feelings for Zoe from him. "You realized you called your sister's lover's family lunatics."

"It may be that as well." Theo laughed. Eva sat back and regarded him. There was a slight twitch at the use of 'lover' to describe herself, but it wasn't disgust she saw on his face. He was just uncomfortable.

"I like you, Eva. You are very honest. I respect honesty." He touched her hand. "The way you were described to me, I thought you were... um..."

"Cold?" Eva tilted her head and smiled. "Aloof? A bitch? I take it you didn't get that description from Father Haralambos."

"Quiet, cold, and aloof were the most common words used. Father H forgot to tell me how beautiful you are," Theo replied a little bashfully. "Young Dimitri thought you had a spell over Zoe."

Eva sat back and laughed lightly at the absurdity of it all.

"Dimitri would make a great old woman." The door to the dining cabin opened, and Zoe walked in with her sketchpad in her hand.

"Hullo." Zoe gave Eva a chaste kiss on the cheek. She also kissed Theo.

"I'm having a severe case of déjà vu." Eva chuckled.

"Yes, so am I." Zoe scowled at the nearly full ashtray. She turned to catch the waiter's eye and beckoned him over. "You still haven't had breakfast."

"No, I was talking to Theo. How's your knee?"

"Feeling better. Evy, you promised me," Zoe gently scolded, and turned to Theo, who was smirking. "What's so funny, Theodore?"

"You sound like Mama," Theo responded with a gentle laugh. He stood up and affectionately ruffled her hair. "Let's eat because I'm now starving."

CHAPTER 32

EVA LOOKED AROUND THE DINING CAR TO FIND they were the only ones in it. Everyone else had got off the train and was having lunch outside, which was a little odd to see. The waiter had come and delivered their order making sure everyone had what they ordered. Theo went to wash his hands, which left Eva and Zoe a moment alone.

"Hey." Zoe bumped Eva's shoulder. "Are you alright?"

"I'm a little anxious," Eva said as she played with her potatoes with her fork.

"About Theo?"

"No. I like Theo." Eva sighed heavily as she gazed at Zoe. "The closer we get to Larissa, it's making me anxious that I'm anxious."

Theo came back to the table and sat down. He smiled at them. "Are you going to play soccer with those potatoes?"

Eva looked up at him and then at Zoe. "I'm not hungry."

"Aren't you feeling well?" Theo asked and stuck a fork in Eva's potato and ate it.

"She's nervous about going to Larissa," Zoe answered, getting a scowl from Eva. "It's alright; he's family."

"Are you anxious to visit your father?"

"No." Zoe shook her head. "She's anxious we get there and then leave."

"Oh." Theo nodded. "That's why you're staying at Thieri's cabin?"

"It's out of town," Eva explained before she took a sip of water. "Larissa is not my favorite place in the world."

"No, I would say it wouldn't be. Where Father H told me that you were coming and where you would be staying, I finished building it."

"You did what?" Zoe asked.

"I built a bedroom and a little kitchenette. I installed a bigger rain tank. I've hooked up a hose where you can get water and a little burner where you can warm it up. I also built a bigger porch so you won't get rained on if you sit outside." Theo smiled. "It's not fancy but..."

Zoe came round the table and put her arms around his neck. She kissed him on the cheek. "Thieri would have loved that!"

"Not that he ever wanted to finish that cabin. He loved to build. I think if he had finished the cabin, he would have demolished it and rebuilt it." Theo chuckled. "You know it belongs to you now, so I didn't get your permission to finish it." Theo took a bite of the lamb stew. "You could kick me out of Michael's house if you wanted to."

"Really?" Zoe grinned. "Nah. Does that mean I get Athena?"

"You saw her?"

"Of course," Zoe replied and then turned to Eva. "I

promised Eva that I wasn't going to ride another motorcycle, but this is different. It's Athena!"

Eva and Theo looked at each other and then at Zoe. "No," they said in unison.

"Why?"

Eva touched Zoe's hand and scowled. "A Promise is a promise, Zoe. The last thing I need in Larissa is for you to get hurt again."

"Hurt? When did you get hurt?" Theo asked.

Zoe looked up at the ceiling in frustration. "I had an accident."

"How did you get hurt?"

"I was in a horrible accident."

"She got hit by a speeding car and smashed against a tree breaking her leg and injuring her hip." Eva shook her head. "She promised me that she wasn't going to ride again."

"Eva!"

"Eva is right, and Athena is way too big of a motorcycle for you."

"No, she's not. I'm bigger than when I last tried to ride her."

"No, you are the same height."

"Theodore!" Zoe exclaimed. "You two are just impossible."

Theo glanced at Eva and smiled. "Yes, we are," he said, causing Eva to chuckle.

The conversation abruptly ended when the train started to move amidst cheering coming from the main cabins.

"Well, Larissa, here we come." Theo clasped his hands together and rubbed them. "Now back to that accident."

"Do we have to?"

"Yes. How serious was it?"

"It was serious," Eva said as she glanced at Zoe. "But we made it through."

"So everything is alright?"

"Yes, I'm fine." Zoe waved her hand in dismissal. "I drew a lot because I wasn't allowed to do anything else."

"I saw you brought your sketchbook. Can I see?"

Zoe gave the book to Theo. "Oh, this is nice," Theo said as he looked up from the first couple of artworks. He flipped through them quietly and then stopped. "Well, this is a bit more...um..."

"Oh, no," Eva said in a panic on seeing Zoe's face and realizing what Theo may be looking at. "Oh, Zoe, tell me you didn't..."

"What?" Zoe asked as she got out of her chair and went around to Theo's side. She looked over his shoulder. "You are horrible." She slapped him across the back of his head as he snickered at his practical joke.

"It's not what you think," Zoe told her relieved partner. "It's my drawing of the Acropolis and you."

Theo chuckled as he turned the pages. "Does she have any of those 'oh no' drawings of you?" he asked Eva with a twinkle in his green eyes.

"Do you honestly think I would let you see the artwork of Eva like that?" Zoe shot Theo a mock glare, which only made him laugh.

"Oh, you are evil." Eva shook her finger at Theo, who just grinned.

"Artists like drawing naked people." Theo shrugged. "You remember Mama did one and we hung it up in the living room."

Eva turned to Zoe with a quizzical expression on her face. "Mama drew me naked on a blanket and hung it up in the living room when I was two years old, which is very different," Zoe explained, shooting an outraged glare at her brother.

"She had a cute backside." Theo laughed. "Do you have any of Eva lying naked on a blanket?"

Eva shook her head at the antics of the siblings. Theo was teasing Zoe, and their banter back and forth made her forget for a moment where they were headed.

"Next stop Larissa in thirty minutes!" the conductor announced as he passed through the dining car.

"Oh, finally!" Theo clapped his hands again. He reached across the table and gently tapped Eva's hand. "You have another Lambros you can count on."

"Thank you," Eva said quietly.

Zoe went over to Theo and put her arms around his neck and kissed him on the cheek. "Thank you, Teedore."

Theo looked up at Zoe and laughed. "I haven't heard that in years!" He looked at Eva to explain. "Zoe took forever to learn to talk. We thought there was something wrong with her because she would barely say two words, but when she was two, she started to talk, and then we couldn't get her to shut up." He grinned at Zoe. "She couldn't say Theodore, so it ended up being Teedore for a long time."

The dining car door opened and Mrs. Muldoon entered. She smiled at the group and approached them. "I thought I would find you here since you weren't in your cabin."

Theo pushed his chair back and rose as Mrs. Muldoon approached. "Della, this is Zoe's brother, Theodore Lambros. Theo, this is Mrs. Della Muldoon. We traveled with her on the ship." Eva made the introductions in German and then in Greek for Theo.

"Yes, hello." Theo offered his hand.

"Pleased to meet you, Mr. Lambros. Would I be able to steal the girls away for a moment?"

Eva translated into Greek.

"Of course," Theo replied. "I'll just go and get their luggage," he added as he nodded to Mrs. Muldoon and left the dining room.

"He's a charming man," Mrs. Muldoon said as she watched Theo leave. She turned back to Zoe and asked, "How's your knee?"

"Oh, fine, sorry for that mad dash out of your cabin."

"It's not every day your dead brother comes back to life, right?" Mrs. Muldoon laughed lightly. "Now girls, my trip with you has come to an end. I wanted to say goodbye before we parted and I don't want to part on bad terms."

"We don't want that either," Zoe answered as she quickly glanced at Eva.

"My job offer is genuine. I do want you to work with me. I want you to think about it. I'm going back to Sydney in two months." Mrs. Muldoon opened her purse and removed a piece of paper. "Contact me when you get back home."

"I will," Zoe replied.

"Eva, I hope you find the answers you need in Germany. Please, give your grandmother a chance."

"I'll think about it," Eva replied graciously.

All three women stood and bid farewell. Eva sighed.

Zoe put her hand on the small of Eva's back. "This is going to be alright."

Eva looked down at her feet and clicked her heels three times. "There's no place like home," she said and closed her eyes. After a moment she opened one eye to look at a bemused Zoe. "Nope, I'm still here."

"What?"

"Remember the movie we saw about Dorothy and the yellow brick road?"

"The Wizard of Oz."

"Hmm, just tapped my shoes and I didn't go home." Eva sighed.

"That's because we are not in the Land of Oz." Zoe laughed lightly. "It's going to be rough, but we will get through this."

"I know."

"Larissa in ten minutes!" The conductor's voice drifted in from the open door.

Zoe put her arm around Eva as they left the dining room car.

CHAPTER 33

LARISSA, GREECE

EVA SAT RAMROD STRAIGHT. She breathed in and out slowly as she tried to calm her out of control thumping heart. She was struggling, and she felt lightheaded and was sweating lightly. It was going to get progressively worse as they neared Larissa. She saw Zoe motion for Theo to leave them alone for a moment, a signal he was quick to obey.

Zoe sat down next to Eva and took her hand. Eva's hands were shaking. "Hey."

"I'm not feeling well."

"I know. Are you cold?"

Eva nodded. "I'm feeling sick and want to throw up."

"It won't be long before we get to the cabin and I'll give you a nice massage, and we can both go to sleep."

"I'm sorry. I'm ruining your time with Theo and—"

"Shh. Stop that. You are not. Theo has plenty of time to

catch up with me. He waited ten years so he can wait a bit more," Zoe reasoned.

"I think I have defective slippers."

Zoe looked down at Eva's feet. "They're brown. I think you needed them to be red."

The train stopped, and Eva heard the whistle blare. The sound of her heart was loud to her ears as she closed her eyes and took a deep breath. "Alright." She got up, adjusted her black cloak, and brought the hood over her head.

Eva and Zoe exited the cabin and found Theo waiting for them. "I'm right here." Zoe put her arm around her waist. "You can do this. I'm right here, and I have my big burly brother right beside you."

Eva glanced at Theo, who brought up his arms and flexed his biceps showing his muscles. She smiled, then stood to her full height and kept her head up.

They went down the steps to the train platform. Eva looked around as friends and family greeted the new arrivals. Nothing had changed in five years—the white stonewashed walls were still flakey, and the smell of burnt oranges permeated the station. She hated that smell. The humidity was already making her shirt cling to her back. How she hated this place. An oppressive weight had settled on her chest that made it difficult to breathe.

"Eva!"

Eva snapped her head up and her face creased into a huge smile on seeing her father headed her way.

"Ah, there they are!" Father Haralambos exclaimed. He embraced Eva and kissed her on the cheek. He turned to Zoe and brought her in for a hug and a kiss. He then patted Theo on the cheek. "You don't get a hug and a kiss."

"I always miss out." Theo bent and kissed the priest's hand out of respect. "I found her, Father."

"Yes, you did. That must have been the longest train trip in the history of Greece!"

"We had goats, we had tracks that were broken, and then we had the train that stopped at every stop," Zoe good-naturedly grumbled.

"How are you?" Eva whispered to her father.

"I'm good, taking care of myself. The nuns are trying to keep me healthy by feeding me too many vegetables, but I'm good," Father Haralambos replied.

"Oh, no," Eva whispered to Zoe, who turned to her in alarm.

"What? What's wrong?"

"Eva!"

Eva made a face and sighed. She turned towards the voice and smiled at the petite elderly lady that had called her. "Hello, Mrs. Kalmias." She couldn't forget Mrs. Kalmias, who had made her life even more difficult during the war and who had hit her with her cane the last time they had met. Mrs. Kalmias was now more stooped over, and fragile-looking than Eva remembered. Eva felt sorry for her—she had outlived her husband and her sons.

"Come down here. I can't even see you all the way up there!" Mrs. Kalmias tugged on Eva's cloak to get her to kneel beside her.

"How are you, Mrs. Kalmias?" Eva smiled.

"I'm old; living hurts. You don't want to hear about growing old, do you?" Mrs. Kalmias patted Eva on the cheek. "I was told you were on this train and I had to be down here when it arrived. It did take a long time, but here you are at last."

"Yes, it took a very long time."

"I want to apologize to you."

Eva was surprised. "Why?"

Mrs. Kalmias sighed. "Some things should not have happened, and I can't get them out of my mind. One of those is that I hit you, my dear child. I didn't know you were working with the Resistance. I thought you were the enemy."

Eva was deeply moved by Mrs. Kalmias' words. No one in this small town had ever apologized to her for the way she was treated during the war, not that they needed to, because she was the enemy. She was part of the Nazi war machine, even if it was by association.

Mrs. Kalmias took Eva's hands in hers and smiled. "When you grow old, there are days when you regret half your life. You have no idea how happy I was to hear that you would be coming back." Eva tried to interrupt, but the old woman put her hand over her mouth. "Father Haralambos was my savior during the terrible war. Such a man of God. It made me extremely happy to find out that you were young Daphne's little girl, and it saddened me because I treated you so harshly."

"Father Haralambos told you I was his daughter?"

"Thanasi told me. He's my nephew." Mrs. Kalmias' revelation surprised Eva. "I loved your mother like my own daughter."

"You knew my mother?" Eva asked, her voice breaking a little with the emotion.

"Your mother and my daughter, Alexandra, were best friends. It saddened me so much to see her leave. My eyes are not working properly, and had they been, they would have seen that you certainly look like your mama. Alexandra and

Daphne were inseparable as best friends usually are." Martha Kalmias' eyes are crinkled. "Will you forgive an old lady for hurting you?"

Eva didn't trust her voice at this point. She nodded. Mrs. Kalmias cupped Eva's face and smiled. "Well, that's one thing I won't have to worry about anymore." She turned to Zoe, who was hovering near Eva. "So, little Zoe, are you taking care of Eva?"

Eva and Zoe looked at each other, wondering how much Mrs. Kalmias knew. She laughed. "My eyesight isn't good but I hear quite well, and what I hear is that you and Eva are taking care of each other in Australia. Yes?"

"We take care of each other, *Yiayia.*" Zoe used the affectionate Greek term 'grandmother' for the old woman.

"Good girl," Mrs. Kalmias said quietly. "Eva, when you have some time, I want to give you a photograph of your mother and my Alexandra." She looked up at Theo and smiled broadly. "Theodore, you take good care of the girls."

"Of course, Yiayia," Theo said as Mrs. Kalmias very slowly made her way out of the station.

"You know, Evy, I've never known that old woman to apologize for anything," Zoe said.

"That's never happened before?" Eva smiled and looked at Zoe in amazement.

Zoe leaned against Eva's shoulder. "Not everyone here hates you," she whispered.

"What happened to Alexandra?" Eva asked.

"She was killed the same day Mama died."

"Don't look now, but cousin Maria is headed our way," Theo said through gritted teeth.

"Zoika!"

"Oh, God, I'm sorry for everything I've ever said about

you!" Zoe groaned. Eva suppressed a giggle as Zoe's cousin bounded towards them. She couldn't quite believe that the two were related. While Zoe was redheaded and green-eyed, Maria's hair was dark, her eyes were a murky brown, and she was slightly taller than Zoe.

"I forgot to warn you," Theo hurriedly whispered.

"Welcome home, Zoika!" Maria made a face when she saw Eva and then turned to Father Haralambos. "Father," she said and bowed down to kiss his hand.

Maria's parents, Dionysius and Keramia, quickly joined her. Dion was a slightly built man of short stature. His grey-peppered brown receding hairline made him look older than his fifty years. Thick black-rimmed glasses framed deep-set dark brown eyes. Keramia was a plump woman with brown hair and brown eyes. She was several paces behind her husband.

"Father Haralambos, how lovely to see you," Dion greeted the priest, and bent down and kissed his hand. "Ah, the prodigal has returned," he exclaimed as he hugged Zoe. He glanced at Eva. He didn't bother to greet her. "Theodore, where is your crazy aunt Stella?"

"I don't know, Uncle Dion. She may have had some patients to see," Theo replied respectfully.

"The least she could do is be here for your sister's return," Dion grumbled. "Are you taking young Zoe to the farm?"

"Zoe is staying at Athena's Bluff."

"All the way up there? Goodness, are you staying up with her?"

"No, sir, Zoe and her friend Eva are staying up there."

"All alone up there? Boy, what did your father teach you? You have to stay at the cabin to protect them!" Dion completely ignored Eva. "Keramia, do you want to say a few words?"

The woman timidly approached Zoe and gave her a hug. "So nice you are home."

"We will see you when you have settled in. I'm now the head of the family and we have much to discuss including your future, Zoe," Dion said as the trio walked away.

Father Haralambos stared open-mouthed at the retreating man and shook his head. "A bull has more finesse."

"I'll kill him before he tells me what to do," Zoe muttered under her breath.

"Try not to kill him, Zoe, we don't want more trouble. Now Theo is going to take you to the cabin. I'm happy that you're both back," Father Haralambos said, and hugged them again. He bid them farewell and walked away, occasionally stopping to wave at someone.

Eva looked down at her feet. "Red shoes," she muttered. Theo picked up their suitcases, and they left the station.

"You two travel light." Theo put both bags down in the middle of the cabin and turned to find Zoe standing on the threshold. "What's wrong?"

"I just don't remember the cabin being so big."

"Oh, that." Theo looked around the cabin. "I told you on the train that I've been working on it since I found out you were coming home."

"Wow," Zoe exclaimed and took a brief tour of the kitchen. She opened the door to the bedroom. It was small but quite lovely. There were two single beds, a small bedside table, and a chair. The beds were made up, and a hand-made bright green bedspread adorned each.

"Aunty Stella made the bedspreads. I think she's color blind." Theo chuckled as he came up behind Zoe and stood at the bedroom door. "She's very excited that you are here."

"She is?"

"Yes, she had an urgent matter to attend to, but she said she would be up to see you tomorrow. Where's Eva?"

"She's outside."

"Why?"

Zoe looked around the cabin before she turned to Theo. "She was shot here. The train station was a trial. All those people... It's really very hard on her at the moment."

"What's the story with the cloak? It's quite warm, and she is still wearing it."

"She wore one like that during the war. She didn't go anywhere without it, even in summer. Made her stand out rather than make her invisible as she wanted." Zoe walked to the window and looked out. Standing on the bluff was the distinctive tall form of Eva. The sun had set, and dusk had descended, but she could easily see her looking out across the valley. "Larissa is one giant raw wound."

"If it's so hard for her, why did you bring her to the cabin?"

"Where were we going to stay?"

"The house."

"It's in the middle of town," Zoe reminded him. "Eva didn't want to stay in town. Larissa is bad enough, but staying there... I wouldn't have been able to get her out of the house."

"How bad was it for her here?"

"She was alone for a long time. Alone, hurt, and miserable," she said. *And suicidal,* she thought. "Imagine being here with no one to love you, to look out for you or to care."

"I know what that feels like," Theo said quietly. "I thought I had lost everyone—Michael, Thieri, Papa, Mama, you."

"Of course. I'm sorry, Theo." Zoe turned to him and put her arms around his waist. She leaned in as they hugged.

"You know how that feels like too, so we both understand how Eva felt."

"Eva lost her mother, but not all her family died. They abandoned her, disowned her. They did things to her that give me nightmares. How she found the strength to trust someone again, I don't know."

"What happened? Why did her family disown her? Was it because she was a lesbian?"

Zoe looked at Theo. "Can you imagine Papa hating us?"

"No, never."

"Eva's did. He hated her so much, he beat her so badly, and he did such horrible things to her. They tortured her for being a lesbian. I just don't understand it. The Mullers are horrible people."

"Well, she's got you, she's got me, Father Haralambos, Aunty Stella, and Te..uh...Uncle Dion."

"Has he always been such a rude man? He didn't greet Eva at all," Zoe said. Her attention was on Eva outside, knowing she was going through extreme anxiety. She wanted to go out and lead her into the cabin. Just the two of them.

"Our dearly beloved Uncle Dion," Theo said dismissively. "You know the good thing about Eva?"

"What?"

"She trusted you, and that says a lot about you, *koukla*. You gave her the strength to trust again." Theo smiled and kissed the top of Zoe's head. "She's a remarkable woman, just like you."

"She's here because of me. She loves me, and she chose to come here so I wouldn't lose my inheritance."

"I'm glad she did that because I would have had to find a merchant ship and work my way to Australia."

"You would have done that?"

"Of course," Theo said as he gave Zoe a kiss on the cheek. "I will see you tomorrow."

"Theo."

Theo stopped at the door and turned.

"Make some noise before you say goodbye to Eva. She's easily startled when someone comes up behind her without her knowing," Zoe said. Theo nodded and left. Eva had gone back to standing on the edge of the outcrop.

Zoe shook her head on seeing Theo 'accidentally' trip over himself and nearly fall, causing Eva to turn at the noise. "I said make some noise, not wake the dead." Zoe laughed.

Eva and Theo talked for a few minutes before he pulled her in for a hug. "I love you, Teedore," Zoe said quietly. She walked out of the bedroom and out the main door to find Eva had gone back to looking out into the valley.

Zoe deliberately stepped on a tiny branch before she joined Eva. She sat down cross-legged on the edge of the lookout, which was shaded by a huge overhanging tree. She beckoned Eva to sit next to her, but Eva stood there with a smile on her face.

"I promise I won't throw you off," Zoe repeated the words she had said six years before and patted the ground.

Eva sat down next to Zoe. She put her arm around her and let her long legs dangle from the edge. "So we are back here."

"It's been an interesting train trip."

"I like Theo," Eva said as Zoe's head rested on her shoulder.

"He likes you."

They fell silent and watched the sky darken. "I'm feeling lost, Zoe. I thought it wouldn't be as bad as I imagined but being here…"

"I know." Zoe took her head and held it tightly. "I promise we will get out of here very quickly."

"I'm happy I didn't jump that morning I came out here alone," Eva quietly said.

"Me too. I'm happy that gun jammed."

"Hmm." Eva nodded. "I thought Athena's Bluff was the place to end it all."

"This was before Father Haralambos told you about being your father, right?"

"Yes. Where were you?"

Zoe pointed to a fallen tree trunk a few yards from the outcrop. "Over there, behind that tree."

"What were you doing there?"

"I had been sleeping in the cabin, and I had come out to relieve myself." Zoe smiled wryly. "I heard someone coming, and I hid."

"I didn't know you were there."

"I thought you had heard me when I was trying to pull up my pants." Zoe giggled. "You didn't, so I stayed put. I was going to kill you that day. I had Stavros' gun. I actually pulled the trigger, but it jammed."

"You fired it? You really fired it?"

Zoe looked into the darkened horizon before she turned back to Eva. "I fired it, and I was surprised you didn't hear my cursing. That blasted thing just wouldn't shoot. That was soon after Mama died. I thought of running at you and pushing you off."

"What stopped you?"

"You walked away from the edge, and Henry came up the pass," Zoe revealed. "Why are we talking about this?"

"Larissa is such a fun place; lots of happy memories," Eva said sarcastically. "I should have died so many times, and yet here I am. Here we are."

"I think we've had enough of the happy memories. It's been a very long day. Why don't we go inside? I'll give you a nice massage, and you can actually get some sleep. What do you think?" Zoe put her hand at the small of Eva's back and rubbed it a little.

"I need to get up and go inside, right?"

"Yes. You are too big a girl for me to carry," Zoe lightly joked as Eva got up, took her hand, and went to the cabin door.

"Can I go in?"

Zoe grinned. "Yes, I think it's okay. I own it." She repeated the line she had said to Eva years before when they first came to the cabin together.

Eva stepped inside and stood in the living room. There was a flokati rug on the floor. "Nice rug."

"Come on." Zoe took Eva's hand and led her to the bedroom and closed the door.

CHAPTER 34

"You're going to be fine here?"

"Yes, Mutti, I'm going to be fine." Eva straightened the hat on Zoe's head. "You are going to Theo's house, and you are going to get some groceries."

"We are only going to be here for a few days."

"What do we eat for those few days? Would you like me to catch a rabbit?" Eva jokingly pointed to the brush around them.

"You wouldn't know what to do with it." Zoe giggled. "Can you skin a rabbit?"

Eva made a face and shook her head. "I don't kill rabbits."

"I didn't think so."

"Come back soon." Eva kissed Zoe lightly on the lips. "Just remember one thing."

"What's that?"

"Don't throw rocks at any girls." Eva laughed when Zoe stuck out her tongue. "This girl fell for you, so those Larissa rocks are lethal," she continued while walking with Zoe down the track.

"Before I forget, Theo said my aunty Stella is at the farm, and we are going there tomorrow."

"Am I going with you?"

Zoe stopped mid-stride and faced Eva. "US. You and me."

"Zoe..."

"Eva Theresa, don't whine. You are coming with me."

"Do I have to?"

"Yes, you have to. It's my aunty Stella, and I want to introduce you to her. From what I remember of her, she's zany, and you will love her."

Eva sighed and kicked a stone, which made Zoe start laughing. "You are precious. The last time I saw my aunty I remember she was just wonderful, even if Papa called her Crazy Stella. She will love you."

"Alright."

"Good." Zoe shook her head, and then stood on her toes and kissed Eva before she went down the track to the village.

Eva slowly trudged up the track, entered the cabin, and stopped. Standing in the middle of the living area was a woman. She appeared to be in her late fifties. Her white hair peeked out from under her bright yellow scarf, and she was dressed in a bright orange blouse with a yellow skirt and pink colored sandals, but it was her eyes that transfixed Eva—they were dark brown, almost black.

"Hello."

"Hello," Eva replied tentatively.

The woman spun and began to look around, which caught Eva completely flatfooted. "I do love this cabin, always have. Thieri would have been so proud of it, had he lived. Helena always did say Thieri had a good eye, but I never thought a cabin up here was going to be of any use other than to walk up all frosty from the cold. You can't tell boys anything anyway."

"Excuse me?"

The woman smiled. "You are probably wondering who I am."

"That question has crossed my mind." Eva leaned against the table and crossed her arms.

"How often do you get women to come into your life like this?"

"Not very often."

"I bet you have the girls falling at your feet."

"Pardon?"

"Ask me who I am. Go on, you know you want to."

Eva regarded her for a moment. Larissa had many a funny character, and this was one woman she hadn't met before. She would have remembered her. "Who are you?"

"Your family."

"Pardon?"

"You sound like one of those new recordings that get scratched, and they keep repeating the same thing over and over." The woman chuckled as she went over to the sofa, tested it by patting it, and then proceeded to kick the base. Satisfied with it, she sat down.

Eva didn't move and glared at the intruder. She wasn't sure who this woman was, and it was just one more unexpected irritant to the visit she didn't need or want.

"What do you want?" Eva asked as she went to the door and held it open, inviting her unwanted guest to leave.

"Where is young Zoe?"

"Who?"

The woman leaned back on the sofa and laughed. Eva was surprised by her reaction.

"Are you lost?"

"Goddess no, I'm not lost. Why on earth would I want to live up a mountain? It's cold and isolated."

Eva just stared at the woman.

"You still don't know who I am?"

"No, I don't, and I don't care either." Eva shook her head. "Please, leave." Eva pointed to the door.

"My name is Stella Nikas-Lambros, but you can call me—"

"Stella...Cra.." Eva stopped just in time, and Stella's face creased into a smile.

"Crazy Aunty Stella," Stella finished Eva's sentence and laughed. "Yes, that is me, Crazy Aunty Stella."

"I'm sorry I didn't know um..."

"What are you apologizing for? It's true."

"You're crazy?"

"No, but it's easier for people to think I am. Makes life so much quieter, don't you think?"

"I wouldn't know."

"Oh, come on, of course, you do." Stella gazed at Eva with a smile. "You seem the type that is very good at not showing people the real you. I know someone else who is just like that."

"You don't know anything about me except for what you hear in the village."

"I don't pay attention to what those silly women say. What's your name?"

"You already know the answer to that question, since you know who I am."

Stella chuckled. "Yes, good point. The village gossips say

you are Eva Muller, the child of the Butcher. What do you call yourself?"

"Eva Haralambos."

Stella grinned. "Your father is Father Haralambos."

"Yes."

"You're very tall."

"Yes."

"And talkative," Stella quipped. Eva continued to stare, which only made Stella giggle. "I do love talking to myself, but maybe you can help me out here and say something other than yes and your name?"

"Why?"

Stella laughed. "Well, that's a new word. Do you know why they call me Crazy Stella?"

Eva smiled despite herself. "Does it have to do with your fashion sense?"

Stella laughed heartily. "What's wrong with my fashion sense? Oh, my Goddess, you are funny. No, it has nothing to do with my fashion sense."

"Your black eyes?"

"I don't have black eyes—they are dark brown." Stella's eyes went wide and then she smiled. "I'm going to hazard a guess that those blue eyes of yours get you as much attention as my nearly black ones."

Eva tilted her head and regarded Stella for a long moment. Stella sighed and shook her head. "Goddess," she exclaimed. "You and Zoe were a little more than friends out there."

"You were spying on us?"

"Yes, I did rather well in hiding myself, considering you can see me from Mount Olympus in this outfit." Stella chortled. "So are you and my niece lovers?"

Eva stayed quiet for a long moment. "Why are you asking a question you already know the answer to?"

Stella grinned. "I like the sound of your voice."

Eva was not expecting that answer and she laughed, which made Stella punch the air in triumph. "You like the sound of my German accent?"

"German? Hmm."

Eva narrowed her eyes. Stella knew more about her than was commonly known. She tried to recall if Father Haralambos had mentioned Zoe's aunt, but she didn't remember any conversation that revolved around a short, crazy, white-haired woman. Eva wouldn't have remembered that conversation.

"Oh, don't give me that look." Stella rolled her eyes. "Zoe looks happy."

Eva smiled and visibly relaxed. She was on a more sure footing when talking about Zoe than about herself. "She is happy."

"That's just absolutely fascinating."

"What is?"

"Your face. Your whole face changes when you mention Zoe's name. Your smile becomes brighter, and your body relaxes. Fascinating."

"Zoe won't be back for at least an hour. She went into the village." Eva avoided talking about her feelings for Zoe.

"Yes, I know." Stella nodded. "You are going to make me spell it out for you, right?"

Eva's answer was to smile and stay where she was.

"You are similar to your aunt, but you're not. You both have that Faber dimple, and you are both tall and gorgeous."

"You are mistaken. I don't have an aunt living in Larissa."

"That is incorrect."

"Oh, I'm pretty sure I don't."

"You are right about one thing—you don't think you had an aunt living in Larissa. She doesn't live in Larissa. Technically she is not *in* Larissa but Farsala..." Eva remained silent. "Oh, you are good at this, aren't you? You are not aware of your aunt, but she is aware of you," Stella continued. "You have a maternal aunt."

"I *had* a maternal aunt. My mother's younger sister died in a fire."

Eva was startled when there was a heavy thud on the door, and then it swung open to reveal Zoe with two large bags. Eva rushed to her side and took the bags, blocking Zoe's view into the cabin. Zoe grinned and stopped Eva by taking hold of her shirt and kissing her.

"Um, Zo..."

"Yes?" Zoe asked as she put her arms around Eva's waist. "You know what I would like to do now? Since we have a bit of time before we head to the farm, I was getting all hot and bothered walking up —"

Stella cleared her throat and Zoe looked at Eva. "That wasn't you."

"No, it wasn't me."

Zoe closed her eyes and buried her face into Eva's chest in embarrassment.

"Oh god, Evy," Zoe said in German.

"Look around me," Eva also replied in German.

Zoe peeked around Eva. "Aunty Stella!" she said and rushed to her aunt. She laughed as Stella hugged her and then tenderly kissed her on the cheek.

"I'm sorry I wasn't here when you needed me, little one." Stella cupped Zoe's face. "I loved her so much, and I love you. Well, your mama would be most proud of you. You have grown into a beautiful woman."

"Thank you, Aunty."

"I prayed for you and for her. I think the Goddess heard my prayer," Stella whispered into Zoe's ear. "You're not so little anymore and you found a beautiful woman to share your life with."

"You know?" Zoe tentatively asked.

"Of course, I know. I'm not blind. I don't see many girls rushing into their friends and kissing them like that!" Stella replied as she turned her attention to Eva, who was smiling and looking at them. Stella turned back to Zoe. "Yes, I know, darling. It's alright."

"You don't..."

"I'm the last person to judge you for falling in love with a woman." Stella put her arm around Zoe and kissed her on the cheek. "She is a little on the mysterious side, but that's alright. I'm not used to Mitsos women being so cryptic."

Zoe watched Eva go into the kitchenette with the bags.

"I'll go and get her from her hiding place," Eva heard Zoe say. She stopped emptying the bag when Zoe put her arms around her waist and rested her cheek against her back for a moment. "So that's your aunt Stella."

"Yes, and I can't believe you didn't warn me."

"Love, you caught me by surprise."

Zoe shook her head and took Eva's hand. She kissed it, and they both walked back into the main cabin, still holding hands.

Eva sat down opposite Stella. Zoe had brought up another chair and joined Eva.

Stella met Eva's gaze. "I was telling your girl about her aunt before you came in."

Zoe turned to Eva with a quizzical look on her face. "I thought your aunt Theresa died in a fire?"

"She did," Eva replied.

"How many aunts do you have?"

"One that I know about."

"Does Eva have another aunt?" Zoe asked. "Where is she?"

"You see, that's how you play the game," Stella gently admonished Eva. "You ask questions, you learn instead of sitting there looking at me with those beautiful blue eyes and giving me a look that you've practiced in the mirror many times."

Zoe laughed. "Was Eva giving you her icy cold stare?"

"Is that what you call it? It works. Very frustrating. Now getting back to my story, which is taking longer than I thought it would." Stella put her hands on her head and straightened her hair. "Where was I?"

"My deceased aunt," Eva replied.

"You don't have a deceased aunt," Stella exasperatedly exclaimed. "Maybe I should start at the beginning."

"That would be good," Eva said icily.

"Is she always this difficult with people she doesn't know?" Stella quizzed Zoe.

"Yes." Zoe gave Eva a little bump.

"Goddess, this is harder than I thought. Now, where was I?"

"Aunt. Not dead," Eva responded.

"Your mother's younger sister, Theresa, did not die in a fire."

"My mother gave me Theresa's name as my middle name to honor her memory."

"Yes, that is true. Daphne loved Tessa so much."

"Did my mother lie to me?" Eva asked as she glanced at Zoe.

"No, your mother was not lying. She believed Tessa had died."

"But she hadn't?"

"No," Stella replied. "Your aunty Tessa is very much alive."

"What happened to her?"

Stella met Eva's gaze. "This is going to sound fanciful, but I'm going to try and explain. Tessa was sent to a lunatic asylum in Athens."

"What for?"

Stella clasped her hands in front of her as she gazed at the floor before she turned her attention to Eva. "She was sent there because exorcism was proven not to work for her, so the only solution was to shut her in a lunatic asylum and for the doctors to treat her for her illness."

Eva stared at Stella as she tried to process what the woman was telling her. Her aunt Theresa was possessed? She felt a heavy weight had settled on her chest, and she wanted to keep herself calm, but she thought she was losing that battle. Theo had been right when he told her Theresa was in a lunatic asylum.

"Exorcism from what?" Eva finally asked when she thought she could talk without it coming out like a strangled cry.

"Demon possession," Stella replied. "What the priests didn't understand was always demon possession."

"What didn't they understand?"

"Tessa is gifted. What we don't understand, we attribute to the supernatural, but that's not always the case."

"If my aunt Theresa is alive, why hasn't she contacted me? Where has she been?"

"That's where you are wrong, my dear girl." Stella reached into her bag and took out a large satchel. "She has contacted you."

Eva's heart began to beat faster. She tried to swallow, but the lump in her throat made it difficult. Eva glanced at Zoe and knew she was thinking the same thing.

"You know what I'm talking about." Stella took Eva's hands. "She has been with you since the day you were born."

"How?" Eva asked. Her voice sounded strange to her ears as if it had come from someone other than herself.

"As I said, Tessa is gifted. Her gift can be a curse." Stella looked at Zoe. "Tessa's gifts are something else."

"What's that?"

"Do you know what astral projection is?"

"Visions?"

"Hmm, not exactly. It is the ability to project yourself in another time and place."

"It was her," Eva whispered as she leaned forward. "It was my aunt that I saw."

"Are we talking about seeing someone as if they were a vision?" Zoe asked the question Eva had already figured out the answer to.

Stella nodded. "It was Tessa. Did you not think that it would be someone who cared about you?"

"Uh... I thought I was hallucinating."

"No, my dear, you weren't. Tessa has a few gifts. One of her other abilities is far stronger, Eva. Do you know what precognition is?"

"You can know the fu..." Eva stopped when she realized what she had just said. "She knows the future?"

"She doesn't know the future, but she does know events that will happen in the future."

"Isn't that the same thing?"

"No." Stella shook her head. "She knows what will happen, but not when it will happen; just that it happens."

"If she is alive and was responsible for my visions as you say, where is she now? Why isn't she here?"

Stella smiled. "Who said she wasn't here?" She turned to Zoe. "Did young Theo tell you I was at the farm?"

"Yes, he said you were at the farm and you brought a patient you were caring for..."

"My patient is Tessa," Stella replied. "We are both staying at the farm. I wanted to come here first, to see you, to talk to you."

"Why didn't she come?"

"We felt it necessary to tell you about her gifts before you met her. Tessa is also an artist." Stella opened the satchel and took out several pieces of paper. She gazed at Eva and then chose a drawing. Stella looked at the picture for a long time and then handed it to Zoe instead of to Eva.

Eva glanced at it quickly and felt an overwhelming fear grip her. She got up from her chair and found her knees were trembling. With the little strength that she had, she ran to the door and out into the night, leaving Zoe gasping at the drawing in front of her.

CHAPTER 35

Eva flung the door open and stumbled out. Her heartbeat beat loudly and it was the only thing she could hear. Everything else was a blur. She wiped the sweat from her brow and took a deep breath. The pounding in her head began to keep rhythm with the beat of her heart. She felt like she was in a pain-filled fog, and gulped to try to get a hold of herself.

"Please, God, help me." Eva moaned. She leaned against the nearest tree, unable to take a deep breath. Her legs felt like molten lead, the pain in her chest increased, and her legs finally gave out, and she slid down the side of the tree and landed with a thud on the gravel. Her head fell back against the tree trunk as she fought to take a breath.

Through the pounding ache in her head, Eva felt Zoe's presence. She knew Zoe was there but couldn't hear what she was saying until Zoe cupped her face in her hands.

"Evy! Look at me!"

Eva tried to focus, but her vision was blurred. Zoe took her in her arms and held her as she took in large gasps of air.

She could hear Zoe talking to her, and she felt like she was outside her own skin.

"Evy, I've got you," Zoe said repeatedly and held Eva against her. "Look at me, focus on me."

"I can't..." Eva stammered as she became more aware of her surroundings. The pounding in her head continued, and she felt hot. She opened her eyes, and through her tears, she could see Stella, who went to the giant drum of water that was used for washing. She took her scarf off her head, dipped it in the water, and handed it to Zoe.

"She's having a panic attack and feeling very hot at the moment. Put this on her forehead," Stella calmly instructed.

Eva tried to move but only managed to fall back into Zoe's arms.

"Are you hurting anywhere?" Zoe asked.

Eva nodded. "My legs feel like lead." Her heart was still racing but not as bad now. The pounding in her head also receded. She felt weak as if she had run up the mountain. "I'm sorry."

"What are you sorry about, child?" Stella gently cupped Eva's cheek. "It is I who should apologize. I'm sorry for hurting you." She quickly looked at Zoe as they both helped Eva up. Eva was feeling a little sturdier. She lent her weight on Zoe, and they made their way back into the cabin.

Zoe quickly glanced at Stella, who hurriedly put away the artwork. She stashed it under the sofa cushion the moment they came back inside. Stella indicated to Zoe she should let Eva rest. Eva and Zoe went into the bedroom and shut the door.

Eva sat slowly on the bed and sighed. "I made a total fool of myself."

"No, you didn't." Zoe took off Eva's shoes. She rolled

down her stockings and removed them. "I am going to have a word with Crazy—"

"She's not crazy. Don't call her that."

"Well, I'm crazy mad, so one of us is going to be crazy tonight," Zoe muttered, and then met Eva's eyes. "I'm scared for you. You've never had such a bad panic attack."

"I know," Eva replied quietly. She took off her shirt. "I'm just going to rest."

"Do you want something to eat?"

"No, I'm not hungry, love." Eva lay down on the bed, and Zoe pulled the blanket up. They looked at each other for a moment before Zoe went down on her knees and kissed her.

Without another word Zoe left and closed the door.

Zoe's anger was building. She faced the closed door, her hand still on the handle, and rested her head on it.

"Take a deep breath and calm down."

"I..."

"Don't react. Just calm down," Stella very quietly said. She took Zoe's hand off the door handle and held it. "Just breathe and don't react."

"That was painful."

"Yes, it was. I'm sorry. I just didn't think."

Zoe turned to face her aunt as she roughly wiped the tears from her face. "Do you know how much courage Eva needed to come to this place? To this cabin?"

"Yes, I know."

"No, you don't." Zoe shook her head as she went into the main living area and sat down. "You don't know."

"What makes you think I don't know?"

Zoe remained sullen. "You don't know Eva."

"I don't know Eva, no, but I know of her and what she has gone through."

"No, you don't."

Stella slid across the sofa and retrieved the artwork. "Tell me what I don't know." She gave it to Zoe.

Zoe looked down at the art. It was so detailed, so vivid that Zoe's nape hairs stood up. If she had been the subject of this image, she would have had a panic attack herself. The room was dark and looked extremely claustrophobic. In the middle of the room was a chair to which a young Eva was strapped, her head held in place by a thick black strap. She had a short thick bar in her mouth. A man stood behind her, but what horrified Zoe, even more, was the look of pain and fear on Eva's face. It was contorted into a silent scream that hit Zoe the hardest. There was also the man at the edge of the art, his hand resting on a square device with knobs. Zoe noticed a date in the corner. Her eyes went wide, and she looked up at her aunt. "This artwork was done on January 20, 1938!"

"Yes, nine months before it would actually happen. Imagine the horror of knowing someone you loved would go through that? Imagine you were that person's beloved aunt. Did she know what Eva was going through? Felt her pain, her fear?"

"Yes."

"Tessa endured that and other shared experiences that were far worse, Zoe. I endured them with her because she is my beloved and she was going through the pain."

"You are a lesbian, like me?"

"I am not a lesbian. I love your Uncle Timothy and I also love Tessa."

"Did Papa know?"

"He knew. Bless his heart, he knew but thought this was a phase I was going through because I had lost my Timothy. Your father loved me."

"Why did he call you Crazy Stella?"

"He thought I was crazy for wanting to work in a lunatic asylum. I really hate the word 'lunatic'—it's an ugly word. He also thought I was crazy because of my dress sense. Not because I loved men and women."

Zoe returned her attention to the artwork. She couldn't take her eyes off Eva's face. The terror was so real, so palpable. "She must have been terrified and in so much pain."

"She was, but you have to remember that she survived that. She survived all of it. They tortured her and she survived. Eva is far stronger than she even realizes." Stella tapped the artwork with her finger. "This was torture."

"They were evil." Zoe pointed to the doctor in the artwork. "That's Eva's uncle."

"I know. Eva had to endure this for months, but she did endure it, and she did not lose her mind. That takes an exceptional amount of courage, internal strength, and a will to survive."

"That's my Eva." Zoe smiled. "She wanted me to come back for the inheritance. She didn't want me to lose anything despite knowing we would be back here. This cabin holds so many terrible memories, but also wonderful memories."

Stella smiled. "When Tessa showed me this, I was so proud of you." She dug through the other art and came up with one. "I remember saying to Tessa that I didn't want to be on the other end of this."

Zoe took the artwork, glanced at it, and then looked up at her aunt. "Wow," she whispered. A teenage Zoe was looking back at her, her face contorted in rage as she fired at a German officer's face. From an artistic point of view, it impressed Zoe. She brought the artwork closer when she noticed the artist had even drawn the scratches on Zoe's face from her mad scramble to reach the major's house, which was going to be blown up during a Resistance attack. "That is incredible."

"When Tessa showed me this, I remember thinking how much you must have loved Eva to go into this cabin to fight for her life. It wasn't to kill in revenge for your mama, but to save her life."

Zoe looked up and blinked rapidly. "I didn't think."

"No, you didn't." Stella held Zoe's hand. "Your heart was telling you what to do and you did it. Now what you should do is go into that room and just hold Eva. Tomorrow you and Eva need to come down to the farm."

"We were going to..."

"Yes, you pay your respects to your mama, to the boys, and to my brother. I've already given him a good talking to, so it's time for some tender, loving words from his daughter."

Zoe nodded. "Did I disappointed Papa?"

Stella shook her head. "No, never. Your papa loved you so much and it would impossible to have him disappointed with you." She lovingly caressed Zoe's hair. "Your father loved you so much." Stella wiped the tears that threatened to spill. "I remember when I came down on your first birthday. You hadn't learned to walk yet, and your papa was doing everything to make you walk to him, but you wouldn't have any of it." She laughed lightly. "Big green eyes and all those red curls. You were his little girl. I remember he turned to say something to me and the next thing we knew, your mama's arms were flapping to get our attention. We turned, and there you were standing, and you took two steps, stopped, looked around, took another two steps, and flopped on the ground. I wasn't sure who was prouder, you with a huge grin on your face, or your papa, who had picked you up and danced."

"I never wanted to disappoint him."

"It's impossible for you to do that. If you think your papa wouldn't be proud of the young woman you have become, you are wrong. All he ever wanted was for you to be happy. Are you happy?"

"I'm ecstatically happy."

"You have made your parents proud. That's all they ever wanted for you."

"Thank you, Aunty."

"You're welcome, darling. Now it's time for me to leave." Stella got up and adjusted her skirt. She picked up her satchel and put it into the large bag. "Go to Eva and comfort her. I will see you tomorrow." She kissed Zoe on the cheek.

Zoe walked her to the door, gave her a last hug, and watched her walk down the track. Quietly, she shut the door and turned off the lamp before she entered the bedroom.

CHAPTER 36

LAMBROS FAMILY FARM - FARSALA

"OH STELLA, THAT WAS SO STUPID." Stella admonished herself. She was using a horse and cart to make her way back to the farmhouse from Athena's Bluff, where she felt she had left Eva with a reopened raw wound and Zoe half-mad with worry.

Stella brought the horse quietly up to the farm. She could see the light from the windows. A moment later the door to the farmhouse opened, and a figure emerged. Her hair glistened in the dim light. Tessa Lambros was a tall woman with waist-length black hair which framed a long face and full lips. Her light gray eyes watched as Stella dismounted from the cart. Tessa leaned against her wooden cane, resting her hand on the silver handle.

Tessa slowly shook her head as Stella looked back and then unhitched the cart from the horse. She took the reins of the horse and led him to the stables without saying a word.

"You're late, Angel," Tessa spoke for the first time. She put her arm around Stella's shoulders and leaned down for a quick kiss. "I was getting a little worried."

"Why are you up and about?" Stella asked. "Didn't I tell you not to put any weight on that knee?"

"Yes, knee hurts, I'll live. What happened to the girls?"

"Tessa, please, listen to me. I'm your partner, but I'm also your doctor. Listen to Dr. Stella, please."

"I do listen to you, Angel, but I've waited thirty years to meet my niece. She's barely twenty minutes from here and I'm getting a little anxious."

Stella shook her head. "I've never seen you so impatient before. I think I like it." She chuckled.

"What happened?"

"We may have a problem."

"What did you do?" Tessa asked as they went inside the house. She closed the door as Stella took the satchel out of her bag. "Oh, no. Tell me you didn't show her the artwork."

"All right I won't tell you."

"I told you that was going to be too much for her to take."

"Tessa, I wasn't thinking, and I should know better and I've worked with shell shocked patients and I should have know better but..." Stella shook her head and put her arms around Tessa's waist. She looked into Tessa's tired light gray eyes. "I caused her pain and that was the last thing I wanted to do."

Tessa led Stella to the sofa, and they sat down. "Did you introduce yourself?"

"No, that was my first mistake. I was intrigued by her; she's not like you and she's not like Daphne. She looks like her mother..."

"We already knew she looked like Daphne."

"It's more than that. Eva is quiet, reserved to the point of being cold. When speaks, there is no niceties..."

"You mean she's blunt?"

"No, it's not bluntness. I'm blunt. She comes across as indifferent. I was a nuisance. Doesn't like personal questions."

"That's was expected."

"Yes but once she lets her guard down, there is so much warmth. She has a quirky sense of humor that peeks out now and then, but the icy persona wins out and the real Eva disappears. I spied on them..."

"In that outfit?" Tessa raised an eyebrow.

"Yes, and I did an outstanding job."

"Those two must be blind." Tessa laughed. "What did you find out?"

"The Eva I met and the Eva that was with Zoe are two very different people. She was playful, loving, and open with Zoe. I couldn't believe it was the same woman."

"Zoe has always been the key to Eva."

"She is, isn't she? Just like you said."

"Why did you show her that artwork?"

"She was slowly coming out of her shell and I thought she might be like you."

Tessa sighed. "You know Eva differs greatly from me."

"I know she is but—"

"But you thought you would convince her I wasn't some lunatic. My guardian angel." Tessa warmly smiled at Stella.

Stella sighed deeply. "As I said, Eva's not an amicable person."

"I did say it wasn't going to be easy. Eva makes it hard on

purpose. Most people would give up trying to get to know her and move on."

"Is that some sort of game she plays?"

"It's not a game, Angel. This is her way of protecting herself."

"Yet Zoe got through those barriers."

"Zoe has more power over Eva than anyone else. If Zoe wanted to, she could kill Eva just using her words as a weapon. Just as deadly as a gun. It would be easy."

"But she won't. You said she wouldn't."

"No, she won't." Tessa shook her head. "What happened when you showed Eva the artwork?"

Stella looked heavenward. "She took one look at it and she fell apart. She was utterly terrified. It was as if she was back there. There was a fragility about her that I never expected, even though I should have known."

"Sometimes what we know and what we get can be very different. What of Zoe? What do you make of her?"

"My darling niece is her father's daughter. She looks like her mother but has all of my brother's steel. The only thing he didn't give that child was his height. His weakness was Helene. Zoe weakness is Eva."

"They both need to heal and they have come to the right place for that." Tessa gazed at Stella and smiled. "We have a lot of work to do before they come here. They are coming, right?"

"Yes, they are coming to the farm."

"What time?"

Stella sighed. "Tessa, darling, can you please go back to being serene?"

"Stella, please..."

"I know, I know you waited thirty years. One more night won't make any difference. We can do the chores tomorrow."

"We need to get Zoe's room ready and—"

"Theresa Rosa Lambros! You are going to drive me crazy." Stella took Tessa's hand and kissed it. "Let's go to bed so that knee of yours can start healing. I told you that horse wasn't going to behave."

"Yes, love."

Stella chuckled and waited for Tessa to pass her through the door of the bedroom. Tessa stopped and turned to face Stella with a wide grin on her face.

"She's really here."

"Yes, she is, and if she's still talking to me after today..."

"You mean there's a chance I won't get to meet her?"

"You will get to meet her; there is no doubt about that. Can you please stop fussing?" Stella led Tessa into the bedroom and shut the door.

CHAPTER 37

Zoe slowly opened her eyes and knew Eva was not beside her. Her hand felt the coldness of the sheet next to her. It was still dark. *Oh, Evy, how long have you been up?* When Zoe had come back into the bedroom, it looked like Eva was asleep, but Zoe knew she wasn't—her body was wound tight, her face tense. Zoe tried to talk to her but all she got back from Eva was either grunts or silence. Eva was not in the right frame of mind to talk so Zoe just put her arms around her and hoped she would at some point fall asleep.

It did not surprise Zoe that Eva couldn't sleep after having the worst panic attack she had ever witnessed. It looked horrendous and must have felt brutal. She shuddered at the memory of Eva's glazed eyes. The image of Eva's tortured face was burned into her mind.

Zoe rolled onto her back and looked up at the ceiling for a moment before swinging her legs over the bed. She shivered since the cool mountain air had dropped the temperature in the cabin. She sat on the edge for a little while and then she picked up her robe and tied it closed. The bedroom door was closed, but she could see the light coming from the main cabin.

Eva raised her head at the sound of the door opening. She had been sitting on the sofa staring at the floor for what felt like hours, oblivious to the cold with just a singlet and panties on. Zoe padded towards Eva, stopped in front of her, and knelt.

"Hey." Zoe took Eva's hands into her own.

"Did I wake you?"

"No."

Eva reached out and brushed red-gold strands from Zoe's eyes.

Zoe rose up and stretched out her hand. "Come to bed."

"I can't sleep."

"You don't have to. Just come and cuddle with me."

Without another word, Eva took Zoe's hand and they both went into the bedroom.

EVA WRAPPED her arms around Zoe and pulled her tightly against her body, loving the feeling of Zoe's overheated skin against her own. They stayed embraced for a long moment before Zoe gently rolled to her side. Eva's arms fell limply to her side, and she stretched out her legs. Zoe crawled up to lay her head on her chest.

"That's even better than going to sleep, isn't it? Good morning." Zoe laughed weakly and gazed into her lover's face. Eva smiled and swallowed audibly. "Do you know where we are?"

"In our cabin."

"I mean do you know where we are right now, here, in this bed."

"I know where we are."

"We could have made love in the living room."

"But we didn't. I needed to replace that memory with this one..."

Eva looked down at the red-gold hair of the woman she loved and smiled. "That was your plan all along wasn't it?"

"That was my plan except my brother changed the layout of the cabin."

"One less horrible memory," Eva finally said and closed her eyes. They were lying on the exact same spot where she had been tied up and shot, the spot where she lay bleeding in Zoe's arms. "I'm tired of hurting. Tired of the bad memories."

Zoe hitched herself up on her elbow. She lightly traced the bullet scar on Eva's upper right shoulder. She kissed it before she captured Eva's mouth. "We just made a better memory," she said as they parted.

Eva rolled to her side, and they were inches apart. She felt behind her back, pulled Zoe's robe, and draped it over Zoe's back, earning her a kiss.

"This cabin is not where I got shot."

"I must be a really good kisser to make you forget that."

"I'm telling myself it's not because there is a far better memory."

"It certainly isn't anymore." Zoe rested her hand on Eva's hip. "It's time to reclaim Thieri's cabin."

"It's not Thieri's cabin," Eva replied. "It's ours."

"Ours." They lay quietly, their hands intertwined. "Evy?"

"Hm."

"I was so scared for you last night. I didn't know what to do."

"You did it."

"What?"

Eva sighed deeply. "You were you. I can't survive without you."

"Yes, you can, but you don't need to."

"No. I'm not as strong as you are, love. I don't have your strength. I see a drawing, and I fall to pieces. I'm... embarrassed."

"You have nothing to be embarrassed about!" Zoe cupped Eva's cheek. "Nothing. You are the most courageous woman I know." She brought Eva's hand to her lips and kissed it. "I saw the drawing. That was just a small taste of what you endured, and my heart shattered into a thousand pieces. How you lived through that, how you even managed to trust again..." A tear slid down Eva's cheek, and Zoe wiped it with her fingers. "You gave me your heart. All that pain and suffering just didn't matter. You opened yourself up to me knowing I could betray you, knowing if I did, it would be the end."

"Maybe that's what I wanted."

"No, you didn't want that." Zoe shook her head. "If you had wanted that, you would have jumped off Athena's Bluff and put an end to it."

"I thought about it."

"I know, but you didn't do it. You didn't give up. You didn't let those bastards win by lying down and surrendering. You fought back."

"Not much good in fighting back when at the sight of a piece of paper, I shrivel up and cower like an infant," Eva said bitterly.

"Is that what you think happened? What I saw in that piece of paper was a terrified woman who was in so much pain that it was unbearable. It hurt to look at it. Your mind and body were shattered. How do you go from the broken teenager having electric shocks run through her body to someone who gave me her heart, her soul, and her life?"

"I don't know."

"I do." Zoe's eyes welled up, and she let the tears spill. "You have so much courage, Evy. They couldn't destroy it; they couldn't break your spirit."

"I'm just tired of hurting."

"I know, but together we will break that cycle. We have to." Zoe gently kissed Eva. "You want to, and I want to, so together we can do it."

"Together?"

Zoe smiled. "Together."

"Alright, but I think we have another problem," Eva said as she reached out and gently touched Zoe's throat.

"What?"

"I gave you a hickey." Eva giggled and kissed the bright pink mark she had left on Zoe's neck.

"Oh, my god." Zoe felt her neck. "What am I going to tell Aunty Stella?!"

"You got bit by a giant mosquito." Eva giggled. "Bzzzzzttt," she added as she kissed Zoe's neck.

"Come on, my giant mosquito, let's get cleaned up. I have to introduce you to my parents and brothers." Zoe tenderly felt the mark on her neck. "I wonder if a scarf would cover that."

"A scarf in the middle of summer?" Eva giggled and rolled onto her back.

Zoe pressed against Eva's body and slid her hand down

the skin of Eva's stomach. "I think the family can wait a bit." She captured Eva's mouth in a long passionate kiss. They parted, gazed at each other, and laughed.

CHAPTER 38

Zoe dried her hair with a towel and marveled at how her brother had stocked the cabin with everything they would need. There were towels, blankets, pillows, and food, although the foray into town to get more supplies did prove to be a trip down memory lane.

Zoe had lost count of how many times she was stopped. Many of those she met hugged her and welcomed her back to town. She avoided the outskirts of town, which used to be a lush field but were now barren land. The land was soaked in blood since the Germans had used the ground as their execution area. Too many of her friends had perished on that once fertile soil. She stopped drying her hair and sighed.

Eva came up behind Zoe and put her arms around her. "Why the heavy sigh, love? What are you thinking?"

"My trip into town yesterday." Zoe turned in Eva's embrace. "There were far too many memories."

"You went past Maragos' field?"

"How do you do that?"

"I have my demons, Zoe, and you have yours. This town

is filled with both of ours. What makes it more difficult for you is that I'm falling apart."

"You haven't fallen apart. You had a bad night, but that doesn't mean you are falling apart."

"Feels like it. I want to be here for you too. I'm sorry if I've made this trip even more difficult for you."

"Are you regretting coming here?"

"No. This is your inheritance, and if we hadn't come here, we would have let the Nazis win. We can't let them win even after so many years."

"For every soul they destroyed, didn't they win?"

"No, they didn't." Eva took Zoe's hand and led her into the living area. They sat down on the sofa together. "Evil was conquered. We conquered it by being alive. I sometimes forget that through the evil we both went through, we are still here."

"We are."

"Since we are here, they didn't win."

"So that's what you were thinking about during our bath?" Zoe smiled and looked down at their intertwined fingers. "Last night was..." She stopped, trying to find the right words. "Your worst nightmare come true."

"No. Aiden was my worst nightmare come true. I feel foolish about what happened with your aunty Stella. I'm thirty years old, and I behaved like a scared five-year-old."

"I don't know of any five-year-old that could have lived through Aiden. There's nothing to be ashamed of."

"I made up for it this morning." Eva put her arms around Zoe and gently rolled her back to the sofa. "I can't believe I gave you a hickey." She lightly traced the bruise on Zoe's neck.

"Oh! I forgot about that." Zoe's hand went to her neck, and she clasped Eva's hand. "What am I going to do?"

"I can give you a matching one on the other side." Eva giggled as she nuzzled Zoe's neck.

"No, I can't explain two mosquitoes biting me at the same time." Zoe pulled away to find Eva's cheeky grin. "Eva, stop."

"I need to finish the job."

Zoe laughed as she disentangled herself from Eva's arms. She stood and looked around the room for the headscarf she had removed after she had come back from town the previous evening. Eva lay on the sofa looking up at her.

A knock on the door made them look at each other. Zoe gave the room a quick look to see if anything was out of place and Eva got up to answer the door.

"Despina!" Eva exclaimed as her former housekeeper greeted her by putting her arms around her.

"Oh, My Lord Jesus Christ, were you always this tall?" Despina stepped back and gazed at Eva. "You are far too skinny for a girl your height! Where is Zoe?"

"Right here." Zoe grinned as she came around Eva.

"Oh." Despina pulled Zoe to her ample bosom and hugged her fiercely. "There you are, little hurricane Zoe. Oh, my dear girl."

"Come in, please." Eva invited Despina into the cabin. She smoothed out the rug with her foot as Despina kissed Zoe on the cheek.

"Zoe, what is that on your neck?" Despina leaned in and took off her glasses. "Hm, those mosquitoes have gotten much bigger since I was last at Athena's Bluff."

Eva turned away and coughed. "They are big over here, much bigger than in Australia."

Zoe's ears had turned a bright shade of pink. She gently slapped Eva's thigh while Despina was busy inspecting the cabin. Eva put her hand over her mouth to stop laughing.

"Young Theo did all of this?"

"Yes, he was busy getting this ready for us."

Despina turned to Zoe with a gentle smile on her face. "One of the happiest days of my life was seeing that boy walking up the street towards me. I thought I was seeing things until he came over and put his arms around me." She sniffed.

"Theo and Despina's son Alexi were best friends," Zoe quietly told Eva.

"Alexi was such a sweet boy. When Zoe was around, oh, Mother of God!" Despina smiled. "He could hardly say two words before he got, so tongue-tied I thought someone had stolen his ability to speak." Her belly laughs made Eva and Zoe chuckle.

"Zoe has that effect on boys," Eva quipped.

Despina smiled. "Tell me what you have been doing."

"Zoe is an artist. She went to university," Eva said proudly and gazed at Zoe. "You should see some of her art—it's just amazing."

"Is that right? Just like your mama."

"Eva encouraged me to go to school." Zoe felt a little shy. "We have a beautiful home in Sydney, and a cat called Ourania."

Despina smiled. "I'm so happy for the both of you."

"How are you?" Zoe asked as she leaned forward and touched Despina's hand.

"Alexi is back." Despina smiled. "He has seen much, and he proudly fought for our motherland. He is the *koubaro* at Thanasi's wedding," she revealed proudly.

"Koubaro?" Eva turned to Zoe with a questioning look.

"Best man," Zoe translated into German, causing Despina's eyes to widen.

"Zoe, darling, you speak flawless German!"

"I wouldn't say flawless, but Eva has taught me," Zoe explained stealing a glance at Eva, who was sitting back on the sofa with a very proud look on her face.

"Mother of God!" Despina exclaimed as she made the sign of the cross and put a hand over her heart. "I never thought I would hear you embrace that language."

Zoe shrugged. "Eva has shown me that it's not about the people, but the Nazis. They were the ones who killed our brothers and sisters and did all those horrible things."

"Yes, yes, of course, but I can't get over the fact of hearing you speak German."

"She's perfect," Eva boasted. "She has a natural flair for languages."

Despina smiled. "You are very proud of her."

"Very proud." Eva smiled.

"Now I will see you both at the wedding? Thanasi has invited everyone, which means all the girls, and I will be cooking at all hours!" Despina chuckled.

"You will." Zoe didn't look at Eva for confirmation.

Despina got up from the sofa. "Well, I will see you then. How long will you be in Larissa?"

"We're not sure." Zoe glanced at Eva, who was smiling politely. "We will probably be here for just a few days."

"Good, I'm sure we will catch up at the wedding. If I don't see you there, I'll be chained to George's ovens with all the food we are making. Come over and say hello to the other girls, alright?" Despina laughed.

"We will try."

"I hear your aunty Stella is in town as well?"

"Yes." Zoe nodded. "We saw her last night."

"Stella is a crazy woman but I love her," Despina said as they reached the door. Eva held it open, and Despina kissed Zoe and then Eva on the cheek before walking out.

Eva stood at the door watching Despina walk away and then sighed.

"Evy."

"Hmm?" Eva turned to find Zoe had found her headscarf and was wearing it around her neck.

"Must protect me from the mosquitoes," Zoe said, which made Eva smile. "Come on, my little mosquito, let's get out of here before we get more visitors."

"Let's do it quickly. I don't particularly like the idea of your uncle Dion or your crazy cousin Maria showing up. Was she always like that?" Eva asked while she donned her cloak.

"Yes." Zoe made a face. "Evy, you're going to be hot in that."

"I'm not hot," Eva answered, turning away to get their bag. "Dion's wife was quiet."

"She suffers from severe melancholy. She is a very nice lady when she is feeling better," Zoe replied as Eva closed the door.

Eva and Zoe walked down the path leading off Athena's Bluff, both lost in their own thoughts. They turned left and away from the town and took the dirt road leading to the cemetery.

Zoe put her hands in her pockets. She kicked a stone along as she walked, her pace slowing when she came to the family cemetery. She stood there gazing at the wrought iron gates for a moment.

"Why don't I stay here while you go and talk to your parents and then I'll come over?" Eva whispered.

"Alright." Zoe nodded. Padding to her mother's gravesite, she was surprised to see a fresh bouquet of flowers placed near the cross. The weeds had been removed, and the grave was well cared for. Zoe made a mental note to thank Father Haralambos for the loving gesture. She had once made a passing remark to the priest that the grave was going to be overgrown with weeds since there was no one to tend to it. Little did she know that Father Haralambos was going to take care of the grave in her absence.

"Well, Mama and Papa, I've come home. Well, not really home, because my home is with Eva now, but you know what I mean..." Zoe sat on the ground cross-legged. She plucked a blade of grass and twirled it around her finger absentmindedly. "You would like her. I know you would. She has the same quirky sense of humor as Michael and she's as tall as Thieri. I think they would have liked her too. I'm sure you know this, but Theo is back. That crazy man. He came to meet us on the train and rode all the way on Athena. He still won't let me ride her. I wish you were still here." She choked back the tears. "I told you I wanted to die when I lost you, but Mama, I found a reason to live."

Zoe lifted her head at the sound of two birds screeching overhead and took a deep breath. "I want to spend the rest of my life with her, Mama, every day of my life, like you did with Papa. She is loving, so kind, and gentle." Her gaze fell on Eva, who was doing a good job of appearing to be relaxing by flicking at a rock with her feet. She kept her gaze fixed on Eva until Eva looked up and was caught. Zoe smiled as Eva shyly looked away. "I'm going to bring her over. Eva said that the dead can hear our thoughts, and I'm really hoping that's true, or else I'm talking to a pile of stones." She shook her head and chuckled softly through her tears. "I know you can hear me and that one day I'm going to see you again, but Mama and Papa, forgive me if I don't want to join you any time soon."

Zoe brushed away the tears and lifted her head to see the village gravedigger going about his business. "You're still alive, Andreas," she muttered. The old man had been the village gravedigger for as long as Zoe could remember.

"Mama, I'm sorry I told you all those hurtful things. I never wanted to leave you alone, but I've learned so much, and I wish you were alive, so I could take you to the places you read about. I'm an artist. See, all that time sketching behind the chicken coup did pay off." Zoe looked down at the grass. "Eva sent me to university, and she worked really long hours to make it happen."

Zoe let out a sigh as she got up from the ground and dusted herself off. Looking again at the white cross that bore her mother's and father's names, she crossed herself. "I love you, Mama." She looked up at Eva and beckoned her over.

Eva quickly walked over and stood next to Zoe in front of the simple graves. Two large white crosses bore the names, Helena Lambros and Nicholas Lambros, etched into the wood.

"Father Haralambos takes care of the graves," Zoe explained.

Eva made the sign of the cross. "Hello, Mr. and Mrs. Lambros, my name is Eva. I just wanted to thank you for raising your daughter, who is kind, generous, and loving. Everything you wanted her to be." She glanced at Zoe, who was wiping the tears from her eyes. "She has helped me through my darkest times. You should have seen her grow up and be happy. I'm sorry you are not here. She has grown into a beautiful woman, very brave, but she's also got a loving heart. Thank you." Eva touched the headstones and bowed her head for a few moments. She then looked at Zoe and held her hand.

"What did you pray about?" Zoe asked.

"I thanked God for your love," Eva replied. She gave Zoe a quick kiss.

"I have two more visits to make."

"Ellie and Artemis..."

Zoe took Eva's hand and led her to the graves of her cousins.

CHAPTER 39

"Now where has that woman of mine disappeared to?" Stella muttered as she stood at the threshold of the kitchen door. Tessa was standing outside, waiting and watching for her niece and Zoe to arrive. She had been scanning the road leading to the farmhouse for over an hour. Stella shook her head at the sight.

"Theresa! You're going to make that knee worse," Stella called out, knowing she was going to be ignored.

"No, I'm not. I'm putting my weight on the other leg. That's what a cane is for." Tessa did not move from her position.

"I'm missing my serene girl! When you see her, please ask her to come home." Stella grinned when Tessa turned and looked at her. "Ah, that got a response!"

Tessa came towards her and smiled. "Stella, darling, I'm going to remind you of this when Thomas brings home another girl."

"I told him that girl was horrible. Why can't he find a

good girl or a good boy? I don't mind as long as they are perfect for our son."

"The problem is, my love, you won't approve of that person."

"Of course, I will."

"No, they won't have what you think Thomas needs." Tessa leaned the cane against the wall. She cupped Stella's face and smiled. "The last time Thomas brought home a girl, you were not very enthusiastic. I think your exact words were, "That woman has crazy eyes, and I don't trust anyone with crazy eyes." Tessa laughed. She lightly kissed Stella.

"Her eyes were crazy."

"It's not her fault she was cross-eyed," Tessa said, making Stella laugh.

"She wasn't cross-eyed. She was not modestly dressed, and the color she chose! Who wears black to meet the mother? Who?"

Tessa laughed. "That's a bit funny coming from a woman with almost black eyes."

"I have never liked anything dark."

"You have dark eyes," Tessa repeated and grinned.

"I can't help my eyes, but it's a choice to wear dark all the time. It's unnatural."

Tessa kissed Stella. "Yes, Angel, it's unnatural."

"Darling?"

"Yes?"

"I think we have visitor's arri—" Tessa whipped around so quickly that Stella didn't have a chance to finish her sentence.

"Where are they?"

"They are just walking down the hill."

Tessa grabbed her cane and walked quickly to the edge of the porch. "How can you see that?"

"Eyes like a hawk." Stella chuckled and buffed her nails on her shirt. "I'm very good at distracting my girl."

Eva stopped at the top of the hill and looked around. There were several houses further down the slope surrounded by cotton fields. It was a gorgeous vista.

"Nice, isn't it?"

"It's beautiful," Eva replied. "Wish I had my camera."

"You mean this one?" Zoe pulled the camera out of her bag. She laughed on seeing Eva's excitement. "Do you love me more than your camera?"

"Of course but not right now..." Eva took the camera and started to shoot several shots of the scenery before her. "I can't wait to develop these."

"You might want to ask the owner of the fields if you can do that."

"Huh?"

"There's a law that says you have to ask the owner of the land if you can take photos," Zoe said seriously.

"Are you sure?"

"Yes." Zoe nodded. "So go and ask."

"Where does the owner live?"

"See that farmhouse that's first in line before the others on the left? That's the owner."

"Oh, alright," Eva said, a little distracted as she put the camera away. "Do you know them?"

Zoe wasn't sure what she loved about Eva's reaction. That Eva was respectful of the law or that she was willing to ask permission and then take more photos. "You are adorable."

"Zoe, I can't use my camera? Is that real?"

"Yes, it's real."

"All right, who do I ask?"

"Me."

"I just asked you, who do I ask?"

"This is like those three idiots..."

"The Three Stooges."

"Yes, them. I own these lands, Evy."

"What?" Eva's eyes widened. "Are you serious?"

"Yes." Zoe nodded. "I own the fourteen fields spread out across the valley right in front of us. I also own the fields next to Athena's Bluff and the mountain."

"All this is yours? I didn't realize how much land you owned."

"We never really discussed it."

"Didn't you mention that the cabin belonged to Thieri? I thought Athena's Bluff was his."

"The mountain is mine and his cabin is on my land. He loved Athena's Bluff, and I gave him the property."

"Oh, that's a lot of property that you own, Zoe."

"No." Zoe shook her head as she took Eva's hand. With her other hand, she swept across the valley before them. "It's ours."

"What about Theo?"

"Theo has another fourteen fields on the other side of the valley. When he turned eighteen years old, Father gave him his inheritance. He did the same with Michael and Thieri. There are another fourteen fields on the west side that belonged to Thieri. I sold six fields that belonged to Michael for the cabin when we sailed to Australia."

"Wow."

"Papa believed in giving his children their inheritance

when he was alive. He didn't believe in leaving everything till the end. Papa was going to give me the fields as soon as I turned eighteen years old."

"Oh," Eva replied as they walked down the dusty road. "You own the farmhouse now, as well?"

"Yes. Theo owns his house in town and I get the cabin and everything else."

"I married a very wealthy woman," Eva teased.

"Yes, if you count dirt as being wealthy." Zoe shrugged.

"Is there such a crazy law about the photographs?"

Zoe grinned. "Yes, the town elders passed it just before the war. It was a bizarre law."

"Those crazy Greeks. Who would want to take photographs of fields?" Eva laughed when she saw Zoe's smirk. "So can I develop my photographs, Miss Lambros?"

"You can, Miss Haralambos, thanks for asking." Zoe gazed at her. "You do realize that if I kissed you now, poor Mr. Papadimakopoulos is going to have a heart attack?"

"Who is that?"

"An old man is looking at us from the second farmhouse."

"How can you see that?"

"Eyes like a hawk." Zoe chuckled.

The easy banter made Eva and Zoe relax. The journey to the farmhouse was going to be emotional for them both. Zoe's anxiety about going back to the farm wasn't lost on Eva, even though she was going through her own turmoil. Zoe had not returned to the farm since her mother's death.

Eva put her arm around Zoe's shoulders and brought her in for a hug. "How are you feeling?"

"I'm nervous. It's just a farm, but I have a knot in my stomach the size of a football."

"I know what you mean."

"I vowed never to set foot in that place again. I just wanted to leave." Zoe's voice broke, and she looked out at the fields.

"We are both facing our demons, love. This place has so many bad memories, but also some good ones," Eva whispered into Zoe's ear. "You have loving memories of your family. It's going to be hard, but you have to remember the good things."

"I do have happy memories."

"Why don't you tell me about them as we walk down there? We both need something to laugh about."

Zoe gazed up at Eva. A smile creased her face as she wiped away the tears with the back of her sleeve.

"I could tell you about the time I put a frog in Theo's bed." Eva glanced down and grinned at Zoe's exuberant and animated storytelling.

They walked down the road a bit more until they saw Stella approaching them. She was wearing a light green shirt with bright pink polka dots and a light purple skirt.

"The woman is color blind," Eva muttered, causing Zoe to giggle.

"Thank the Goddess you have arrived. My normally very serene wife was very unlike herself." Stella kissed Zoe on the cheek.

Eva stood up straight. She was feeling a little bashful. "Darling, I can't kiss you all the way up there. Bend your knees," Stella asked jokingly.

Eva did as she was asked and Stella put her arms around her.

"I'm sorry for last night," Eva whispered.

"I think the apology should be from me to you, darling. I

wasn't thinking. It's my fault." Stella took Eva's hand and held it. "We can talk about this some more at the house because if I keep you out here any longer, your aunt Tessa will be jumping out of her skin."

"Why don't you go to her?" Zoe suggested, gently pushing Eva ahead. Eva glanced back and walked purposely towards the farmhouse.

Tessa tried to calm the butterflies in her stomach as she watched Eva approach. She put her hand over her mouth and was transported to another time and place. For a moment she thought her sister was heading her way. She was aware of what her niece looked like through her visions and art, but seeing her in person was entirely different.

The resemblance to her sister was unmistakable—the hair was dark, almost black, straight and long, just the way her sister wore it. Even from this distance, she could see Eva's light blue eyes. Tessa was the same height as her niece. Tessa smiled at the way Eva carried herself with grace. Even the gait was Daphne's. "Oh Daph, she is you all over," she whispered.

Eva smiled, causing Tessa to gasp. For a brief moment, she was going to call her sister's name, but she stopped herself in time. Eva's smile transformed her face and transported Tessa to the last time she had seen her sister. Daphne was leaving the asylum to go back home. It was going to be the last time they would see each other, even though neither of them knew that. *Oh Daph, you created a beautiful child. I bet she also sounds like you.*

Tessa dropped the cane and opened her arms, inviting Eva into her embrace. Eva rushed the last couple of steps and melted into her embrace. They both started crying at the same time.

"I'm your aunt, Tessa." Tessa cupped Eva's face with both hands and looked into her eyes. "I have waited thirty years to meet you, Eva Theresa. Waited thirty years to tell you how much I love you and that you are loved. I'm your blood, and there is nothing they can do to change that."

"I'm Eva. Hello, Aunty," Eva managed to say, although it came out more like a garbled mash of unintelligible noise.

"Eva Theresa," Tessa said the names proudly. "I love the sound of that. My sister honored me with naming you after me." She reached out and brushed the tears from Eva's cheeks.

Eva nodded and swallowed audibly. "My mama loved you so much."

Tessa's heart skipped a beat on hearing Eva's voice. "You sound so much like her. She had the same soft voice, so gentle." Her tears continued to fall. This time it was Eva who reached out and wiped her aunt's cheek.

"Thank you for saving my life," Eva whispered and smiled shyly. Tessa shook her head. She felt like her heart was going to explode right out of her chest.

"You saved your life, darling. I just helped a little." Tessa took both of Eva's hands and held them. "Now before we get too emotional." She laughed. "Let me meet your gorgeous redhead."

Eva looked back at Zoe. "That's her."

"She looks so proud of you that I think she's going to burst," Tessa whispered into Eva's ear.

"Yes, that's my Zoe, although she doesn't have her auntie's fashion flair," Eva replied. Tessa laughed and beckoned Stella and Zoe over.

Tessa watched as Zoe quickly walked over, her hand slipping into Eva's and gently squeezing it.

"Hello, my name is—"

"Aunty Tessa." Zoe didn't stand on formalities and embraced Tessa. Tessa laughed and nodded. She looked at Stella over Zoe's shoulder.

"Goodness, you are a tiny one, aren't you?" Tessa stroked Zoe's cheek. "Very brave, loving, and beautiful. I'm glad we are finally meeting, Zoe."

"Well, that was quite emotional," Stella said softly. She cupped Tessa's cheek. Tessa took her hand and kissed it. "You should have seen her all morning," Stella said lightly. "Are they here yet? What are our girls doing? Did they get lost?"

"Now, now, I wasn't that bad."

"You put my eyeglasses in the icebox," Stella quipped, making everyone laugh. "Trust me, girls, that is not like Tessa. She is usually very calm, but the prospect of seeing her niece today just made her giddy." Tessa and Eva were looking at each other. "Now, Theo said he would be around later."

"We had Despina drop by the cabin. She was Eva's housekeeper during the war." Zoe kept up the conversation while Eva was acting shyly towards Tessa and Tessa just gazed at her with a smile.

"How was that like?" Stella asked, and looked at Zoe with a knowing smile.

"It was good. Eva liked Despina."

"Is that right?" Stella smirked.

"You know, I really love the color of the sky—it matches your shirt." Zoe threaded her arm through her aunt's elbow. "It has that really nice green and the polka dots really do give it a nice glow."

Zoe and Stella looked at each other and then at Eva and Tessa, who were very quiet. They shook their heads.

"Evy," Zoe came up against Eva and took her hand. "Did you hear what I just said?"

"Um." Eva shook her head.

"It's alright. It wasn't anything important. Do you want to help me find my Oliver Twist book?"

"Is that the one Theo brought you back from Thessalonica?" Stella asked.

"Yes."

"Where did you hide it?"

"Under the chicken shed," Zoe replied. "Come on, Evy, let's go find my book."

"Alright." Eva was led away by Zoe to find the book.

Stella sighed. She glanced at Tessa's tear-stained face and put her arm around her waist. "Darling."

"Yes, Angel."

"Our babies are home." Stella's own voice broke as she held Tessa in her arms.

"Welcome home, love," Eva whispered. She cupped Zoe's face and kissed her tenderly.

Zoe buried her head into Eva's chest and wept as Eva rubbed her back. They stood there for a while trying to come to terms with the emotional events over the last hour.

"Oh, I'm going to run out of tears by the time we get back home." Zoe wiped her eyes with the back of her hand.

"As long as they are happy tears." Eva sniffed.

Zoe took Eva's hand, and they walked around the courtyard, passing the chicken shed. Just under the brushes and the wooden supports for the shed was the book. Zoe stared at it for a few moments and then dropped to her knees.

With trembling hands, Zoe picked up the damaged book. It was a little waterlogged, barely held together, the pages stiff with mud. She turned the pages over, barely able to make out the inscription written inside. She tried to swallow the lump in her throat.

To my favorite sister, Zoe, may you always have more than Oliver did! – Love, Teedore.

Eva pulled Zoe into her embrace, stroking Zoe's chestnut hair as Zoe wept anew. She held Zoe slightly away from her and gazed into her eyes. "You always will have more than Oliver ever did. Welcome home, love."

CHAPTER 40

"This is the kitchen." Zoe whirled around the large room. A long bench that held a sink stood against one wall with a large window. It overlooked the side entrance to the farmhouse and also had a view of the fields and Mount Ossa in the background. In the middle of the room was a long table. The other side of the room contained another long bench and cupboards. On the wall were hooks for pots and pans.

"Wow, I love it," Eva said.

"Do you cook?" Stella asked. Tessa was leaning against the bench. Stella noticed Tessa's eyes never left Eva. She smiled and made a mental note to tell Tessa that it was a little creepy for her to do that. On the other hand, Eva was doing the same thing. She would quickly glance at her aunt and then, on being noticed, there would be a shy smile, and she would turn back to what Zoe was talking about.

Stella found that Zoe was fully aware of what was going on but kept on the commentary regardless, occasionally throwing in some nonsense to see if Eva was paying attention. Only once did Eva respond with a puzzled look. Stella wondered if Zoe was used to Eva being distracted and found an amusing way of dealing with it.

Eva smiled shyly and shook her head. "We found out pretty quickly that I'm not very good at it."

"It's alright. I cook, and we won't starve."

"We would if I cooked," Eva quipped.

Stella smiled. Eva was starting to relax and allowed for the easy banter between herself and Zoe to shine through. Stella glanced at Tessa, whose smile was permanently etched on her face.

"Stella is the cook in our house," Tessa said. "If you asked her nicely she may make my favorite dessert."

"If *we* ask her nicely for your favorite dessert?" Zoe chuckled. "What's your favorite?"

"Galaktoboureko." Tessa put her hand on her heart. "That desert is just so creamy."

"I think I can do that," Stella replied. Tessa and Eva smacked their lips.

"Oh, now you've captured Eva's heart. She loves that. She likes to try every Greek pastry shop to find out which one is the creamiest." Zoe laughed.

"Ah, you have a sweet tooth," Tessa said, making Eva smile. "I love sweets and would eat them more than I do."

"Why don't you?" Zoe asked.

"Stella is a meanie." Tessa pouted. "Now that Stella has said she will make it, I'm much happier."

"Does that mean you will listen and rest your knee?" Stella asked from across the room.

"Yes. I'm getting Galaktoboureko." Tessa blew Stella a kiss.

Stella shook her head and laughed. She turned to Zoe. "Why don't you show Eva your bedroom? Theo painted—"

"He didn't paint everything, did he?" Zoe looked at Stella in alarm.

"No, darling, he said if he did that wall, you would kill him." Stella chuckled.

"What was that?" Eva asked.

"I'll show you." Zoe took Eva's hand and led her out of the kitchen.

Stella watched them leave. She turned to find Tessa's gaze was on her. She lightly laughed and crossed the kitchen. Tessa very quickly sat down on the counter. "Look, I'm sitting."

Stella shook her head. "You've been standing now for hours, and that knee has got to be hurting."

"It is a bit," Tessa admitted as she reached out and brought Stella to her. "I couldn't feel it earlier." She opened her legs, wrapped them around Stella's body, and captured her lips for a long passionate kiss. "Hello," she said as they parted.

"Kissing me won't make me forget about this knee." Stella kissed Tessa's hand. "But it helps." They gazed at each other and laughed at the same time.

"Sorry," Tessa apologized. "I know I should be listening to you but..."

"I know, you've waited thirty years to see her." Stella smiled. "What do you make of young Eva?"

"She's shyer than I thought she would be. Was she like this at the cabin?"

"She was shyer than now. Once Zoe came back, she let her do the talking."

"I want them to stay here, Angel. They have to. They don't have a soul to look out for them."

"They do now, and we are not going anywhere." Stella smiled. "We won't abandon them."

"Let's go and ask them."

"If they stay here, you have to stop staring at Eva all the time. Your eyes never leave her."

"I know but..."

"Yes, you have been waiting thirty years."

"No." Tessa shook her head. "She reminds me so much of Daphne that I find myself almost calling her that."

"She does look like Daphne, but there is something different."

"There's a deep sadness there, Angel. I can feel it. She does look like Daphne so much. Now I know why Panayiotis said he couldn't believe his eyes when Muller arrived with Eva. He nearly called her Daphne himself."

"With everything going on, I forgot to ask you about Panayiotis' visit last night. I never really got the chance to meet him. Was he glad to see you?"

Tessa nodded. "He was delighted, and for a moment I thought he was going to cry."

"What did he say?"

Tessa gazed into Stella's eyes. "He couldn't say much, he was with a young fellow who drove him out here. He said he will come by later and then we could talk."

"I look forward to meeting him. Now did you get any inkling if young Eva is gifted?"

"I tried to read her but I couldn't."

"What do you mean you couldn't? I know you were distracted and all but..."

"No, it's not that. I just couldn't get anything. If she is

gifted, she's blocking me but if she's doing that, then her reaction was a lie when you revealed my gifts."

Stella paused for a moment before she shook her head slowly. "No, that reaction was real. It was a full panic attack. I've seen too many panic attacks to know that was real."

"Maybe I was distracted. I'll try later." Tessa replied. "I don't think she is gifted because of her reaction."

"What if she doesn't know she's gifted?"

"No, she's now thirty years old, that's too old not to know you a gifted. It may have jumped the generation again."

"I'm going to send a telegram to Aunt Irene and let her know Eva is here. She did say the house will be ready for them by the time they get to Berlin."

"Eva will want to meet her once we tell her about Irene."

"I have no doubt that this will happen."

Zoe pushed the door and entered her bedroom for the first time in eight years. She looked around and her eye caught a photograph that was prominently displayed. She bent down and picked it up.

A pang of overwhelming sadness gripped her heart as she gazed at the smiling faces of her parents. They were seated, and in her mother's lap was their five-year-old daughter. With shaking fingers, Zoe traced the picture. Eva put her arms around her and held her as she cried against her chest.

"Is everything going to make me cry?"

"Yes, love, we are going to cry rivers of tears," Eva said

quietly as Zoe held up the photo. "They are beautiful people."

"They were."

"That's you?" Eva pointed to the little girl in the photograph. "What a cutie." She kissed Zoe. "We are going to have the most beautiful children in the world," she said. Still holding Zoe, she picked up another photograph. Zoe's three brothers were holding her aloft.

"Your brothers were big boys. You don't resemble Michael or Thieri, but you do look like Theo."

"We can't have everyone look alike." Zoe giggled and wiped her eyes. Taking a last look around the room, she spotted her favorite doll. "Gypsy," she said softly.

"I don't want to be nasty, but that is an ugly doll."

Zoe looked at Eva. "Her name is Gypsy."

"This is one hideous doll, Zo." They both broke up laughing. "Why did you name her Gypsy?"

"She reminded me of a gypsy fortune teller I saw once at the fair who had that expression on her face." Zoe chuckled and then kissed the doll. "Michael found her at some market, and I felt sorry that she was ugly."

"Looks like someone really didn't want her to be pretty. This is really a very sad doll."

Zoe looked around the room. The walls were light beige and the baseboard was a deep maroon. The window had lace curtains over a heavy drape. She pulled it aside and looked outside. She smiled when she saw Mount Ossa in the distance. On the far right, there was a row of dolls next to a large stack of books and an easel.

Eva was standing stock-still in front of a wall that was one giant mural of Mount Ossa and the valley. "Oh, wow."

Zoe came up to Eva and put her arm around her waist.

"Mama and I worked on that. Well, Mama worked on that and I added the top of Mount Ossa. She was such a talented artist."

"She passed it on to you." Eva smiled and kissed the top of Zoe's head.

"Evy, look." Eva turned to where Zoe was pointing. In the middle of the room was a queen-size bed. "I know where that came from."

"I hope that's not your parents' bed."

"It's not my parents' bed."

"How do you know?"

"It's the bed we used for guests. I know it because if you see here," Zoe said and pointed to the side of the headboard which had a small carving of a monkey, "I drew that on there." Zoe assured Eva, who was looking at the bed rather suspiciously. "We had a spare guest room with a double bed."

"Are you sure?"

"Yes. I wouldn't sleep in my parents' bed. That would be just a little too much."

"It would be like having them looking over our shoulder when you get mosquito bites." Eva grinned. She kissed Zoe, the kiss becoming passionate. "I love you so much. You are the best thing to ever happen to me," she said as she lowered Zoe to the bed. Eva brushed her fingers across Zoe's soft lips. She smiled and captured Zoe's mouth. Zoe moaned, and they parted, both breathing hard, knowing they couldn't go further.

"God, I love you," Zoe whispered as Eva gazed into her eyes. Zoe tangled her hands through Eva's dark locks and kissed her.

"Girls, Tessa and I—" Stella flung the door open and stopped.

Eva yelped and reacted quickly by jumping up from the bed. She practically fell into the nearby chair. Zoe's face went a bright shade of pink as she lay on the bed and pulled the pillow from under her head. She covered her face with it and groaned in embarrassment.

"Oh, dear," Stella said softly. Tessa came up behind her, oblivious to what had transpired.

"What's the matter?"

"I didn't knock."

"Oh, Angel." Tessa gave Stella a look before she went over to Eva and put her hand on her shoulder. "Please, excuse my Stella; she was born in a tent."

"What I wanted to ask you both before I rudely interrupted the kissing, was if you would like to stay here tonight."

Eva nodded and looked at Zoe, who had taken the pillow off her face. "That would be nice."

"You can actually test out the bed properly. I don't think there are any mosquitoes, but you never know," Stella teased, earning herself a wry smile from Eva and a mortified look from Zoe. "Please, resume your kissing," she added.

"Come on, let's get out of here." Tessa chuckled and closed the bedroom door.

Eva looked at Zoe and they both started laughing. "Oh, dear god." Eva put her hand on her heart.

"Why did you jump? You were blocking her view of me rather nicely." Zoe laughed when Eva came over and resumed her place. "Hello."

"This bed squeaks."

"Yes, it does." Zoe cupped Eva's face. "I know how to make it stop."

"Oiling the springs?"

Zoe chuckled. "No."

"How did you find this out? Did you have a chance to test it out?"

"No. Michael showed me after he—"

Eva quickly disengaged herself from Zoe's arms and scrambled off the bed. "Michael slept here?"

Zoe rolled her eyes. "You're just too funny. Michael and his girl did not sleep here. Papa would have kicked his backside." She took Eva's hand and pulled her back to the bed. "What I was going to say before you did your roadrunner impersonation is that Michael showed me how to make the bed not squeak."

"Oh." Eva grinned. "Do you want to stay here tonight?"

"Yes." Zoe nodded. "Does it make you uncomfortable staying here?"

Eva shook her head. "This is your home."

Zoe stroked Eva's cheek. "That isn't the question I asked you. Does it make you feel uncomfortable, especially with Stella and Tessa in the same house?"

Eva shook her head. "She's my aunty. I want to get to know her."

"Alright then. We stay."

"We lock the door."

"We will also lock the door," Zoe repeated as she tweaked Eva's dimpled chin. They looked at each other for a long moment. "You are just so adorable," Zoe said and brought Eva down for a kiss.

EPILOGUE

Eva was leaning against the wooden railing on the front porch of the farmhouse. She brought her cigarette to her mouth and took a drag before she exhaled. She watched the smoke rise and drift off into the slight breeze.

The beauty of the full moon casting its glow across the fields was lost on her. Her mind was on the unexpected revelations that the trip to Larissa had brought. She knew this trip was going to be emotional, and it had lived up to that expectation, but a new complication had arisen.

Eva turned towards the sound of Zoe's voice inside the farmhouse. Zoe's laugh at something her aunt was saying made Eva sigh. Zoe—the young girl she had met so many years ago, the angry child who had blossomed into a beautiful, caring, loving woman.

Eva had come to Larissa in 1942 a broken woman, and now, eight years later, she was with the woman who had taken that damaged soul and given her so much to hope for and a future.

Eva could see Zoe through the window. "I love you so much," she whispered.

Eva's attention was drawn to the woman sitting on the sofa listening to Zoe. Her long black hair cascaded down her shoulders. Her eyes crinkled in delight at something Zoe had said.

Her aunt was alive—a woman Eva and her family thought had died in a fire before Eva was born, a woman with extraordinary gifts, a woman that could project herself across time and see the horrors Eva lived through long before they happened.

Who was Theresa Rosa Lambros?

What other gifts did this woman possess?

Why was Theresa here and what did she want from Eva?

So many questions ran through Eva's mind. None of those questions were going to be answered that night.

Eva's thoughts were interrupted when Zoe opened the door and stuck her head out. They smiled at each other for a moment before Zoe came out and joined her.

"It's been a rough day," Zoe exclaimed.

"I don't think this will be the last rough day we have, love."

"I know. I'm not sure what's going to happen..."

"Maybe we can ask my aunt Tessa, and she can tell us." Eva put her arm around Zoe's shoulders.

"How does that work, Evy?"

"I don't know, and I'm not sure I want to know either."

They remained silent for a moment. Zoe smiled at Eva. "I guess we will find out, won't we?" She took Eva's hand and held it.

"As long as you are with me, love, I'm ready to face

whatever comes our way," Eva said before she kissed Zoe lightly on the lips.

The End - Continued in Book 4: Awakenings

OTHER NOVELS BY MARY

Eva and Zoe Intertwined Souls Series

Enemy At The Gate (1940-1942)

In The Blood of the Greeks (1941-1944)

Where Shadows Linger (1947)

Mabel of the ANZACS (1948)

Promise is a Promise (1948-1949)

A Widgie Knight (1950)

Hidden Truths (1950)

Awakenings (1950)

No Good Deed (1951)

Nor The Battle To The Strong (1956)

Non-Fiction

In the Blood of the Greeks The Illustrated Companion

ABOUT AUSXIP PUBLISHING

WWW.AUSXIPPUBLISHING.COM

AUSXIP Publishing is an Australian based publishing house. We publish quality stories with strong female characters that inspire, strengthen and enrich the soul. To build up, to create a sense of achievement and most importantly to entertain. We love reading about strong women who change their world. Come with us on our journey and discover your next favorite book!

AUSXIP Publishing Newsletter
https://newsletter.ausxippublishing.com

AUSXIP Publishing Store
https://store.ausxippublishing.com

Social Media

Facebook:
https://facebook.com/ausxippublishing

Twitter:
https://twitter.com/ausxippublish

Instagram:
https://instagram.com/ausxippublishing

Made in the USA
Monee, IL
28 April 2026

49136495R00207